Angels of the Mourning Light

A Novel

Frank E. Bittinger

iUniverse, Inc.
New York   Bloomington

Angels of the Mourning Light
The Third Book of the Scarabae Saga

Copyright © 2009 Frank E. Bittinger

iUniverse books may be ordered through booksellers or by contacting:

iUniverse
1663 Liberty Drive
Bloomington, IN 47403
www.iuniverse.com
1-800-Authors (1-800-288-4677)

Because of the dynamic nature of the Internet, any Web addresses or links contained in this book may have changed since publication and may no longer be valid. The views expressed in this work are solely those of the author and do not necessarily reflect the views of the publisher, and the publisher hereby disclaims any responsibility for them.

ISBN: 978-1-4401-4558-2 (pbk)
ISBN: 978-1-4401-4556-8 (cloth)
ISBN: 978-1-4401-4557-5 (ebook)

Printed in the United States of America

iUniverse rev. date: 5/26/09

Special Dedication

For my tattooed cowboy in the black hat.

Thank You

L. Ron Hubbard: for providing the way to happiness and the means to clarity.

Milan and all my friends at Celebrity Centre International: for showing me distance means nothing when you share a foundation of belief and for strong friendships.

Amber, JJ, David, and everyone at the Boston Church: for your incredible friendships and for being there for me in my journey up The Bridge.

Flo and everyone at the Founding Church in DC: for your friendship, for our chats, and for always being there for me; I promise we will have visits more often.

The IAS: for being the Force for Freedom on this planet; working together we can and will reach a state of Planetary Calm. I have such respect for the work we do.

Kirstie Alley, Leah Remini, Jenna Elfman, and Catherine Bell: for making me laugh and entertaining me when nearly everything in my life was turned to ash.

Heather Lloyd, publicist extraordinaire: for being my friend and for taking such great care of me; together we reach the stars, doll.

Laura Meese: for designing the fantastic cover you, the readers, see on the front of this book; Laura, you are a true artist and your work is awesome.

Sarah Moses: for being the editing force behind my manuscript--you rock. If you find any errors, blame her! Just kidding, Sarah. (Seriously, blame her.)

R'Chel and Cole, my sister and brother-in-law: for taking us in after the fire and giving us a home until ours was restored, for making us feel at home, and for enduring Chiffon when the demon would come out—you are the best ever. To everyone out there: make sure you visit Stormsong.org for all your skull candle needs.

Nancy Stallings: thank you, my friend, for having the courage to share your story of the supernatural with the world; it is with pride I call you friend.

My Mother: as I might have mentioned before, I would not be here without her—you can read this one, Mama; I left out all the dirty parts…those will be in Book 4.

A special Thank You to my friend Savannah Russe: I am so thankful you came into my world and I look forward to knowing you for a long, long time. You are a true talent and I love reading your books. Your friendship and advice are invaluable to me.

Angels of the Mourning Light

The Third Book of the Scarabae Saga

Frank E. Bittinger

Prologue

She floated adrift on a sea of pain; it rolled in and ebbed like the tide. Sometimes the pain was a raging agony; other times a rippling discomfort. Her body had grown accustomed to the mega-doses of painkillers. They only reduced the pain for a small window of time, never killing it like promised. No more treatments or surgeons for her. Only a matter of time. The battle had lasted for years. Finally, she refused to die in the sterile hospital. Instead, she demanded to be allowed to go home and live out her final days in surroundings she knew.

"I'd like to see my son," she told the caregiver.

The older woman smiled and said, "He's here. That boy never leaves your side. He's a good boy."

Barely thirteen years old, the boy should have been doing something else—anything else—instead of standing deathwatch, but he never dared to stray far from his mother. He had to be forced to go to school or else he'd spend the entire school day with her. As it was, he'd sneak out of bed at night, tiptoe into her room, and curl up in the big chair by her bed.

Many times he'd heard her cry out from pain in the middle of the night; he had wiped the tears from her eyes and placed a cold towel on her forehead, doing what he could to make her feel better. But nothing much except the heavy dosage of medication the doctor prescribed made her feel better. The medicine didn't make her so much feel better; it just made her hurt a bit less.

He didn't curse God because his mother suffered, but he found himself praying less and less, because he felt his prayers went unanswered. He'd heard people talk about how her suffering cleared her path to heaven, but he didn't think that made any sense. Why would you have to endure agony to get to peace and love?

Stirring from the chair, he went to her bedside and held her hand in his. Her skin was always either cold and clammy or sweaty and burning.

"I'm here, momma," he said.

"Why aren't you out with your friends?"

He shook his head. "I don't feel like going out today."

"You can't stay cooped up in here with me all the time," she said, stopping to draw a labored breath. "A whole wide world out there waiting for you. You better go and experience it before it passes you by."

"Uh huh, and it'll wait for me," he said. "It'll be there when I'm ready. I've got all the time in the world to go explore. Years to go through caves and up mountains and diving in the sea," he said, repeating the things she'd told him.

The corners of her mouth turned up. "Don't count on it. Wasting time's a sin, because you don't know how much you have." She stared, not at him, through him. "It goes by so quickly; the good times seem so far out of reach when…"

She came back to him, focused her eyes on his. "You're too young to be held prisoner here with me." Her body tensed, and he knew from experience the pain assaulted her. "I need you to know two things. Two important things you have to know so you can live life to the best of your abilities."

"Momma, don't talk like this," he said. "I don't like it."

"Now listen to your mother. Two things you need to know, okay? So you better hush and let me tell you so you know."

"Okay."

"You need to make the best life you can. Make the best. No one will hand you anything; you have to decide what you want and then go after it."

"Okay, I'll try."

"And you need…" Her breath caught as she tried to breathe through this fresh assault; the struggle was evident on her face. "You need to know," she battled to say, "I love you, my son. Never forget. Never question my love for you. My love for you is bigger than the universe and it will go on forever and ever, through eternity. You understand? There is no end to my love for you, son. It is infinite."

"I love you, too."

Her eyes moved from his to stare over his shoulder. Something in the room had changed. It didn't turn cold or hot, or get really dark or light. Turning around, he saw nothing. When he turned back to his mother, she was still staring the same as before. He didn't know what she was seeing. Her eyes were focused on the corner of the room. He saw shadows but he couldn't see anything else.

"Momma?"

No response.

"Momma?" he grabbed her arm with his other hand.

Still no response.

And then all evidence of pain and suffering fled from her face. She looked like she had when he was younger, before she got sick. Before the word Cancer changed everything. She looked so beautiful; her face was so full of love and life, and he couldn't remember the last time he saw her looking like that.

She breathed deeply with no struggle. Whatever she saw did not scare her. It must have brought her peace and comfort.

Because she smiled.

And then the light faded from her eyes.

* * * * * * * * * * *

It rained the day of his mother's funeral. He'd wanted the day she was laid to rest to be sunny and warm and beautiful. But he would always remember the overcast sky and the falling drops of water.

Those drops helped camouflage many tears that day.

He stood beside his aunt under her somber black umbrella, only half-listening to the minister's words about being called home and the glory of everlasting life. The people standing around with their wet eyes and their pressed-together lips didn't scare him, but they made him feel so alone.

Looking at the ground, he didn't want to see anybody or make eye contact in case they would try to offer him comfort. The hugs and the pats on the head or the back made him so uncomfortable. It didn't help ease his pain, or help him understand. He didn't care that the people around him were supposed to rejoice because his mother had been called to receive her eternal reward.

He'd have much rather had his mother with him instead of having to face life on his own so soon. Not that he wanted her to hang around, writhing in agony from the disease eating away at her insides. He wanted what he saw on television: he wanted a happy, healthy mom who would be able to do things with him like camping and bike riding and rollerblading in the park on sunny afternoons.

The water drops dripped down his face. He couldn't tell if they were the rain or his own tears. Tears and rain both looked the same when he wiped them away with his hands. He wanted it to end.

He wanted a normal life. He wanted a mother who was a dynamo and who would stay with him until he was old enough for a family of his own.

But it was never meant to be.

No, he didn't understand any of it at all.

For most of his life he would wonder why. Why, after so many years of pain and suffering, why did she smile at the end?

He didn't see a thing when he looked.

What did she see?

PART I

Grave Ruins

Chapter One
Present Day

Zenk Mortuary and Mausoleum provided the perfect backdrop for an elegant funeral service. Sprays of flowers in burgundy, mauve, and white—with the appropriate amount of greenery—burst forth from urns placed around the room and from vases on the walls. Chandeliers, one on either end of the twenty foot room, and sconces were designed to replicate antique gas lights. The brass and glass lights, neither gothic nor gaudy, added a glow to the room. Silk paper covered the walls from the chair-rail up to the crown molding, cherry wood panels from the chair-rail down. Carpet, its pile thick and lush, felt soft underfoot.

Austere it was not.

People, more out of confusion than stupidity, mistakenly believe mortuaries and mausoleums are one and the same. Of course they have one major thing in common: both are technically places for dead bodies.

Basically, a mortuary is where the dead are housed while awaiting burial or cremation. It's a stop on the way, *not* the final resting place. The word "mortuary" comes from the Latin "mortuus" meaning "dead."

And a mausoleum is a place, usually elaborate, which houses tombs—where bodies or ashes are entombed. It *is* the final resting place. The word "mausoleum" comes from a name, from King Mausolus of Halicarnassus. Upon his death, his wife-sister-queen commissioned a tomb so grand it became one of the Seven Wonders of the Ancient World.

Micah understood the difference.

For a man like Micah Graves, an obsession with death was certainly understandable. A name such as Graves would seem enough of an excuse, but the circumstances surrounding the final moments of his mother's life was truly the deciding factor. Over the course of the last twenty-three years, Micah attended over four thousand funerals, which averaged out to be about three and a half funerals each week. Most of those funerals, roughly ninety-eight percent, were for people with whom he was not acquainted.

Micah knew the ins and outs of the funeral business. He knew the difference between remains and cremains. His collection of In Remembrance cards, while not the envy of all who saw it, was cause for amazement. In fact, he should have found employment in the field of mortuary science.

Today's voyager into the great hereafter: Eighty-seven-year-old Clara Stark. She'd been making French toast, her favorite breakfast food, when it happened. The cinnamon spilled all over the counter. As she cleaned it up, she accidentally inhaled some. The resulting sneeze caused Clara to smack her head on the countertop. The blow knocked her unconscious and she expired shortly thereafter on the kitchen floor of her quaint bungalow.

A neighbor called the police when Clara failed to show for a scheduled game of gin that evening. Not only were they shocked to find Clara dead, they were stunned to find her as naked as the day she was born.

Clara, reclining in her casket, looked as demure and lovely as any living lady. The huge purple bruise, where her forehead had connected with the countertop, was artfully covered by a thick layer of pancake make-up. Her tight curls had been teased and fluffed and hairsprayed into a gray nimbus. Everyone commented on how lifelike she appeared.

Micah wouldn't know; he'd never laid eyes on her before in his life. He knew the story of her demise from gossip he'd overheard.

"A pleasure to see you," Edgar Zenk, EZ to his friends, said to Micah, "as always. Did you…" he gestured towards Clara with his eyes.

"No, no," Micah said. "Just here to pay my respects."

"Of course," EZ smiled. "The members of her weekly gin game arrived earlier, with refreshments."

"Here? That's unusual. Is it even sanitary to…" he wiggled his eyebrows.

"Eat with a corpse in the room?" EZ finished for him. "Yes, it is. Unless they plan to lay out a buffet on the casket, that is."

"Appetizing thought."

* * * * * * * * * *

He enjoyed strolling around viewings, listening to the stories people told each other, sharing in the memories. Dozens of friends and family turned out for Clara's memorial service. Clara's gin cohorts laid out a buffet worthy of a king; Micah surveyed the two tables laden with food from main dishes to soups, salads, and desserts. People gathered to fill plates and then stood in groups reminiscing with each other; exchanging memories made them feel better.

Several times people asked Micah how he knew Clara and he gave them his standard line, "We didn't know each other as well as we would have liked, but I couldn't miss paying my respects."

Over the last twenty-odd years he'd been attending funerals, Micah had yet to find the answers for which he looked. Never once did he witness a soul hovering around the casket or hanging near the ceiling. No ghostly voices whispering upon the wind.

But he never thought of ending his search, not until he found the answers he sought.

A familiar face nearly eclipsed by one of the potted weeping fig trees caught his attention. Someone he'd seen at various funerals.

When EZ walked by, Micah caught his arm and asked, "Do you know the guy over by the tree?"

EZ looked and nodded his head. "He's another one like you."

"What do you mean?"

"Comes to funerals. Pretty regular, but not as often as you."

"I remembering seeing him a few times, but I wasn't looking for him."

"No reason you would have been."

"What's his name?" Micah asked.

"Can't help you with that one, my friend. I don't know."

"Thanks."

The friendly undertaker smiled and walked away.

Micah decided to take it upon himself to get to the bottom of the situation. He walked nonchalantly over to the potted plant and nodded to the guy. Just about six-two, medium build, and dark blond hair.

He extended his hand, "My name's Micah, Micah Graves."

The man grasped the offered hand and said, "Graves, huh? I know you."

"Yeah, we've run into each other at a couple of these."

"I'm Lucian Sterling; call me Luc. Good to meet you."

"Did you know Clara Stark?"

"No, you?"

"Huh uh. I, uh, come to a lot of funerals, but I don't necessarily know the deceased every time."

"Sounds like me," Luc said, turning to Micah. "Why do you come? I mean, I know why I do, but you can't be here for the same reason."

"If I told you, you might think I'm crazy."

"Try me."

"All right," Micah said. "For more than two decades I've been coming to these places. Looking for answers is the easiest way to explain it, I guess. You?"

Luc smiled and nodded. "The same. Guess we're two of a kind. I'd make a reference to the two peas in a pod thing, but it's too corny."

"Tell me your story and I'll tell you mine," Micah said. "We can go for coffee, that way we could have some kind of privacy."

"Sounds good. There's a café down the street a couple blocks; we can walk there and come back for our cars."

"Okay, let's go."

* * * * * * * * * * *

Cup of Jo's began as a hobby for JoAnna McKinley, but soon became a major attraction for the people of Rain Falls, Maryland. Rain Falls, situated in the western part of the state, lived up to its name with an average rainfall of 50 inches per year.

Micah and Luc seated themselves at one of the wrought iron café tables arranged outside on the sidewalk. The waitress came over and asked if they would like menus.

"I don't need one, thanks," Luc said. "I'll have a black coffee, please."

"Of course. And for you, sir?" she asked Micah.

"For me, a cup of tea, please. Cream and sugar."

"Be back soon." She smiled and walked away.

"I've never been here before," Micah said.

"No? It's a real nice place to come and unwind, to think about things. But we came here to talk about this funeral thing we have in common."

Laughing, Micah said, "The list is very long, my friend. I've been to just about four thousand."

"Holy Christ." Luc's eyes got big. "That's a lot of funerals. I haven't been to more than a couple dozen."

"But I've been at it longer than you have."

"Yeah, I guess so. Why do you go to them?"

And with that question, Micah told him about his mother and his search.

Just as he was finishing, the waitress came back with their drinks and placed them on the table. "Enjoy, gentleman. If you need me, just wave your hand if I haven't checked back with you. Okay?"

After adding cream and sugar, Micah took a sip of his tea and said, "Your turn to tell me why you go to all the funerals."

Luc thought for a minute to formulate his answer before he spoke. "For me, this all started with a car accident. Four years ago. My fiancé, Karen, and I were coming home from celebrating my thirtieth birthday." He stopped to clear his throat. "Up to that point winter'd been mild. No big storms or anything. But that night it was cold; I think the temperature actually hit zero or got damned close to it.

"Anyway, we'd gone out to celebrate. Drinks, dinner, and a movie. I can't even remember what movie we saw. On the way home, just after eleven, we hit black ice and the car spun out of control. You ever have a car wreck?" he asked Micah. "Maybe not a bad one like mine, but any?"

"Yes, I totaled a car in the winter, but it was during a storm when it hit the ice. It rolled end over end and side over side."

"You hurt bad?"

"Weird thing about that," Micah said, "the car was completely totaled, the roof crushed down so far it buckled the seats. But I escaped with no broken bones, not a single scratch on me."

Luc smiled. "I wish I could say that. Like I said, our car spun out of control, did a couple doughnuts on the road before slamming sideways into the guardrail. We bounced off the rail and spun around another time or two before slamming head first into the side of the mountain. I remember thinking it wasn't how other people described it. Wrecking, I mean. For me, the time didn't speed up; it slowed down, like a movie sequence. Was it like that for you?"

"Yeah, it felt like every second was dragged out to four or five. I watched it all happen in slow motion, like a movie."

"Our car wasn't totaled. The front end and the driver's side were banged up pretty good, but I found out later it could've been fixed." Luc took a drink of his coffee before continuing. "My next memory is waking up in the hospital. Dad sat beside the bed. He told me I'd been out of it for about a week. I asked about Karen, but dad said I needed to rest and wait for the doctor to come in and explain everything. I knew right then it couldn't be good news."

Luc wiped under his eyes and blinked several times. "When the doctor came, I think I already knew what he was going to say before he said it. My back was broken, one leg, and a couple ribs. I had a concussion and six of my teeth had been knocked out. My left eyes was black and I was told I was so goddamned lucky to be alive. Oh, and by the way, Karen didn't make it. He didn't say it like that, but he may as well have. It didn't hurt any less to have the news broken gently. Sometimes I think it should be delivered like the bandage theory: do it quick and it will cause less pain. Making me wait for the doctor only added to my misery."

"I'm sorry to hear that," Micah said. "Even after years have passed, it still hurts. The pain only lessens, it never goes away completely."

"Yeah. And me being out for nearly a week robbed me off the opportunity to go to her funeral, to see her laid to rest. She got put in the ground while I stayed chained to a hospital bed. I never had the chance to say goodbye. Like I could have gone in the condition I was in anyway."

"No closure."

"No nothing," Luc said. "I spent months, over six, rehabilitating and going to therapy. I had to fight so hard to get back to me, to rediscover who I was, that I lost who Karen is…was. A year passed before I had the chance to go to her grave. I brought dahlias, her favorite, and tried talking to her to sort out my feelings, but I felt like an idiot standing there talking to a marble monument. Three times I visited her gravesite—long enough to come to the conclusion there were no answers waiting for me there. She didn't speak to me from beyond the grave. If she had, I'd probably gone running back to therapy. Nothing happened for me. No closure. I feel like I'm hanging there, you know? I'd been out of the hospital for about three months when I went to the first funeral. Some guy in his sixties. I don't remember his name. Weeks, maybe a month, went by and I didn't feel the urge, but it did come back. Eventually, I began gravitating towards them; I felt drawn to them."

"Happened the same way with me," Micah said. "One funeral turned into two, then three, and before I knew it—thousands. Now, it makes me feel if I don't go to them, makes me somehow feel left out."

"Even more empty; I know the feeling. All those funerals and we finally met someone we can relate to."

"And now we sit here, complete strangers, pouring out our stories to each other."

"Yeah, but it does make me feel somewhat better. Two kindred spirits coming together, like it was meant to be. I do feel better."

"Me, too."

The waitress came by to check on them. They both said they were fine, so she left them to their conversation.

"Did you realize you were going to so many?" Luc asked. "Or was it a case of you waking up one morning and having it dawn on you? 'Whoa, this is number four thousand'?"

Micah grinned and shook his head. "Not exactly. I knew I had been to a great many services, but I had no idea how many. I just sat down one day and the thought popped into my head. I did the math. Turned out to be a lot. Actually, it was a whole lot more than I thought it would be."

"Is this where I admit something to you and sound like a loser?" He laughed and looked away for a moment.

"You won't sound like a loser. Tell me."

"Every night I write down whose funeral I've been to along with other details in a journal, what I saw and what I felt, emotions," Luc said. "It's all so I can look back and reflect. Maybe help me figure out why I do it."

"Sounds like a good idea to me. I should learn from your example and keep my own records. Be difficult to backtrack now, but I could start with Clara Stark. She could be the first name in my own journal."

"Maybe sometime we could compare our experiences."

"And start carpooling."

"This could very well be the beginning of a macabre relationship, Mr. Graves, I can feel it."

Micah lifted his cup. "A toast then, Mr. Sterling."

"To us."

"Yes, to us."

They touched cups and toasted their new-found friendship.

Chapter Two

"Hey, Graves," the voice called on the answering machine. "I know you're not still in bed. It's after eleven, for God's sake. Wake up. Answer the damned phone. Hello. Are you in there?"

Micah rolled over and cussed under his breath before picking up the cordless phone beside the bed. "What do you want, Sterling? It's before the crack of dawn."

"Dude, dawn was hours ago. I don't know how you can still be asleep on a beautiful day like this. Get up and enjoy what the world has to offer."

"Beautiful day? I wouldn't know. The drapes are closed. Don't you know sunlight burns the flesh of my kind?"

"Crawl out of the coffin, my friend," Luc Sterling said. "If you wouldn't stay up all night you could be out of bed at a normal time."

"Leave me alone. Don't you have to work?"

"No. It's Saturday, and you're wasting it by lying in bed all day. Rise and shine."

"Rise and shine, my ass. Why do you have to bother me?"

"We got a funeral to attend. The poor guy didn't have any family, so I doubt many people show. Show some respect. Get out of bed, get dressed, and I'll be over to pick you up in an hour."

"Go away. I'm going back to sleep."

"You better be ready when I get there. Don't make me throw you into the shower. I'll do it. Get out of bed, Graves!"

Micah turned off the phone, tossed it on the floor, rolled over, and pulled the blanket up over his head. The low drone of the air conditioner in the window started to lull him. He would have fallen back asleep if Sia, his black cat, hadn't jumped up on the bed and draped himself across Micah's covered head.

"Why does the entire world conspire against me?" He threw the blanket back and Sia rolled off the side of the bed. On the floor, the cat looked up at Micah and meowed his indignity before proceeding to groom his front paw.

Micah leaned down and spoke to the cat. "I feed you, clean your litter box, and keep the fleas from sucking your blood and you repay me by taking Sterling's side. Go live with him, see if he treats you half as good as I do. Ungrateful git, that's what you are. See if any more treats make their way to you. Haul your ass to the store and buy them yourself."

He bit the bullet and crawled out of bed. The minute his feet touched the floor, temptation to crawl back under the covers hit him, and he reconsidered the decision to get up. Deciding against curling up in the warm bed, he stood.

"So not fair," he whined. "Why must I be the martyr? Sacrificing sleep for a good deed. Where's my reward?"

After turning on the CD player in the bathroom, he stripped off his boxer shorts. Once in the shower, the cold water shocked and then revived him. He slowly added hot and turned off the cold until the bathroom filled with steam.

"That's the stuff," he said as he stretched and enjoyed the hot water drumming against his skin. Singing along with Alice Cooper, Micah poured gel on the shower puff and lathered up his body. Fifteen minutes in the shower did wonders for his sleep-deprived state. He rinsed his body, turned off the water, slid back the curtain, and was reaching for a towel when he heard the thunder coming from the direction of the front door.

Micah wrapped the towel around his waist and went to answer.

"You're early."

"I thought I'd have to drag your ass out of bed or we'd be late," Luc Sterling explained. "You're dripping."

"Observant, aren't we? I'm wet. I was in the shower when you tried pounding down my door. The shower is where I go to clean off."

"No need to be pissy, Graves. You going to invite me in or do I have to stand here all day?"

Micah slammed the door and walked back towards the bathroom.

Luc let himself into the house and closed the door behind him.

"Funny, my friend."

"Yeah, funny's what I was going for," Micah said over his shoulder. "Keep your pants on, Sterling; I'll be ready in fifteen minutes."

"Damn, and here I was looking for a reason to get naked."

* * * * * * * * * * *

Twenty minutes later, they were in Luc Sterling's car on the way to a funeral.

"Man, just let me say, you look like hammered shit."

Micah shot him a look. "I didn't get enough sleep."

"Don't sweat it, that's what they make coffee for."

"I don't drink coffee."

"I forgot. Then buck it up, Graves, we're going to see a dead body."

Micah pulled his sunglasses down over his eyes and leaned his head back against the seat. After a couple minutes of silence, Luc reached over and lifted the glasses.

"What?"

"Just checking to make sure you didn't nod off on me."

"I hate you."

Luc laughed. "No, you don't. I'm your best friend."

"With friends like you, I'll never get any damned sleep."

"Go to bed at a decent hour and you'll get all the sleep you need."

"Sterling, you are getting on my last, in-need-of-rest nerve. Knock it off before I knock you out of this car."

Luc snorted. "You are a real cranky-ass when someone wakes you up."

Micah smacked him on the side of the head and said, "I rue the day I ever met you. You disrupt my peaceful existence."

"Peaceful existence, huh? You're a recluse, a hermit. I just try to drag you out of your shell long enough to have some fun. Life's full of fun. Better wake up and smell the coffee before time wastes away. It's a sin to waste time, my friend."

Smiling, Micah said, "My mom used to say something along those lines."

"Heed those sage words of advice. Now, don't you feel better?"

"I still hate you for waking me up before the crack of dawn."

"Hate me all you want, but there's one dead body coming up."

"Show a little respect."

"But he'd want us to joke instead of stand around bawling our eyes out."

"You are so full of shit. You never even knew the man."

"What's your point?" Luc asked.

"The point is you have no idea what he'd want."

"You didn't know him, either."

"Neither one of us did."

"Then how can you say he wouldn't want us to joke and remember the good times?"

"Therapy and Jesus would do you wonders, Sterling. Throw in some Prozac, too, while we're at it."

"Life would be boring without me in it, Graves, so boring."

"Boring, but peaceful. Where the hell are we going anyway? Where is this funeral? Timbuktu?"

"It's in New Mystic and it's not that far," Luc said. "Maybe fifteen minutes."

"At Sanctuary?"

"Uh huh."

"Damn, that's a nice funeral home." Micah whistled. "Of all the funerals I've been to, I don't recall ever having been there."

"Yep, old guy must've had some money."

"What did the obit say about him?"

"His name was Edgar Wagner. He passed away peacefully in his sleep at the age of ninety years old. Mr. Wagner was preceded in death by his wife of forty years, Mrs. Edna (nee Winthrop) Wagner, age eighty-two. Edgar Wagner lived his entire life in the town of New Mystic, attending church at St. Sebastian's on Clearfax Drive. His hobbies included whittling animal figures and playing Solitaire."

"Sterling, you sound like you're announcing him at a debutante ball."

"What about his not having any friends?"

Luc pretended to think about it. "Did I say he had no friends?"

"No, but…"

"Stop putting words in my mouth. What I said was he had no living family, because he and the wife never had children. I felt sorry for the guy."

Fifteen minutes later they pulled into the parking lot of Sanctuary. There were six cars in the lot, including theirs.

"Told you there wouldn't be a big turnout."

"It's still early. When does the service start?"

"About ten minutes."

"Cutting it close." Micah looked at the mortuary and smiled. "I get a kick out this being smack dab in the center of town."

"Morbid is the word that comes to mind for me. Building a town around a funeral home is just weird."

"The town was probably here first. This building isn't hundreds of years old, so the town couldn't have sprung up around it."

"It's still creepy. Didn't you ever see *Phantasm*, Graves?"

"Be on the lookout for silver spheres flying around," Micah whispered.

"Dude, that's so not funny."

* * * * * * * * * * *

Once inside Sanctuary, all joking stopped. The mausoleum was indeed lavish and overwhelming. A vaulted ceiling, painted with realistic images of celestial bodies and edged with gilded molding, was supported by towering black marble columns veined with gold and crowned with more gilded molding. A huge chandelier hung from the middle of the ceiling, its purpose more to highlight the painted ceiling than to illuminate the foyer. Black marble also made up the walls and the floor, giving a cold feeling to the place.

Riese Nicholson, the man in charge, strode toward them, introduced himself, and ushered the two into the chapel. There were only two other people, older women seated down front, in the chapel.

After viewing Edgar Wagner's urn, the two friends seated themselves and took in their surroundings.

"Oak floors and walls, it's like we're in a room-size coffin. A burgundy-lined, room-sized coffin," Luc whispered to Micah. "Christ, this place really does give me the creeps."

"You've never been here before. If you think that's the only strange thing about this place," Micah whispered back, "look around."

Doing as he was told, Luc couldn't figure it out. "What?"

"How many funerals have you been to?"

"Couple dozen, I told you. Why?"

"How many of those had some sort of religious overtones, icons, anything?"

"All of them." He thought about it for a minute. "I still don't get it."

"Even if this were a nondenominational service," Micah explained, "you'd expect some kind of icon hanging around. A picture of Jesus, a cross, a statue of a saint. There isn't one crucifix or Star of David in here anywhere. Not even a plain wooden cross. It's utterly void of any iconography."

"Uh huh, I see what you mean."

Micah started to speak, but was interrupted by Riese Nicholson, who stood behind a wooden structure that could be construed as an altar and faced the four mourners, his hands clasped behind him. The silver urn rested atop the altar.

"Sanctuary honors the wishes of the departed, and it was the wish of Edgar Wagner for his loved ones to reminisce and laugh in lieu of a religious service."

This isn't right, Micah's mind screamed. He didn't know Mr. Wagner, but he felt this was not what the man would have wanted.

"This doesn't feel right to me," Luc leaned over and whispered.

"You must've read my mind."

When no one rose to come to the altar and share memories, Mr. Nicholson said, "Allow us to proceed to the final resting place." He picked up the urn and walked down the center of the chapel and out the door.

Nicholson stopped at a square opening in the wall of the mausoleum and placed the urn inside.

"Here may he rest," he said.

"Here may he rest," the two women echoed.

* * * * * * * * * * *

"And that wasn't in the least bit bizarre," Luc said once they were safely in his car and back on the road. "Riese Nicholson could have been on *the Addam's Family*."

Micah laughed. "What about those two women down front? You think they were professional mourners?"

"Equipped with their own veils and hankies. Talk about macabre."

"An experience to treasure forever," Micah said. "You hungry, Sterling? There's a pizza joint around here somewhere."

Luc leaned back in the seat and pulled his sunglasses down over his eyes. "I could eat, if you could."

"Three Sisters Pizza is a couple streets over. They have the best pizza."

"I'm starving; I'd eat ketchup smeared on cardboard."

"Such a gourmet," Micah laughed. "I think we can do better than that."

"You buying?"

"It's your turn."

"Nope, it's yours."

"Thought it was your turn. I bought last time, after the Deacon funeral."

Luc shook his head. "That wasn't the last time. I bought after the Lander funeral. We haven't been out since then."

Micah thought a moment before speaking. "Yeah, you're right. It's my turn. Seems like I'm always the one paying."

"You're mister money-bags."

"Like you don't pull down a hefty salary at the magazine. Big shot editor."

"That's Mr. Big Shot Editor to you."

Micah glanced at him. "Then you won't mind picking up the tab, Mr. Big Shot Editor. Even if it's not your turn."

"I guess I walked right into that one, huh?"

"More like ran headfirst."

"Hey," Luc jolted up and pointed out the window. "You just drove by the pizza place, Graves."

"Yeah, yeah, yeah. Don't wig out on me. We'll circle back around. You won't die of starvation in five more minutes."

"Maybe not, but I gotta go to the bathroom."

Micah stopped the car in the middle of the street. "Get out."

"What?"

"You heard me."

"This is not funny," Luc said.

"Get out."

"No. This is my car."

"I don't care. Get out."

"There's a car coming." Luc pointed through the windshield at the car coming down the street toward them.

"It'll go around us."

"Graves, you're crazy. Get going before you cause a wreck."

"Not 'til you exit the vehicle."

"I am not getting out," Luc said. "The car's getting closer. You better get us moving. Or I swear to God…"

Micah hit the gas and laughed the whole way down the street. He was still laughing when they came back to Three Sisters and parked.

"You are one seriously messed up man."

"Maybe I am, but it freaked you out."

"Damn, remind me not to get on your bad side."

Micah pointed a finger at him and said, "Serves you right for waking me up so freaking early."

Luc walked away and said over his shoulder, "Let it go, man, just let it go."

Chapter Three

"Pizza always hits the spot, especially after a weird funeral service. Ties never were my favorite article of clothing," Luc Sterling said as he loosened his. He sat on the sofa in Micah's apartment and promptly propped his feet up on the coffee table. "I don't see why you have such a fascination for them."

Micah walked by and shoved his friend's feet to the floor. "Because I like them, that's why. You want a Coke?"

"Ice in mine," his friend said. "Can't see how you drink it warm."

After pouring the soda, Micah sat down beside his friend. "What are your plans for tonight?"

"Nothing major. I thought I'd hang out with a friend and watch a movie or three."

"Any particular friend in mind, Sterling?"

"Yeah, I got this one friend who stays up half the night who wouldn't mind my company. And since you're letting me hang out with you I'll be generous. You can pick the first movie."

"You'll keep your lips shut and watch whatever I pick?"

Luc swallowed a mouthful of Coke and nodded.

Micah chose a DVD and slid it into the player. When the movie's opening theme began, Luc started shaking his head violently.

"Graves, not this one."

"Huh uh," Micah countered. "You said my choice. You said you'd keep your lips shut and watch. So, watch."

"That was before I knew what it was."

"Just watch it."

Luc threw himself against the back of the sofa, arms crossed. Micah attempted to ignore him. It was night in the movie. The camera panned across the water, toward bright lights and laughter. Music played as people amused themselves up and down the boardwalk.

"I cannot believe you are going to submit me to the two Coreys, dude. Cruel and unusual punishment. I know my rights."

"You have the right to remain silent and you have the right to be hit in the back of the head. Take your pick."

Scenes changed. A mother in a station wagon with her two sons.

"Quit pouting." Micah slowly let out a breath. "It's a vampire movie; you like vampire movies."

"Not this one. I liked it until the Coreys saturated the market. They were in every other movie ever made."

"A bit of an exaggeration, don't you think?"

"No."

"There's nothing wrong with *The Lost Boys*. It's an awesome movie; the only thing that would've made it better would have been to have Lita Ford on the soundtrack."

"I don't wanna watch it."

"Suffer."

"I like *Vamp* better." Luc reached for his glass of soda before turning to Micah. "Did I ever tell you I met Grace Jones?"

"About three times."

He took a drink and said, "She was cool. Signed my…"

"She signed your t-shirt, I know. Would you rather watch Grace tear the hearts out of people?"

Luc smiled.

"You act like a baby when you don't get your way."

"Nuh uh."

"Yeah, that's a mature response," Micah said, getting up to change the DVD.

Luc stuck his tongue out at him.

"Boy, if I had known what a pain in the ass you'd turn out to be, I would have never introduced myself to you."

"But then you never would have known the joy of having me in your life."

Micah looked at his friend on the sofa, who blew him a kiss. "Yeah, it's been a real joy," he said. "Right up there with genital warts."

"Funny. What a sense of humor. Are you going to change the damned disc before the end of this movie or what?" He drained his glass and got up to go to the kitchen for more. "You want anything while I'm out here?"

As he switched DVDs in the player, Micah muttered to himself, "I curse the day you were born, Sterling."

"What was that?" Luc called from the other room.

"I said you should make us some popcorn," he said as he put the new DVD in.

"Great idea. You got any of those flavored toppings left? I liked the barbecue best. The white cheddar tasted like mold."

Micah walked into the kitchen and said, "And how much mold have you been eating to know what it tastes like?"

Luc was looking in one of the cabinets. He closed the door as he turned around and said, "Dude, everybody's eaten a slice of bread or a piece of cheese that had a spot of mold on it."

"Not everybody."

"Don't tell me you never did."

"Nope."

"Not even when you wanted a sandwich and only had two slices of bread left?"

"Not even then."

Luc shook his head. "Where are the flavors for the corn? I can't find them."

Micah pointed to the cabinet over the stove. "And the popcorn's in there, too. Make whatever flavors you want and then maybe we can watch the movie in peace."

Pouring the kernels into the popper, Luc talked over his shoulder. "Did I tell you about the woman who submitted an article to the magazine?"

"What woman?"

"You know who I'm talking about," he explained. "The one who keeps trying to get herself into the magazine. This time she wrote an article about Camry Park. It's all about the family picnic she had there and how disgusted she was by all the used condoms and needles she saw around the statue of General Augustus Camry. She's on her soapbox in the article, saying how the park's in a state of disgrace and how she can't enjoy an outing there without exposing her family to the unsavory elements of our society."

"You going to run it?" Micah asked.

"I don't know. May get me some flack from the owners if I print something like that. They much prefer happy stories about the community."

"An image of the statue of GAC covered in used prophylactics and hypodermic needles would tend to throw most of the people around here into hysterics."

"That could be the cover photo!" Luc laughed. "You think it would be our biggest selling issue so far?"

"Could be the issue that gets your editorial butt kicked out the door." The kernels started popping and Micah grabbed a bowl out of the cupboard. "Is it worth risking your job to expose the seedier side of our community?"

"If the community is so protective of the park and the statue," Luc said as he added flavoring to the popcorn, "why doesn't someone clean up the trash instead of leaving it strewn all over the place?"

"Because becoming full of righteous indignation over an article airing dirty laundry requires less energy than actually cleaning up the park." Micah helped himself to a handful of popcorn. "You seem to dwell on the darker side of things when you write."

Luc unplugged the popper before speaking. "What makes you say that?"

"Come on," Micah said. "In the premiere issue, your cover story was the Swann-Griffin Aquarium tragedy. You devoted nearly half the magazine to it."

"Because it was big news. Ever hear the phrase 'if it bleeds, it leads?' Journalists live by it. And besides, didn't it hit home?"

"It was too close to home, Sterling. Not just in the same state, in the same county. It happened barely thirty miles away," Micah pointed out.

"And the people here are counting their blessings it didn't happen here. People are the same every where you go, my friend, whether it's in Cumberland, New Mystic, Grantsville, Idol, Eden Heights, or another city in some other state. Wherever you go, you see the same kinds of people."

"Maybe. But if that's how you feel, why did you move here?"

"You know why. They offered me the job heading the magazine a year ago," Luc said. "I would have been a fool to turn it down."

"Please, you could have found a job anywhere in the world. Why don't you go all the way and turn the magazine into a full-blown tabloid? You can dig up all the dirt in the tri-state area and run it for the world to see."

"I was only making a joke about the cover photo." Luc picked up the bowl of popcorn and grinned. "Do we have to have come to blows right now or can we go back to watching movies?"

"Let's change the subject."

"Okay." Luc popped a kernel of corn into his mouth. "Did you know approximately four thousand people each year are hurt by their toasters? Did you know in the last twenty years over two hundred people were killed by their toasters?"

"No, but I can go you one better," Micah said. "Did you know each year roughly forty-four thousand people are hurt or maimed by their toilets?"

"Shit."

"No shit."

Luc laughed. "And what about what's his name? The mortician guy?"

"Nicholson."

"Riese Nicholson," Luc said. "What a piece of work. He sure put the fun back in funeral, didn't he? Scared the living daylights out of me."

Micah shared the laugh before reaching for a handful of popcorn. "Are we okay now?"

"Yeah, let's watch *Vamp*."

"You so have to get over this Grace Jones fascination," Micah said. "It's not healthy. Maybe you should see a therapist."

Luc laughed. "Like you are so stable yourself, he who collects funeral cards."

"Everybody has to have a hobby."

"And Grace is mine."

Chapter Four

Monday morning Micah was greeted by the ringing of the phone as he unlocked the doors to his antique shop, the Sacred Scarab. He walked quickly to his office and picked up the cordless phone.

"Sacred Scarab, may I help you?"

"Micah?" the voice asked. "It's barely ten-thirty. I didn't expect you in before noon." David Cordone, one of his big-ticket customers, always on the lookout for a piece to add to his collection.

"Leslie needed the day off so I came in. What can I do for you?"

On the other end of the line, Cordone coughed before speaking. "Never get old, my boy; it's no damned fun at all."

The man hit eighty-three on his last birthday, but Micah said, "You have decades to go before you're old."

"Flattery'll get you mentioned in my will. I'm calling today to ask you to keep your eyes and ears open for something for me."

David Cordone possessed an appetite for antiquities, so Micah was intrigued. "And what might that be?"

"A statue. Very unique. You'll know it if you ever lay eyes upon it."

Micah sat on the edge of his desk and said, "What kind of paperwork do you have on the object?" Cordone kept his files up-to-date; he knew who owned what and who might be putting what up on the auction block. He had his finger on the pulse because he had a wish list of items he wanted to add to his collection.

"Well, therein lies the difficulty," he answered. "I don't even know for sure if the statue is in the country much less who might have it."

"Uh huh, I can see where that could be a problem. I can't make you any promises, but if you fax me a picture, I'll definitely see what I can find out about it."

He heard Cordone expel a breath—the man's constant companion was his oxygen tank. "The best I can do is fax you a sketch I had made."

"Sometimes a sketch is just as handy as a photo."

"I'll have my assistant fax it over this morning."

Micah reached for a pencil. "Why don't you tell me more about this statue and I'll make some notes; then I'll put my nose to the grindstone and see what information I can find out for you."

"A word of warning before I describe the item: Don't be too quick to think me senile when you begin your research."

He laughed. "I'd never think you'd gone around the bend; you're one of the most sensible people I've met. What makes you say that?"

"Because most people do not believe the statue exists; they believe it to be a myth," Cordone said.

The answer threw Micah for several seconds. "So," he said, "you would like me to see if I can find the whereabouts of a mythical statue?"

"But it does exist," Cordone insisted. "I was lucky enough to see it with my own eyes many years ago when I was a young fool."

"And that's how you know it's real and what it looks like. What exactly is it?" Micah asked.

"The statue itself is approximately a foot tall, maybe a few inches more. A winged ankh with a scarab beetle nestled in the oval of the head of the ankh."

Micah made a note of the description. "So we're looking for an Egyptian artifact."

"Not technically, my young friend."

Micah frowned. "The ankh makes me think it would be Egyptian in origin."

"Unless the Egyptians originated from somewhere else," Cordone said.

Cordone coughed again. "Surely, since you traffic in artifacts from ancient civilizations, you've heard the myths, the legends."

"Of?"

"The lost city of An'khyr. The basis for Atlantis."

Searching his thoughts, Micah drew a blank. "I can't recall anything about… what did you call it again?"

"An'khyr."

"I know about Atlantis, but I can't say I've ever come across a reference to An'khyr," Micah said slowly. "But before we go into all that, do you know if the statue was unearthed in Egypt and if it was, when?"

"I can't say for certain. Why?"

"It's important because prior to 1858 there was no control over the selling of antiquities. It wasn't until 1983 the Egyptian government passed a new antiquities law stating that any cultural artifact unearthed in that country after 1983 belonged to the country of Egypt," Micah said.

Cordone inhaled sharply. "I recall this law. My aged mind hasn't lost all its usefulness. Let me see. Yes, it means any object taken out of Egypt illegally, or what you would say was without legal title, from 1970 on and residing in any country that has recognized the convention must be returned to Egypt. Basically, everything before the specified time is free game. Like closing the barn door after the horses have escaped, if you ask me." The sound of Cordone's deep breaths came over the line. "Whew. That was a long speech for someone like me to get out. But to answer your question: that particular law does not apply to the statue I seek."

"Okay. That's one hurdle we don't have to jump," Micah said. "You said you actually saw the statue yourself. When did you see it?"

"As a child, back in the thirties. I remember it like it was yesterday," Cordone said. "Magnificently carved. I knew even then it was something special."

Micah shifted the phone to his other shoulder. "I'm sure it was. What do you remember about the statue?"

"Everything. I can close my eyes and see it as plain as if I were sitting here staring at it. The majestic wings, the scarab."

"David, you said it may have originated somewhere other than Egypt; you stated it may very well have come from the lost city of An'khyr. What makes you so sure? After all, the legend of Atlantis has never been proven and here we are talking about the legend that inspired the legend of Atlantis." Micah stopped for a few seconds. "I don't know what to think."

"I swear to the stars the statue exists. And I have devoted most of my life, since I first saw it, to researching An'khyr and finding the statue again."

"What happened to it after you saw it?" Micah said.

"It was sold to a private collector," Cordone answered. "He died in a mysterious fire that summer and the statue disappeared."

Twirling the pencil in his fingers, Micah asked, "Why enlist me in hunting for the statue now?"

Cordone said, "Because I have, over the ensuing years, come close numerous times to seeing it again."

"You said earlier you didn't know if it was in the country at this time."

"At this time is correct," Cordone said. "I have recently come across a snippet of information that leads me to believe the statue will eventually make its way here or will be brought here; I believe it will be put up for auction, possibly in the guise of an estate collection."

Intrigued, Micah asked, "What makes you think such a thing, David?"

Cordone answered simply, "The signs all point to it."

Before Micah could ask what he meant, David Cordone said, "You must forgive me, my young friend, but I believe this old body is telling me I need to have a bit of a rest. We'll have to continue this discussion at another time. My assistant just faxed you a copy of the sketch; it should come through any time now. We'll talk of An'khyr another time."

Before Micah could say goodbye, Cordone had hung up the phone. The fax machine on the occasional table buzzed to life and began to print. He walked over and grasped the paper coming out.

Rendered in black and white was the sketch of the winged ankh statue Cordone had promised.

The old guy wants me to chase a legend, he thought, *but if he says he's seen the statue himself...*

* * * * * * * * * * *

Later in the afternoon when the phone rang Micah wondered briefly if David Cordone had rested enough and was calling back.

"Sacred Scarab," he said.

"Micah, my friend," the female voice said. "This is Vanessa Archer."

He smiled because he was genuinely fond of the proprietor of Archer's Antiques. "Nice to hear from you, Vanessa. How's business in New Mystic?"

"Very good, thank you. And how is that blessed feline of yours?"

"Sia's doing well. He has a vet appointment in a week or so, but other than that he's a spitfire. What can I do for you today?"

She laughed. "I'm calling to ask if you heard about Johanna Edensburg's estate finally going on the auction block?"

"I did. Will you be going to the auction?"

"Yes, but only as an observer."

"You mean you aren't tempted to bid on a few things for yourself or your shop?" He laughed.

"Nope. Got a feeling the merchandise will be a tad ritzy for me and my shop. But I'm calling to ask if you would be going and if you are may I hitch a ride with you."

"Sure thing. Lansington's in Cumberland will be packed to the rafters for this auction," Micah said. "Collectors from D.C. and the rest of the country will come."

"Who are you kidding? I bet collectors from all around the world will fly in for the occasion. Johanna's collection was the envy of many a person."

"Tell me about it. Her jewelry alone could take up the better part of a day on the block," Micah said.

"Highly doubtful her jewelry will be up for grabs," Vanessa said. "I believe the lot will consist of her South and Central American artifacts."

Micah took a sip of his soda. "I never could understand why she was fascinated by the sacrificial and ceremonial daggers of the Aztecs, Incans, and Mayans."

"She saw the beauty in them, I suppose. There will be several statues, as well," Vanessa said. "Some Egyptian, some Roman, some Greek. You may be interested in some of those for your clients, Micah."

He scratched his cheek before responding. "Quite possibly."

"Be all mysterious." She laughed. "The second auction is the one I will be interested in."

"The furniture. I understand she had a lovely Victorian bed."

"Yep. And if I have my way, I'll be getting that for one of my customers. You do know Storm Cassavettes?" she said.

"Of course. We met briefly after the terrible tragedy at the Swann-Griffin Aquarium." Micah remembered he was intrigued by the personality of the man: more than confident but not quite arrogant. "Very nice fellow."

"Oh, he's a sweetheart once you really get to know him. We'll have to invite you over the next time Storm, Nannette Dupres, Khris King, and I get together. You'll simply fall in love with his home, Micah."

"From the bits you've told me about," he said, "I'm sure I will."

She laughed. "Anyway, I just wanted to call you up and chat for a few minutes. We have a few weeks before the auction, how about we make our arrangements later because I know you have work to do."

"It was good to hear from you, Vanessa."

"Always a pleasure." She hung up the phone.

He picked up the sketch once more and looked at it. As if the research for antiquities wasn't difficult enough, the tracking down of an alleged myth might prove to be too much.

But he put the winged ankh out of his mind as he busied himself with readying the paperwork for several pieces his client Xavier Hunsford would be driving down from Grantsville to pick up later that same afternoon: a piece of a Roman tablet, several coins, and a small chalice.

* * * * * * * * * * *

After Mr. Hunsford collected his packages, Micah decided to call it an evening since it was six o'clock. Sia was happy to see him when he returned home; the black cat rubbed against his calf as soon as he walked into the house.

"You really happy to see me or do you just want some treats?"

The cat looked up at him and meowed loudly.

"And just think, you've seen more of the world than most people," Micah said. Sia had come to the United States from Egypt after a brief stop in Romania and Iraq. The cat had been saved from a life, and probably an early death, on the streets of Cairo by a kind Middle Eastern doctor who took the cat with him when he traveled first to Constanta, Romania, then to Kirkuk, Iraq, to visit family before returning to the States. Micah had adopted the cat because Sia didn't interact well with the other cats the doctor's family owned. The doctor bid Sia a fond farewell but knew he would have a good home with Micah. The black cat lived with Micah ever since, becoming his constant companion.

Micah gave Sia a few treats which the cat alternately growled and purred over while he snacked.

Yawning, Micah said, "Tired, but I still have work to do. Time to supplement my income."

He went into his home office and sat in the chair behind the desk. Micah penned a moderately successful paperback series of bodice rippers under the pseudonym Iamma Trampp. Preferring to keep his identity under wraps, he was able to utilize his creative outlet to the best advantage. No book signings. Readers desiring an autographed copy of one of his bawdy books could either mail a copy to him for him to sign and send back or they could purchase a copy already inscribed from his website.

Sia padded softly into the room and jumped to his regular position on Micah's lap. The cat would curl or sit there for hours while Micah worked; Micah would absentmindedly stroke the cat's fur when he stopped to ponder or read something he'd written.

"What do you think, buddy?" he asked his feline companion. "Is this new idea worthy of Ms. Trampp's name?"

The cat looked into his eyes and meowed.

Micah laughed. "You always say it's a good idea. This romance business is easy enough to write about; it's all make-believe. If only it were that easy in real life: intriguing and still wind up with a happy ending."

He continued typing, his fingers caressing the keyboard. But try as he might to concentrate on the story, his mind returned time and time again to David Cordone and the winged ankh statue and, before he realized, he had written the hunt for a supposedly mythical statue into the plot of the book. The dark-eyed Romany woman with the raven hair and the blond Englishman with the green and gold eyes were soon pursuing a statue of their own from the mountains of

Romania to the London museum; hot on their trail, a cadre of foot soldiers loyal to an evil man intent on capturing the statue and wielding its dark power.

Two hours later, Sia shifted and broke Micah's concentration.

"Wow. This story is shaping up to be something else, don't you think?" He read the last few lines he'd written. "I think it'll capture the imagination of Ms. Trampp's readers. And it could catapult me into the Romance Writers' Hall of Fame."

Sia stretched and looked up at Micah before jumping to the floor and walking out of the room.

"You could have just said you didn't like the idea," he called after the cat.

Before calling it quits for the night with his writing, Micah saved the manuscript to disk. He never forgot the sinking feeling in his stomach the night his computer died, taking with it the completed manuscript for his first novel, three days before the publisher's deadline. Working from a rough draft of the manuscript and trying to remember all the changes he'd made nearly drove him insane, that and the lack of sleep over those three long days and nights.

An image of the winged ankh statue floated to the forefront of his mind. Crystal clear, it mesmerized him for a few seconds until he shook his head and stood up.

"Chasing shadows," he muttered. "An old man's fantasy."

But Cordone had been adamant about the statue existing. And he claimed to have actually seen it. He couldn't be imagining the entire thing, could he?

I'll have to do a bit of research on my own before I decide it'll be worth my time and effort to go any further; dig a little deeper before I write it off and move on.

Old Man Cordone was a good customer; Micah didn't want to dismiss him without giving him a chance.

No need to jump to conclusions or make a decision right at this moment, he told himself. *Mr. Cordone has certainly led me on what I thought were wild goose chases in the past and he's always delivered the goods.*

Always a business man, Micah's thoughts soon turned to Lansington's auction of Johanna Edensburg's collection. Quite a few of his clientele dabbled in daggers; some were of course more serious collectors than others. He could find more than a couple treasures at the auction. In addition to serving clients through his shop Sacred Scarab, Micah also went to a number of auctions on missions from his clients who either couldn't or didn't wish to attend the auctions themselves.

"I'm a glorified personal shopper," he joked to friends.

Micah had made good friends through his business dealings, one of which was Vanessa Archer. The two dealers dealt in two separate trades. Micah preferred the more high-end items of ancient civilizations while Vanessa's passion was furniture and ornamental objects.

Still, the two had struck up a friendship that led them to attending various auctions together, a lot of times in Vanessa's pick-up.

The doorbell rang, breaking Micah's train of thought.

"Gotta be Sterling," he said as he made sure he'd saved the document he was working on. "Hold your horses, I'm coming."

He made it to the front door just as it opened and Luc Sterling walked in.

"Dude, you look half asleep," Sterling said.

"If you're going to walk in, why do you bother ringing the bell or pounding on the door?" Micah asked.

"To give you ample warning to get your clothes on before anybody sees you nekkid," he said as he shut the door.

"You're a pain in the ass," Micah told him.

"A royal pain?"

"A common pain."

Luc made himself at home, getting a soda before taking a seat on the sofa. He leaned forward and picked up a photo album from the top of the coffee table.

He opened the cover before saying to Micah: "Graves, you really have to stop looking through these like they were a stamp collection. It's depressing, and that's something you don't need."

"It's my collection," Micah said.

Placing the album back on the table top, Luc said, "One thing to collect memorial cards, another to sit and look through them. You said yourself you can't remember each funeral because you've been to so many. Why do you put yourself through it night after night? Throw them away."

Micah sat down and formulated his answer. "I look through them in the hope I'll remember seeing or feeling something at one of the funerals that will help me find the answer I'm looking for."

Luc breathed audibly. "Your mom."

"Why she smiled right before she died." Micah smiled weakly at him. "I know it sounds weird."

"Hey, no weirder than why I've been cruising funerals, my friend." Luc tipped his can of soda in Micah's direction. "It's what drew us to each other. And I guess if it helps you to go through these things," he gestured toward the albums, "I suppose I can't burn them. But I wish you wouldn't force yourself to do it every day of your life. Can't be good for you"

"Like I said, I keep hoping I'll remember something."

Luc leaned forward and said, "What exactly are you hoping to see? You never really explained what you mean."

Micah shrugged. "I don't know. A clue, maybe."

"Well, Hardly Boy, I can tell you this: clues in this life are few and far between. You could be looking until it's your time to go."

"A sign would be nice."

"A sign of what?"

"Something to tell me my mother went to a better place, a place where her suffering ended."

"From what you've told me about her smile," Luc said softly, "my guess is she was going to where there is no more pain."

Blinking tears from his eyes, Micah said, "I'd like to think so."

"But isn't that what it says in the Bible? There will be no more hurt? Don't you believe an angel came to spirit her soul to her reward?"

"I don't know exactly what I believe," he answered.

"Seems to me, and don't bite my head off when I say this, you might be looking more for something to believe in than why your mom died with a smile on her face," Luc told him. "I'm not saying it to piss you off or anything but did you ever consider that? Not finding the answer you've been looking for might mean you're not asking the right question."

Micah smiled. "You may be onto something. I could be making myself depressed for nothing."

"Let me ask you one question."

"Okay."

"Does it help you to sit here for hours on end scrutinizing these memorial cards?" Luc asked. "Does it provide any relief?"

Micah grimaced instead of answering.

"Guess that's my answer. Basically, you're torturing yourself. You understand?"

Micah nodded.

"Then don't you think you should wean yourself off these albums? I'm not asking you to throw them out or anything. Just slowly stop the obsession."

"I agree," Micah said. "We can still go to funerals and search for the truth."

"Absolutely, my friend. And I think you'll have more luck at a live, pardon the expression, funeral than with these."

"I do have a life to lead and I've spent way too many hours pouring over those cards hoping for a divine revelation."

"My thoughts exactly." Luc took another drink of his soda. "So what's on the books for tonight? Dinner and a movie?"

Micah stared at him.

"Okay, okay. I can take a hint. You got better things to do than spend every waking, non-working minute with me. I should be doing some editor-type thing anyway."

"Magazines don't edit and publish themselves. Speaking of which, did you ever come to a decision on the story about Camry Park and the statue of General Augustus Camry?"

"GAC? Lovely sound, isn't it?" Luc laughed. "To answer your question: yes, I did come to a conclusion."

"And?"

"You'll have to wait, along with the rest of the general populace, until the magazine comes out."

With that, Luc left and Micah burst out laughing.

Interlude

She awoke with a sense of urgency. At first, she'd thought her bladder had received a call from nature. Over the course of the last few months, as the baby grew inside her, her body had changed or reacted in ways she never thought possible. She made more trips to the bathroom on an hourly basis than she ever did in a day pre-pregnancy. But her bladder wasn't the culprit this time.

Maybe someone had rung the doorbell. She eased herself into a sitting position and slowly stood. Being nearly seven and a half months along, she still hadn't adjusted to the awkward balancing act called "walking while pregnant."

"You should be twins," she said to the child sheltered inside her. "You eat enough for two, and I'm certainly big enough to house twins."

Her swollen ankles complained, a feeling to which she'd grown accustomed, so she ignored the complaints as best she could. A peek through the sheers revealed no one on the porch. Opening the door anyway, she leaned out to see if anyone lurked in the shadows.

"Nope," she spoke again to her unborn child and shut the door. "Your mama's gone crazy."

A few steps later, a wave of dizziness washed over her. Nausea soon followed. She leaned against the nearest wall for support. Pressing her forehead against the cool, smooth surface, she waited for the sensations to abate. Her stomach heaved and emptied its contents onto the floor. She needed to lie back down on the sofa and wait for it to pass.

The headache hit her with full force before she took five steps. The world around her looked out of focus. It was devoid of color; in its place were shades of gray. Her eyes went to the rooster clock on the wall as it crowed the hour. One in the afternoon and the gray tones made it feel closer to late evening.

She'd never felt this sick before in her life. Even her morning sickness paled in comparison. The headache throbbed behind her eyes; all she wanted was to lie down, close her eyes, and ride it out.

In the corner of the living room, away from the windows, the figure took shape. She saw it from the corner of her eye and turned.

A man.

"Who are you?" she demanded. "How did you get in here? What do you want?"

"I've come for the child, Miranda," he said.

"What?" A spasm erupted within her and she clutched her belly. "No!"

"Yes," the man said. "He is a life not meant to be."

"Are you Death?"

He blinked and said, "In a manner of speaking."

She was scared.

The man reached out a hand. "There's no need to have fear."

She shook her head violently. "Get out. My husband is on his way home."

"Your husband is out of town," he said. "There is no need to lie when I know the truth. Fate cannot be denied."

She gasped and fell; her body was numb. The man came to kneel beside her and placed his hand upon her abdomen.

Barely above a whisper, he said, "This small soul not meant to be; come now, child, and come with me. Cry not, small one, for loss of life. Just reach out to take my hand; feel the warmth in my touch and I'll guide you to the Mourning Light."

Miranda's eyes fluttered shut and she realized when she woke she'd have no memory of the man who came to take her unborn child. A tear spilled from the corner of her eye and softly traced its path. Grief was the last emotion she had before the dark claimed her.

Chapter Five

The obituary attracted his attention. He couldn't imagine what it must feel like to have your child die, a part of you die. Micah slowly shook his head as he continued reading. *Did she feel him die? Did she know what was happening to her and her unborn son?*

A service was to be held at the Grace Memorial Building in Rose Hill Cemetery. Wasn't it a requirement for all towns and cities to have a cemetery named Rose Hill or some derivation of it? One small service to celebrate one small life before the urn was placed in the columbarium.

He reached for the phone and dialed the number for Luc's office.

"Did you read the obits today?" he asked as soon as his friend answered the phone. "Did you read it?"

"Obits? I need a better clue."

"The obituary for the baby," Micah explained. He heard Luc turning what sounded like pages and assumed his friend was looking through the newspaper.

"Found it. Gimme a second." Luc Sterling whispered softly as he read. "That's sad. Their hearts must be broke, the parents."

"It almost reminds me of Barbara Eden."

"How do you mean?"

"Her baby died in utero," Micah said as he folded his newspaper, "and her doctors explained to her, for sake of her own health, she would have to carry the baby to term. She literally carried a dead child, all the while having to endure people coming up to her and asking about the baby or making the usual comments people make when they spy a pregnant woman."

"That is one of the most incredible things I have ever heard," Luc said. "How do you know about it?"

"I saw it on her *E! True Hollywood Story*. It was on late one night and I couldn't sleep, so I thought I'd waste an hour watching television." After pausing for a second, Micah continued. "She's always been one of my favorite actresses but, after seeing that, I have a whole new respect for the woman."

"And seeing the obituary for the baby made you think of Barbara Eden?"

"Not really. The obituary made me think we should go and pay our respects."

Luc made a sound on the other end of the phone. "More like it made you think you should go and see if a sign will be given unto you."

Micah couldn't deny the accuracy of the statement. Instead of answering, he curled the newspaper in his hands.

"I see I hit the nail on the head," Luc said. "But I understand. Two o'clock on Thursday—tomorrow. I'll go with you, unless you're too mad at me."

"No, I'm not angry," Micah said. "I actually called to ask if you wanted to come along, since you're my funeral-going buddy."

Laughter came from the phone. "Something about that statement seems inherently wrong. One of these days, we are going to have to invest in some heavy therapy."

"One day," Micah agreed, "but not today, or any day soon."

"Rose Hill's not too far from your place, so how about I swing by and pick you up about quarter 'til? We'll have plenty of time to make it there."

"Sounds like a plan."

"Just don't get your hopes up too high," Luc advised. "I don't want you disappointed and getting even more depressed."

Micah bristled a little. "I don't get depressed."

"Yeah? What do you call it?"

"Disappointed about covers it." He rubbed a hand over his face. "I've been searching for what feels like forever; I'd just like some verification. Something."

"And one day you'll have it," Luc assured him. "Trust me."

* * * * * * * * * * *

David Cordone called again that afternoon.

"Micah, my boy," Cordone said after they'd exchanged pleasantries. "I know I haven't given you much time to make any progress before I touched base with you, but I figured an intelligent young man such as yourself would have some nugget of information to do an old man's heart good."

"It's only been three days so I don't have much to report," Micah admitted, reaching for the folder on his desk. "Mostly results from internet searches."

He heard the old man draw a ragged breath before Cordone spoke. "Anything is good. What do you have?"

Micah opened the folder and began to share the information. "Not a whole lot other than speculation. Most of the information I've come across regarding the winged ankh statue purports it to be an object of complete fiction, a myth."

"Yes, many believe it to be such."

"But there are those who believe it to be real."

"We are few and far between, my young friend," Cordone said. "But we are out there, searching for it, waiting for it to make itself known."

Micah paused. *Twice now Cordone has made reference to the statue making itself known. Did he believe it had the ability to remain hidden, only to surface when it chose?*

"What else have you uncovered?"

"Not much. One article I found referenced a collector, one Abraham Caligaria, who died when a fire broke out in his home back in the early thirties."

"Caligaria, that would be the man who had possession," Cordone said.

"The article stated he was a collector of what were termed crypto-artifacts—objects that could not be attributed to any known civilizations," Micah continued. "After the fire and in later years, it came to light that what remained of his collection—what survived the fire—consisted of fakes, hoax artifacts, and his reputation suffered."

"Yes, yes," Cordone said irritably, "I know all about the mermaid skeletons and the alien remains and the like. But the man did possess several genuine artifacts, among those few was the statue I am so interested in obtaining."

"The accidental fire that took his life—"

"Accidental fire, my ass," Cordone interrupted, "Caligaria was murdered."

"Nowhere did I see anything claiming he was murdered," Micah said.

"He was murdered by a person or persons unknown for the statue, if not by the statue itself."

"What do you base this on?" Micah asked.

"I base it on the fact the fire was awfully convenient."

Sitting down, Micah said, "That would be why it was ruled accidental."

"Arson cover-up," Cordone asserted.

Micah sought to change the direction of the conversation. "You've said you have come close numerous times over the years to laying eyes on the statue again. Tell me what you mean."

Cordone took a labored breath before speaking. "In the late 1970's I happened to be in Budapest, a stop-over visit on my way back from Egypt, to visit a colleague. He'd been making noises over the course of several months about coming into possession of something I would be very interested in, in his words. I could get no other information out of him. All he would say is the object was something from my past, and I should pay him a visit and he would end the mystery."

The story had captured Micah's attention. "What happened?"

"Once in Hungary, I phoned my colleague to tell him I was on my way. He told me he eagerly awaited my arrival. He did allow one thing to slip: he said he was excited to see the look on my face when I saw the *statue*."

"Obviously referring to the winged ankh statue," Micah said.

"Of course, that was and still is my opinion."

"Why didn't you get to see it?"

Cordone's breathing had become even raspier than normal. "Because when I arrived at my colleague's home, it was impossible to enter. The house was conflagrant. Reduced to rubble and ash in a matter of hours."

"And your colleague?"

"Trapped inside and burned with the house and all its contents." Cordone was silent for a moment. "This is but one more example of my coming close to seeing the statue again, only to be deterred."

"What happened the other times?" Micah asked.

"Twice more I thought I would see it, touch it," Cordone answered. "Each time it was not to be. Each time fire reigned. So you see what I mean when I say these accidental fires are not accidents?"

He understood where the old man would see a conspiracy. "Yes, I do see how you could come to such a conclusion. But do you believe it is to keep you from coming into contact with the statue?"

"Of course not," Cordone said. "At least, not to keep only me away. My belief is the time for the statue to surface had not yet come."

"But now you believe the time may have come?"

"Yes, I believe it may have come," Cordone said. "The signs all point to it."

Again with the signs pointing to it.

"Which is why I have contacted you and assigned you the task of tracking down and obtaining the statue for me."

"I'm doing my best," Micah assured him. "I only wish I had more to go on than a handful of internet articles."

"Have faith, my young friend," Cordone told him. "When the time is right, you will find you have all the knowledge you need to perform the task I have assigned to you. I have faith in you."

The old man's labored breathing traveled over the phone lines. Micah didn't want to press him, but he needed to ask another question before he ended the conversation.

"You've mentioned An'khyr," he said, "and I would like to hear a little more about it. I've yet to do any research on that end and I thought you could give me some background so I know what I'm supposed to be looking for."

Cordone laughed, a low garbled sound. "Yes, my body failed me before I could fill you in on the subject." He coughed several times before continuing. "I believe I mentioned An'khyr was the truth behind the fable of Atlantis."

"Yes, sir."

"A civilization built upon magic as much as science. In fact, magic and science were held in the highest regards. An island paradise, much like the myth of Atlantis, where the citizens lived in harmony. Exotic creatures, including many extinct today, imported from all parts of the world roamed the wonderful city. It is my understanding the An'khyrians held ocean life in the highest regard—building massive aquariums for all to marvel at the specimens."

Micah interrupted him. "Much like what is attributed to Atlantis in the folklore."

"Very much so. It has been speculated," Cordone continued, "that supernatural—preternatural, if you prefer—creatures lived alongside mortals."

"Such as what exactly?"

"Vampires, practitioners of magic, wereanimals, among others," Cordone said. "All living together in the city. Lavish gardens and temples decorated with precious metals and stones. Truly a paradise on earth."

"Was the destruction of An'khyr much like what is said to have happened to Atlantis?" Micah asked.

"Very much, but with one exception," Cordone said. "Instead of angering the gods and being destroyed, the magical structure of the city was eaten away—destroyed by a horrific force: the Scarabae.

"It is believed," Cordone continued the history lesson, "in certain circles, that citizens of An'khyr who had been in other parts of the world along with the survivors who escaped the destruction of the city were responsible for seeding the great civilizations of the world."

"Meaning," Micah said tentatively, "civilizations such as Egyptian, Greek, Roman, Aztec, Incan, et cetera?"

"Correct, my boy."

"And An'khyr is the civilization to which you attribute the statue of the winged ankh?"

"Also correct," Cordone said. "We believe it to be one of the few, if not only, surviving relic mankind has discovered."

"That's why you prize it," Micah said. "Because it's truly one of a kind?"

"For one reason," Cordone answered. "And because it almost certainly is a key to something."

"Key?"

"A key quite literally," Cordone said. "The statue itself is flush on the back, flat. Like it was made to fit into a specific spot. And knowing civilizations like those we spoke of were fond of such keys, if you will, I believe our statue is also a key."

"To what?"

"Of that I have no clue as of yet," Cordone said. "Let us take one step at a time, shall we? The first being we locate the statue."

"I'm taking a lot on faith here," Micah admitted.

"Sometimes all we have is faith."

Micah thought about merely shining the old man on, not wanting to waste precious time to chase a shadow, but something told him Cordone didn't believe he was sending him on a wild goose chase.

"Of course, I will be compensating you on time spent," Cordone told him. "I don't expect you to spend your time on me for free."

"That is a mighty gesture on your part."

* * * * * * * * * * *

Research had a way of consuming your time. Micah had spent nearly three hours surfing the worldwide web in search of references to the lost city of An'khyr.

"Where's Leonard Nimoy when you need him?" he muttered. "Busy with the Loch Ness Monster and the Yeti probably."

He glanced at the pile of paper on the left side of his desk—information he'd printed out. It was about four inches in height. Patting the top of the stack with one hand, he knew he had nothing much to go on. Most of the information was a rehash of things David Cordone already told him.

What fascinated him the most were the articles concerning the number of close similarities between the Egyptian civilization in Africa and the Aztecs and Incas in Central and South America. For groups of people with a vast ocean between them, many aspects of their cultures were nearly identical: from their temples and religions to their studies of astronomy and other sciences. Magical beliefs, very similar in nature, played important roles in most of the ancient civilizations.

"It may all be a conspiracy theory," Micah said to himself, "but the hard evidence is difficult to deny. I can see where people would think these cultures descended from a common one."

And just as dumb luck would have it, he spied the word *Scarabae* in the article he was reading.

How do you like that?

The author of the article, in a brief paragraph, described the Scarabae as "an unknown force that literally and secretly ate away the magic the city of An'khyr was built upon and used to protect itself. The damage was too vast to be repaired and the city was destroyed."

Micah searched for any footnotes the author may have made, any points of reference, but there were none.

"Ain't that a bitch?" he said. "To find mention of it and then hit a brick wall. But if I found one thing on it, I'll find more."

He printed the article and added it to the growing pile on his desk before shutting down the computer so he could close the Sacred Scarab for the night. Tomorrow would be emotionally draining. Funerals always sucked away his energy. Maybe it was because of the way he'd build it up in his mind, promising himself each time this would be the time he'd find the all important clue.

Maybe Sterling is right, he thought. *I need to just let it go, quit pursuing it so vehemently, and then maybe something will happen.*

Too much heavy thinking. Like the famous literary character said, tomorrow was another day and he'd think about it then.

Micah double-checked to make sure everything was in order before turning out the lights and closing up shop. Leslie would open in the morning as usual and take care of business until he came in after the interment.

Chapter Six

Lightning split the sky and the crash of thunder echoed. The overcast sky made everything feel dark and moody. Large drops of water fell and splattered everywhere. Another day of Rain Falls living up to its name.

It reminded Micah of his mother's funeral.

Normally the rain made him sleepy and he wanted nothing more than to curl up in the blankets and dream the day away.

This Thursday, however, he was up earlier—but not that much earlier—than his usual crack of noon-thirty and in a mood as dark and foul as the day outside.

"Shit. Damn. Hell," he cussed in the shower when the hot water mysteriously and suddenly cut to cold.

Grabbing for the faucets to turn off the arctic blast, he slipped on the slick surface of the tub and fell sideways out of the tub, taking the shower curtain with him. He landed on the tiled floor, wrapped up in the clear plastic.

And cussed some more.

"Piss. Bitch." He attempted to stand while the profanities spewed from his mouth. And whacked his head off the side of the sink. "Motherf—"

Sia peered around the corner and stared at him.

"I know, I know," he said, still on the floor and rubbing his head. "No more f-bombs. I promised."

The cat opened its mouth as if to answer and then closed it, apparently deciding silence was a virtue, and walked away.

"No, don't worry about me," he called after the cat. "I'm fine, really. Just maybe a subdural hematoma. No worries. I don't need you to call 9-1-1. But thanks for offering." Rubbing what he would swear was an apple-sized knot rising on the side of his head, he tried to stand and decided maybe it would be better to sit a while longer. "It's probably a tumor," he said, and then realized the water was still running.

He reached over to turn the faucets off. When the water splashed his arm he felt the heat: the hot water was back.

"Son of bi—" A great clap of thunder stopped him before he could finish the swear word. "Yeah, I get it: no more bad cuss words."

He turned off the water so he could stand and hang the shower curtain back in place. "Good thing it didn't tear." Once again Sia made an appearance.

Micah glared at him. "Don't even think about asking for a treat after leaving me for dead on the floor," he said, "Or I'll pick you up and give you a bath."

The cat sat down in the doorway and bathed his front paw, all the while staring straight at Micah.

He laughed. "I'm just kidding; I know you had nothing to do with it. Or did you? You were plotting my death so you can collect the insurance money?"

The cat turned and stretched, raising its tail high in the air.

"I know that means 'kiss my ass' in cat language, Sia." Micah leaned against the wall. "Which I don't have to put up with."

He hung the shower curtain in place and put down several towels to absorb the water on the floor before climbing back into the bathtub to finish his shower.

* * * * * * * * * * *

By the time Micah finished his shower and picked the wet towels off the floor, he discovered the clock had sped up and it was now close to noon. Later than what he thought it would be, but he still had plenty of time to finish getting dressed.

He turned the television on and switched the channel to one of the 80's music stations. Joan Jett was singing about how much she loved rock and roll.

"Thank God for satellite radio," he said. "Keep us safe from Top 40."

Walking into the closet, once a spare bedroom, he scanned the clothes hanging on the racks. He looked at his suits, about thirteen of them, before selecting a new gray jacket and pants. He needed a shirt; a plain white one would do nicely. Next came the ties. Micah's collection had officially reached the one hundred mark a few days earlier when he bought numbers ninety-nine, one hundred, and one hundred one. He reached for the ties, allowing the cool silk to glide over his hand like water from a mountain stream, before choosing a medium pink one to go with the suit.

In the living room, the music changed; the opening synthesizer caught Micah's ear. One of his favorite 80's songs: "Take On Me."

"A-Ha." He laughed and started singing along with the Norwegian band as he began to get dressed.

Sia sauntered into the closet and made it plain he wanted something to eat.

"Didn't I fill your bowl with food last night before I went to sleep?" he asked the cat. "Go eat that if you're hungry; I'm not giving you treats this early."

The cat obviously didn't like those comments; he dug his claws deeply into the carpet while looking at Micah.

"Don't even think about it," Micah warned. "How much carpet do you think I'm going to let you destroy?"

Sia sat down and pulled his claws from the carpet. He meowed.

"If you give me five more minutes," Micah promised, "I will give you a treat or three. But only if you quit ripping out pieces of the carpet. Agreed?"

The cat looked at him and blinked.

"I guess that's my answer."

He buttoned his shirt and put on his tie before heading to the kitchen to get the promised treats. Sia followed him, weaving around his ankles in proverbial cat fashion, and rushed into the kitchen to sit in front of the refrigerator.

"You need to remember who's in charge around here, my furry friend," Micah said. "Because it's not going to change unless you get a job and start contributing to the purchase of treats."

He bent down and held out a treat to the cat who began sniffing suspiciously at it.

"Like you don't know what it is," Micah said. "Like you don't wolf them down every chance you get. Be a good boy and just eat it."

Sia stopped sniffing at the treat, looked up at him, and walked away, leaving the treat in Micah's hand.

"I see how it is, your majesty. I am at your beck and call; I'm only here to serve you." He stood and put the treat back in the bag and the bag back in the cupboard. "See if you get any more today. Don't ask again until tomorrow."

As Micah went to finish getting dressed the song on the satellite station changed: Robert Palmer singing about how he didn't mean to turn someone on.

By twelve forty-five, Micah was fully dressed and searching the kitchen for something quick and easy to eat for breakfast. He found frozen pancakes in the freezer and popped two in the toaster oven. Music floated in from the living room and he recognized another one of his favorite songs, one of the two that could be his personal anthem: "Don't Pay the Ferryman" by Chris De Burgh—a song he knew was not about paying the cost of the ride until the ferryman gets you to the other side of the River Styx. It seemed to sum up Micah's quest for answers.

He shared his pancakes, smeared with butter and strawberry preserves, with Sia. The cat daintily ate each tiny piece Micah cut and held out for him.

"Better than those treats, huh?"

After they finished their breakfast, Micah went to his computer to check email. He pressed the space bar to turn off to aquarium screensaver and accessed his account. Fans of his paperback romance series often sent emails asking all sorts of questions, if he was lucky. On days when his luck didn't hold out, the emails contained way more information than he ever wanted to know about someone's sex life. Some of the fans were a bit eager and liked to share things from their private lives in case she—his pseudonym Iamma Trampp—found it interesting or needed an idea or two for one of her books.

None of those today, please, he said to himself.

The emails were of the former variety instead of the latter, so he graciously emailed back a somewhat form letter from Ms. Trampp saying how wonderful it was to hear from her loyal readers, thanking the fan for taking the time to send her an email.

Often he worried about some overzealous fan discovering his true identity, because his worst nightmare was the loss of his privacy. That and the loss of the modest income he received as the author of those bawdy bodice rippers. The money certainly did come in handy, even though he made a nice living owning and operating the Sacred Scarab.

By the time Luc walked through the front door at one-thirty, Micah was singing along with his second anthem.

"It may be her last night of sadness," Luc said, "but you have only happier days ahead of you, so don't go getting all depressed."

"Hey, 'Don't Fear the Reaper' is a classic, dude. How can you pick on such a song?"

Luc shrugged. "Maybe it's the cow bell."

"It's a cult phenom," Micah said. "It's not technically an 80's song, but she likes to play it every once in awhile."

"You ready to go soon or do I have to wait around while you finish primping?"

"I am ready, or I will be as soon as I put on my shoes," Micah answered. "What's the rush? We got a few minutes before we have to leave."

"Just don't want to be late; I know how you are about being on time for a funeral."

Micah walked by him and said, "It's not the funeral, remember? It's the placing of the urn."

"Same difference."

"You say tomato," Micah called over his shoulder, "and I say round red object into which a small explosive device can be inserted to blow unsuspecting salad bar patrons to smithereens."

Luc stood there shaking his head slowly before speaking. "You're sick, man. Just sick. Only your demented mind could come up with something that wicked."

"You have any plans for this afternoon?" Micah called out from the other room.

"I need to get back for a staff meeting," Luc answered. "Wouldn't normally be a big deal but there's a big shot in from corporate and so I have to be a good editor and be on time and all that."

"Is he here to read you all the riot act?" Micah asked as he walked into the room. "Or did you do something good to make him come bestow hugs and kisses?"

"Profits and circulation are up," Luc explained, "so I guess he's here to tell us what a wonderful job we're doing."

"Blah blah blah," Micah said. "He could've sent that in an email."

"I think it's a smoke screen and he's really here to see how I run the place."

Micah nodded. "Sounds more like it to me. You better be on your best behavior."

"I don't have anything to hide. Well, maybe three or four skeletons." Luc looked at his watch. "And speaking of skeletons…"

"Yeah, let's go."

* * * * * * * * * * *

The interment of the urn in the columbarium was short. Only four other people besides Graves and Sterling attended: the priest, the parents, and an elderly woman who could have been anyone from a grandmother to a friend.

Since it was such a small group, the two friends felt as if they were intruding, so they didn't stay long.

On the way back to the car, Luc broke the silence. "That was about as awkward as anything I've ever been involved with."

"I know. I thought there'd be more people or else I wouldn't have suggested we come," Micah said. "Even though they weren't rude, I felt like we crashed a private moment."

"They didn't give us dirty looks or anything; the older woman looked over and gave me a small smile."

"I saw that,' Micah said, "but I still felt wrong being there."

"Yeah," Luc agreed. "I felt it, too. Maybe because it's a child. That's always harder on people."

They walked back to their car. On the way out of the cemetery, Micah said, "I'm surprised there are any available plots left in here as old as it is."

"They may not be available," Luc pointed out. "They may just be waiting to be occupied. The families might have bought them generations ago."

"Good point." Micah rubbed his eyes. "Since you have your meeting, I guess I'll go into work; I need to go to the post office anyway."

"Isn't there some big estate auction coming up soon?" Luc asked.

Micah nodded. "Johanna Edensburg's estate will be up for grabs at Lansington's. Did I tell you I'm going with Vanessa Archer?"

"Uh-huh, the lady who owns the antique shop in New Mystic," Luc said. "She sounds like a riot."

"She is," Micah said. "One of these days you'll get to meet her and she'll tell you the story about how she got her cockatoo Chiffon. You'll never believe it."

"I take it she didn't go to her local pet store and pick out a bird."

"Far from it." Micah laughed. "You'll have to wait and hear her tell it because she tells it better than I can."

"One of these days," Luc agreed.

"I have an idea." Micah reached to turn on the air conditioner. "Why don't you go with the two of us to the auction? You'll finally get to meet Vanessa and you may even find something you like for that dismal house of yours."

Luc rolled up his window and said, "Ask me about it tomorrow and I'll look at my schedule; I'll be able to tell you if I can go then."

The two friends were silent for a few moments before Luc spoke.

"Have you ever seen a ghost?"

"A ghost?" Micah was surprised by the question from out of the blue. "Nothing I can say for certain was an apparition. Why do you ask? Have you seen one?"

Luc shook his head and said, "No, I was just asking because I'm thinking about a story for the October issue about ghosts, maybe interview people who claim to have seen them or people who investigate hauntings. For Halloween."

"There are a lot of historic houses, buildings, and places around you can write about, it doesn't necessarily have to be about ghosts," Micah explained. "I remember hearing stories growing up about a stone house in Grantsville where people have had experiences you could classify as paranormal. What about that for a start?"

"A stone house. Any idea which one it might be?"

"Not exactly, but I know people who live in Grantsville who might know what I'm talking about; they could also give us more leads on other places to check out.

And there are dozens of old cemeteries around where you can take atmospheric pictures for your article, old mausoleums and grave stones and such."

"Sounds like a plan," Luc said as he pulled over in front of Micah's. "Here we are. I gotta get to the office, so I'll probably talk to you tomorrow if you call to remind me to check my schedule about the auction."

Micah got out of the car and said, "Thanks for going with me."

"No problem. See you later." Luc waved as he pulled away from the curb.

* * * * * * * * * * *

Micah went to the Sacred Scarab. Leslie, his assistant, seemed to have everything under control.

"You're early," she said. "I wasn't expecting you for another hour or so."

"I thought I'd catch you engaged in untoward activity if I came in early." He grinned. "No, the service was rather short and Luc had to get to work, and I didn't have anything else to do."

"So you thought you'd come in and catch up on all the paperwork on your desk."

He nodded. "You must be psychic. And I have to go to the post office, too. No better time than the present."

They walked to the office where they continued their conversation.

"Today's been slow," Leslie said. "I made it through more than a few chapters of the latest Iamma Trampp book. There were a couple older women in to look around and we had a delivery. I didn't unpack it but it should be another one of the funereal masks Winston asked you to procure."

Compiling three stacks of papers and invoices on his desk, Micah said, "He'll be thrilled when I tell him we've managed to get six of the seven he wants."

"And you'll be thrilled to cash the ample check he writes you."

"But of course, Leslie; don't you know money's the name of the game?"

"Avarice doesn't suit you, Micah." She laughed. "I've been meaning to ask you how the research David Cordone asked you to conduct is going. Gotten anywhere?"

Micah paused before answering. "It's going to take a lot more than I thought. There's a good bit out there about An'khyr, the amount of mythology is amazing. The hard part is wading through it and weeding out what amounts, basically, to fan fiction. Hours and hours of tedious reading, let me tell you."

"No mention of the statue?"

"There have been literally dozens of items mentioned, but like I said," Micah told her, "there's a great deal to wade through. So far I've only found a few things that may prove useful to finding out if the statue actually exists."

Leslie placed her hands on her hips. "So you still think it could be the figment of an old man's imagination? Mr. Cordone always seemed of sound mind to me."

"Never said he wasn't, but his memory may be faulty," Micah explained. "I'd have to write him off if I hadn't come across a couple articles concerning some of the accidents he told me about."

"The fires?"

"Yes." Micah began stuffing envelopes and sealing them. "According to what I've read, the accidents did occur. There was no mention of our statue, but then I didn't expect there to be. And it does lead me to believe him, I can't explain why."

"Maybe because you've seen other legends or myths or whatever you want to call them become reality," Leslie said. "Troy, for instance, and the Hanging Gardens."

"True. Didn't Shakespeare write something about more things in heaven and earth?" Micah said.

"I believe he did."

"All I can say is I am willing to do the research and see what I can come up with," Micah said, "and not merely to appease a valued customer and friend, but because I think it would be the coolest thing in the world to be the person who brings to light an artifact from a culture thought to be nothing more than a legend."

"Glad to hear you say that." Leslie smiled. "David Cordone, on a respirator or not, is a sweet man with a wise and level head on his broad shoulders. I simply cannot imagine him concocting a scheme like this in order to monopolize your time and send you on a wild statue chase."

He stopped shuffling papers; he looked up and said, "Which is why I am going to continue my efforts to investigate and see what I can come up with."

"I know. I just wanted to make sure you got my point."

"I got it," he said. "And now I need to run these things down to the post office and get them into the afternoon mail. I'll be back." With an armload of envelopes, Micah left the shop and stepped out onto the sidewalk.

Sunlight warmed his face as he made his way down the street, greeting people as he walked. Thoughts of events from the last few days filled his head. Images of the winged ankh statue floated through his mind. Bits of conversations between himself and Luc Sterling and David Cordone whispered in his thoughts.

He crossed both Eaves Avenue and Austin Boulevard and continued his trek to the post office.

Not paying attention, he failed to notice the "Don't Walk" sign flashing in front of him on Escape Street. Still immersed in his thoughts, Micah stepped off the curb and into the path of a Transit Now Authority bus. The bus driver blared the horn and slammed on the brakes; the sound of screeching tires filled the air.

A hand reached from behind him, grabbed the back of his shirt, and pulled him up onto the sidewalk. Envelopes flew out into the street and were scattered even more as the TNA bus breezed by.

"What the f—?" Micah gasped.

"You better watch where the hell you're going, dude," the voice said, cutting off Micah's profanity. "And you better watch that language, too."

Micah stood on the curb breathing heavy and surveying the sight of Luc Sterling standing in front of him. "What are you doing here? You're supposed to be in a big magazine meeting."

Luc laughed sarcastically. "I think a better question would be where was your head? You walked right in front of that bus. Didn't you see the sign flashing, see the light change?"

"All that's a moot point at this juncture," Micah said as he got his breathing under control. "Besides, it's a common enough mistake and I haven't come to any harm."

"Because I was here to drag your ass out of harm's way. Where were you going anyway?"

Turning to stare at the envelopes strewn across the pavement, Micah said, "The obvious answer would be the post office." He turned back to Luc. "And you never did answer my question."

"Which was?"

"Why aren't you at the meeting? You were in a hurry to get there earlier."

Luc shrugged and said, "It was canceled. Something about the guy from corporate was detained in Baltimore and wouldn't be able to make it in until later in the week."

Looking back out into the street Micah said, "I guess as long as you're here you can help me gather up all those envelopes. You think the post office will still accept them?"

Luc stepped off the curb and picked up the closest one before answering. "The ones with tire marks on them may not be acceptable."

"When it rains," Micah said, "it pours. This is just great. Now I have to redo most of these before I can mail them."

"Don't get all pouty," Luc told him. "I'll help you out since I have the rest of the afternoon free. Shouldn't take us but a half hour."

"That's not the point. Damned drivers should watch what the hell they're doing or they'll run over half the population."

Luc held out the envelopes he'd picked up. "I don't think it was so much the driver's fault, my man. After all, you're the one who blew off the 'Don't Walk' sign. That poor dude was just going through a green light. He sure as hell didn't expect somebody to come sauntering out into the street."

Micah stopped to take a deep breath as he considered what his friend said to him. "I guess. Just feels better when you can blame your stupidity on someone else. Takes the burden off you."

"Consider yourself lucky. Could've been you spread out across the intersection instead of a paper storm." Luc leaned down to pick up another envelope. "And wouldn't that have been a big mess."

Micah grimaced at the thought. "Funny. Hey! Grab that one before it falls down the grate."

Luc chased the errant envelope, grabbing it a second before it reached said grate. "Indiana Jones couldn't have done it with more grace." He waved the runaway envelope in the air.

"Thanks. Now we better get back to the shop and redo these so I can take them to the post office before it closes."

The two walked back down the street in silence for several minutes before Luc spoke.

"Seriously," he said. "Tell me what you were thinking about that was so absorbing it almost got you splattered."

"Nothing in particular," Micah answered as he sifted through the stack of envelopes he held.

Luc barked a short laugh. "You are such a bad liar. It was that damned statue again, wasn't it?"

"What if I was thinking about it some more? It's an interesting subject. Who can blame me?"

"Sometimes I wish Cordone had never mentioned it to you. You're damned close to being obsessed with this. And for what? You don't even know if it's real."

Stopping, Micah looked at his friend. "It could very well be."

"It's a figment of an old man's mind, I tell you." Luc held up his hand to stop Micah from speaking. "Don't tell me about those sites you found on the internet. You don't have one shred of physical evidence the statue exists. You are building a case on theory and stories people with a whole lot of extra time on their hands wrote. I double-dare you to present to me something concrete, completely factual. You can't because you haven't found a solitary piece of evidence. Admit it."

"The situation bears looking into, Luc, whether or not it turns out the statue isn't real. That's not the point."

"No, the point is you've found something to replace your endless and morbid fascination with memorial cards. Admit it," Luc demanded.

Micah started walking again. "I'm not admitting any such thing," he said over his shoulder.

"Tell me one last thing," Luc called after him. "Is Denial a nice place to live?"

Micah didn't justify his friend's question with an answer.

"Redo those envelopes your damned self," Luc muttered as he followed.

Chapter Seven

When Micah's friend Mama Starr called him from the cab of her truck while she drove down the Pennsylvania Turnpike Saturday morning, he was a bit shocked. After all, he hadn't expected to hear from her for about another week because her run was supposed to take her out West.

"You need to look up Gravity Hill on the internet," she told him. "I just saw a sign for it and remembered I always wanted to go there, but I never knew where it was exactly. C'mon, you know you'll find it fascinating. They probably have a website; everybody has a website."

"Gravity Hill," Micah repeated, typing it into the search engine. "They do have their own website, and they're considerate enough to provide detailed directions." He printed out the page and glanced over it before laying it on his desk. "Hey, it's in Bedford County, that's not too far from here and won't take long to get there if you really want us to go. Hey, if you saw a sign for it, you must be close."

Her laughter traveled over the distance between them. "Close enough to be at your place tomorrow. I thought I'd park the bobtail and we'd go experience Gravity Hill for ourselves."

"Nice to be thought of."

"You don't have any plans, do you?" Mama Starr asked. "If you do, that's okay; I know this is short notice."

"Nah, I don't have anything too important," Micah said. "The shop's usually closed on Sundays unless I've made special arrangements."

"I'll be rolling in before the crack of noon, maybe 10:30 or 11," she said. "So you can get a couple or three hours of work in before I get there."

"Seriously, I don't have any pressing engagements. And besides, you know I seldom make it into the store before eleven on a work day."

Mama Starr's cell phone cut out and he couldn't hear what she said.

"Repeat that, I didn't get it," he said.

"I said, then I guess it's a date." She told him he could invite his friend if he felt like it.

They said their good-byes and hung up.

* * * * * * * * * * *

Over breakfast Sunday, a late breakfast at noon, Micah and Mama Starr discussed Gravity Hill.

"I did more research on Gravity Hill after I got off the phone with you. According to some websites, it's not such a unique phenomenon."

"You mean there's more than one?" Starr asked. She speared a slice of French toast with her fork.

"Yes, and they are all mostly named Gravity Hill, Anti-Gravity Hill, Mystery Hill, Magnetic Hill, or something just as quaint," he said. "From what I understand, you can find them pretty much anywhere, from Oregon to Maine. All over the world actually; there was a long list of places."

"Okay, so it's not unique." She shrugged and reached for her glass of water. "Big deal. We can still go and see what it's all about. Don't you want to roll up a hill? Backwards?"

Micah laughed. "That would be the point: it's an optical illusion. It tricks your eyes into seeing something other than what is really there or what is really happening. We won't be rolling uphill."

"Whatever." She waved her hand. "We can still go and see for ourselves. Did you find out how these hills work?"

"Uh huh. It's all about not being able to see the horizon, not having the horizon line to judge the slope of the area in question."

"And in plain English this means what exactly?" she asked.

"Let me see if I can explain this correctly," Micah said. "Without the horizon, it's easy to become disoriented. Things you would normally use to judge the slope of, say, a road—like trees or telephone poles—may actually not be perpendicular to the ground; they could be leaning, causing your visual reference to be offset. You're thinking it's one thing and it's really another."

She stared at him. "I suppose that's the plain English version." She took a bite of toast before continuing. "So the point is the road looks like it goes uphill when in reality it's going downhill?"

"Yep. And that explains why vehicles roll uphill when you put them in neutral. It's not a miracle."

"Do you think knowing the scientific explanation will take the joy out of it? I don't want it to be ruined."

"Not at all," Micah said. "I think it'll be awesome. Something we haven't seen or tried before."

She tilted her head. "It's a bit like knowing what your present is before you unwrap it Christmas morning. Knowing what it's all about sort of takes a bit of the bloom off the rose, if you know what I mean."

"Who's to say there isn't a true Gravity Hill out there somewhere? A place where the law of gravity is disobeyed and cars really do drift uphill. Just because no one has discovered it yet doesn't mean it doesn't really exist. There are more things in heaven and earth and all that jazz."

"Yes, Virginia, there really is a Gravity Hill," she said and smiled. "I suppose things can't always be what they seem. You should write an article on it for your friend's magazine." She glanced at her watch. "We better get a move on. It's, what, forty minutes away?"

"Give or take a couple minutes. We'll be there in plenty of time to experience the sensation," Micah said. "Oh, I did forget to tell you there is supposed to be two places on this road where you can experience the dazzling defying of gravity. I bet there's a sign proclaiming that somewhere along the road."

"Well now, this place must be practically an amazement park."

Micah placed a bit of scrambled egg in front of Sia. "I only hope there's not a ton of people there, what with this being Sunday and all. We might be wading into a hundred or thousand sightseers converging on the same spot."

"Quit being so negative," Starr scolded. "I honestly don't know what gets into you sometimes; you know you like people. It's going to be lovely. The spot is probably out in the middle of nowhere, and if there are people, we'll be nice and wait our turn like good people do in public."

"We'll pretend we have manners."

"Exactly."

"Should I bring along the camera?" Micah asked. "Just in case there is any phenomenon we need to capture on film: UFO landing, ghost in the mist, or a phantom floating in the field."

"Little green men will be the least of your worries," Starr told him. "I could leave your ass out there to walk back."

He stood and smiled. "I'm too lazy to walk back; I'd just kick back and wait for the next car and bum a ride. It's hard to say no to a face like this."

"Okay, cowboy. Load up so we can move out. You did print off the directions?" Starr said. "I don't want to get lost and spend most of the day driving around looking for Gravity Hill."

"I know how to get to Bedford, Starr," Micah said. "From there, it can't be too hard to find if we follow the directions, which look pretty straight forward and simple. We'll be fine."

"Uh huh. I'm sure that's exactly what Mr. Donner told the rest of the party." She smiled wide, showing her teeth.

"Get in the car."

Just as Micah said, it didn't take more than twenty minutes or so for the friends to make it to Bedford County in Pennsylvania.

"Don't the directions say we have to find Route 30 now?"

"We're on Route 30," Starr pointed out.

"Are you sure?"

"I am a truck driver, I do know how to read a map," she said dryly. "We are on Route 30. Keep driving. We're going to Schellsburg; it's about seven or eight miles west of here."

They found their way to Route 96 and drove towards New Paris.

"But we don't go all the way to New Paris," Starr said. "We drive until we come to a bridge, and we turn before the bridge. It's not supposed to be very far. I think this is it."

"This?" Micah said. "This is not a bridge, it's two planks and a rail. I've seen bigger bridges built in dental work."

"Shut up and turn left. Here, on Bethel Hollow Road."

Micah blew out a breath. "We're going to get lost and killed in the woods. Our dismembered bodies thrown for the wild animals to feast upon. Bones used for furniture. I saw this movie."

Ignoring him, Starr continued with the directions. "We go six-tenths of a mile and bear left at the 'Y' in the road. Are you watching the odometer?"

"Yes. Six-tenths of a mile."

"Keep your eye out for the 'Y.' Do you see it yet?"

"Trees. I see trees. Trees everywhere. Coming up on six-tenths, so it should be here any second."

Starr pointed straight ahead. "That's got to be it."

They stayed on what would be considered the main road and drove for the recommended mile and a half and looked for the stop sign.

"I don't see a stop sign," Micah said. "Do you?"

"Yes."

"Where?"

"Right in front of you."

"It's facing the other way. How am I supposed to know what it is?" Micah said.

"It's facing the other way because it's for the traffic coming the other direction, and you should know what it is because of its shape," Starr explained. "Don't you know how many sides a stop sign has?"

"What is this, math class?"

"Drive and look for the letters 'GH' painted on the road."

"*General Hospital?*"

"Gravity Hill, boy."

"There they are," Micah said. "We made it."

He pulled over to the shoulder, put the car in park, and looked around. "There's nobody else here. Surprise."

"And you thought there'd be a crowd."

Micah grinned at his friend and then said, "Let's pull over, shall we? That way we can get out, walk around, and take a look before we engage the experiment. Better to be safe than sorry."

"Listen to you," Starr said as she took off her seatbelt. "Engage the experiment. I mean, you sound like the host of a fourth-rate science show on public access television. It's not really much of an experiment; the car will either roll uphill or it won't. Engage the experiment my patoot."

But Micah wasn't listening. He'd already gotten out of the car and was scoping the lay of the surrounding land.

"Hey, you want an apple?" he called. "There's a tree on this side of the road loaded with fruit."

Starr turned to look across the road at him, just in time to see him bite into one of the apples. "For God's sake, boy, don't eat any of those. Where are your brains? They could have worms in them for all you know. You want a colony of worms living in your intestinal tract?"

Micah tossed the apple over his shoulder and spit out what was in his mouth. He walked back across the road, wiping his mouth on his sleeve. He spit again and wished he had some mouthwash.

"What would possess you to start eating roadside fruit out in the middle of nowhere? You don't have a clue."

"Apples are good for you," was his only defense.

"So are antibiotics."

"Okay, okay. Are we going to have a look around or are we going to stand here assigning blame?"

"Then get your butt moving so we can try this before a mob does show up," Starr said. "I'd rather not be rear-ended by an oncoming vehicle while we're coasting backwards up the hill."

"Looks like we have company," Micah said as the sound of engines reached them.

Two motorcycles and their riders came into view; they came to a stop a couple yards from Micah and Starr.

"Is this where stuff is supposed to roll uphill?" the first rider asked.

Starr nodded. "Yes. We were about to give it a try ourselves."

"Sorry," the second rider said. "Didn't mean to interrupt."

"No problem," Micah assured them. "You guys go ahead."

"You sure?"

"Absolutely," Starr said. "That way we can see what happens when you do it, so we'll sort of know what to expect when we do it."

"Thanks," the first rider said.

The first rider then pulled up to the GH painted on the road and turned off the engine of his motorcycle. He balanced as best he could and waited. Slowly but surely he and his motorcycle began to drift up the slope. Once he reached the top of the hill, he walked the motorcycle back down to where his friend waited.

"Dude, that felt so weird. You give it a try now."

The second rider positioned himself the same as the first and the experience was repeated: he and his motorcycle coasted seemingly uphill, against the pull of gravity. He turned to wave when he reached the top. When he came back down the hill, he stood shaking his head.

"What did I tell you?" his friend asked. "Weird, right?"

He nodded. "At first, I didn't think anything was going to happen even though I just saw you do it, but then the bike started rolling. I never felt anything like it before in my life."

"We can say we did it," his friend said. "And now why don't we get out of here so these folks can have their turn?"

They said good-bye, mounted up, and rode off.

Starr looked at Micah and said, "Let's take our turn now before anyone else shows up and makes us wait."

"I'm driving."

"We can each take a turn. Just get back in the car."

Micah drove back onto the road and pulled up to the spray painted GH. He put the car in neutral and let up on the brake. And then they waited.

Nothing happened.

"What the...?"

"Here it goes," Starr said.

The car began to coast backwards up the hill.

"Can you feel that?" Starr asked.

"Yeah, it's picking up speed."

"It feels odd, almost like something's pushing us," Starr said. "I know it's an optical illusion, but it feels weird."

Micah agreed and applied the brake because they had coasted to the "top" of the hill. "What next?"

"My turn," sang Starr. "Pull back down so we can trade places."

After they switched places, Starr sat in the driver's seat and said, "Here we go, baby, hold on."

And they coasted up the hill for the second time.

"You want to try the second spot?" Micah asked whenever they reached the top.

"Might as well since we're here already."

About that time, the two heard the unmistakable sound of a car approaching. The cherry red Plymouth came into view, the sound of "Christine Sixteen" from the 1977 KISS album "Love Gun" blaring from the open windows.

Starr and Micah got out of their car and stood by the rear fender.

The Plymouth's driver parked the car. She opened the door and as she got out she swung her long, thick mane of flame red hair over her shoulder like an 80's hair band video vixen. She turned and reached back into the car to pick something up before motioning the other occupant to exit the vehicle. The man and woman walked over to Starr and Micah.

"Hello there, I'm Harley," she said, holding out her hand. In the other hand she held a model of a racehorse. She held up the horse and said, "This is Ingmar. And this," she gestured to her male companion, "is Royce. It's nice to see someone else is here to enjoy Gravity Hill."

"I'm Micah and this is my friend Starr. This is our first time here, and so far I think we're having a blast."

Hands were shaken all around and Royce said, "We try to come down here once a month in the summertime, and we enjoy meeting the different people who come to coast uphill."

Mama Starr asked the new arrivals, "So, do you buy the rational, scientific explanation for the hill or do you really believe there's a little more here than meets the eye?"

Harley tossed her fiery mane and laughed. "I can buy the explanation on this hill because maybe we are actually experiencing an optical illusion, but I do not believe the second hill—just down the road a bit—is an illusion." She shook her head, sending her hair flying in the air. "Nope, we've used a level and the telephone poles are straight up and down, not slanted in any way, so I believe the second hill is actually a true Gravity Hill where you coast uphill. Wait until you try it; the entire experience just feels different than this one."

As he turned to look in the direction Harley had pointed, Micah said, "You've really used a level to determine the telephone poles aren't slanted?"

"Yep," she grinned. "I don't believe the absence of a view of the horizon line causes us to be fooled into thinking the slope is up when it's really down. The second Gravity Hill is for real."

Royce nodded his agreement.

"We haven't made it down to the second hill. We haven't been here long at all, and we've only seen two other people," Micah said. "Is it as good as the first? I mean, will it feel like we are coasting uphill?"

"Did you get a funny feeling in the pit of your stomach when the car started rolling uphill?" Royce asked.

"Yeah."

"You get the same feeling at the second hill," Royce explained, "only it's more intense, and you really feel like something is pushing the car up the hill. Like Harley said, the entire experience is intensified."

"If you wait until we get a few pictures of us and Ingmar," Harley said, "we'll go down to the second hill with you, if you don't mind. I can't wait; it'll be fun to experience with our new friends."

Mama Starr told Harley and Royce she and Micah would be pleased if they'd accompany them.

"Would you mind if we took some pictures of the two of you?" Harley asked. "We'll be happy to send you copies in email or snail mail, whichever you prefer. We enjoy keeping a photo album of the people we meet here at the hill, and we occasionally keep in touch with each other."

"Not at all," Micah assured her. "We'd be happy to have our pictures taken, since we forgot our own camera."

Royce clapped his hands and said, "Excellent then. Let me take the pictures of you and Starr first. And then, if you don't mind, would one of you take photos of Harley and me?"

"You'd better let me do it," Starr said. "This one," she pointed to Micah, "can break just about any device he comes in contact with."

They all posed for pictures and everyone had a picture taken with Ingmar the model racehorse—Harley insisted Ingmar would love to be photographed with his new friends; she said he had an album for the picture she took of him and his friends, in places all over the country.

No one else happened onto the hill until they were getting in their cars to drive the yards down to the second site. A compact car with four blue-haired ladies inside came to a stop. A window rolled down and the blue-haired lady driving poked her head out and asked:

"Is this where we roll backwards up the hill?"

Micah said, "Yes, ma'am, you've found the spot."

"Thank you, young man," she waved before pulling her head back inside the car.

He opened his mouth to say "You're welcome" but realized the lady had put the window back up and wouldn't be able to hear him anyway.

So he got into the car with Starr and the two of them followed Harley and Royce down the road to the second Gravity Hill where they repeated the experience of coasting against gravity up a hill. Everyone wanted a turn at the wheel. Starr wanted another turn in the driver's seat.

* * * * * * * * * * *

After Micah and Starr had said goodbye to Harley and Royce, and promised they would attempt to keep in touch, they drove off in search of a place to eat.

"How about that charming inn a few miles down the road?" Starr suggested. "It's supposed to be colonial and all that. I forget what it's called."

"Then it should be easy to find," Micah said. "Do you think there'll be a sign?"

Starr gave him a side-ways look. "Don't be smart, boy; it'll only get you a smack. On another subject: Harley and Royce were interesting, weren't they? Not everyday you run across people as colorful."

"They certainly were. Although, I thought Ingmar rocked and I hope Harley does email the pictures of he and I together. I'll send you copies and then you can hang them in the cab."

Suddenly Starr pointed. "Look. There it is."

They pulled into a deserted parking lot.

"Doesn't look like they're open for business." Micah said. "You know, on account of there being no other cars around and all."

"I think I'll have to agree with your observation," she said. "And I do believe I see a note on the door. Let me just run up there and see what it says." She got out of the car and leaned down to say, "I'll be right back."

As Micah waited for her, his thoughts turned once again to the statue David

Cordone had asked him to attempt to locate. Lost in his thoughts, he didn't hear the car door open or Starr speak.

She poked him in the shoulder. "Are you in there? I said, the note on the door said 'Closed Temporarily Due to Family Emergency.' Makes me curious to know what the emergency is."

"Great," he muttered. "Where do you want to eat now?"

She shrugged. "We can always find some place or we can wait until we get back to your place. You pick."

"It's been hours since breakfast and I'm practically starved. Listen, you can hear my ribs poking through my skin."

"Oh, bull," she said. "It hasn't been 'hours' at all. Well, maybe two and a half. You act like you haven't eaten in twelve. You're nowhere near starvation, boy; you exaggerate."

"You wanna find some place to eat or not?"

"I could use a snack," she admitted. "How about a nice little eatery? The kind with outdoor tables, maybe in a garden setting."

"That should be readily available to us in this part of Pennsylvania, Starr," Micah said. "Wanna cruise around a bit and see what we can find?"

She nodded her consent. "Hey, don't you have to be up before your typical hour tomorrow?"

"Yep. Sia's got an appointment at the vet's for his check-up."

"Meaning shots," she said. "I bet he's gonna love that."

"Doesn't every cat like to be poked in the ass with needles?" Micah said. "He hates it with a passion and he always seems to know where we're going, even if I lie to him and say it's for treats."

"He's gonna be pissed."

"He'll forgive me after a day or six, he always does."

"I know I'll hate crawling out of bed by five in the morning so I can be back on the road," Starr said. "But I do love my job. Just imagine, I get paid to travel back and forth across the country. You've seen the pictures I have from the states I've driven through. I think you have presents from most of the places I've been. Like the frog I got you in Winslow, Arizona. Remember when I called you and said I was standing on the corner. Took you a while to get the reference."

Micah laughed at the memory. "But the point is I did get it."

They drove around and drove around, passing all kinds of antique shops and curio stores, until they finally spotted what appeared to be a little eatery. Potted trees and hanging plants, wrought iron tables and chairs.

"Bingo," Starr called excitedly. "I told you we'd find something quaint. Stop, stop, stop. Perhaps they'll have Bee-sting cake."

Micah parked the car and said, "Just get out."

Chapter Eight

The next morning, Micah rolled out of bed way before his accustomed time and stumbled bleary-eyed into the bathroom. Sia followed him, vocalizing the entire way.

"Yeah, I know you know why we're up so early," Micah told him. "Quit bellyaching about it because it has to be done."

He opened the shower curtain and stepped into the tub. "The things I do for you, cat," he said before pulling the curtain closed and turning on the water.

The water hit him, and felt as cold as he thought liquid nitrogen would feel; it woke him up completely before changing to hot.

"To paraphrase Terri Nunn," Micah called over the sound of the water to Sia, who sat on the edge of the tub, "it takes my breath away."

Sia meowed in response.

After he'd showered and dressed, Micah picked up his cat. Holding Sia in his arms, he said, "I know you'll hate me for most of the week, but, buddy, this is something we gotta do. A needle in the butt once every year or two makes you legal. You don't want to go to the pound because you don't have your rabies vaccination and those other requirements, do you?"

The cat looked at him and made his whiskers wiggle.

"You think that now," Micah said, "but you'll be mad as sin after you get poked by the needle. No worries, you'll still be able to sit in the window like you like to do while I'm gone. We may have to get you a pillow, but you'll still be able to sit in the window and keep your eye on things."

He put the cat down and went to grab the kitty carrier. He didn't like confining the cat to the plastic and mesh contraption but the vet's rules were inviolate and they strongly discouraged bringing an uncrated animal into the animal hospital. He'd done it once and was reprimanded by a nurse before he'd made it three steps into the lobby.

The cat carrier rested, door open, on the carpet, and Micah looked around for his cat. Sia was nowhere in sight.

"C'mon, good little kitty, come to me," Micah cajoled. "Come here and get into you oh-so-comfy carrier. We have to be on our way."

Not a creature stirred. Micah surveyed the living room. "Where are you?"

Nothing.

"I know you're here somewhere," he said, "because I shut all the other doors."

He squinted, like a gunfighter about to take a shot, and stared at the sofa. Something moved. The movement was slight; nonetheless, it was movement.

Micah got down on his knees. "Are you under there?"

No response.

"If you're under there, it would behoove you to come out and get in your comfy carrier. I thought we discussed this and you understood."

He leaned down and peered beneath the sofa. Sia peered back at him.

"You know," he reasoned, "this is going to happen, one way or another." *Am I really going to threaten the cat with doing it the easy way or the hard way?* "There are two ways we can do this."

Sia meowed and rolled onto his back, unsheathing his pearly daggers, as if to demonstrate his opposition to the trip to the veterinarian's office.

"Why do you always act like this? Is it genetic?" Micah wanted to know. "Do all cats act all cuddly up until the moment of departure only to go all Krueger when it's time to get into their carriers?"

Seizing Sia by the scruff, Micah gently worked the cat out from his hiding place. Once out, Sia curled up in Micah's arms like a baby trying to take a nap, eyes closed and purring to beat the band.

Not so easily fooled, Micah took the opportunity to put his pet in the carrier and close the door. Sia apparently was not happy his ruse hadn't worked. He began to vocalize his abject misery by howling as if someone were trying to torture him to death.

"Will you knock it off?" Micah peered into the carrier. "I have to take you out in public and you can't have people thinking I'm hurting you."

Sia ceased his howling.

Until Micah walked outside with the carrier, that is. As soon as Micah closed and locked the door behind him, Sia let loose with the horrific howls and the sound echoed all around them.

Hurrying to the car so he could unlock it and shove the cat carrier inside before a mob of do-gooders could descend upon him demanding he free the cat, he nearly tripped over his own feet.

Once inside the vehicle, with windows up and doors locked, Micah stared into the cat carrier. Sia stared back.

"What the hell was all that?" Micah's voice cracked. "Good God, you could've had me arrested for animal cruelty or something. I already explained why we have to go to you and I thought we had an understanding. Seems like only one of us had the understanding and the other one had a psychotic break."

Every once in a while, during the entire drive to the vet's office, Sia would let out a long "ooowww" sound that made the hair perk up on the back of Micah's neck.

"That is as eerie as all get out, cat," Micah moaned. "Must you?"

Sia turned around and around inside the carrier before settling down, face pressed as close as possible to the mesh door.

"Don't look so pathetic," Micah said. "This is the same visit we always make. You'll be back home in no time flat."

* * * * * * * * * * *

Once at the animal hospital, Micah parked and carted the cat carrier into the lobby. He checked in at the front desk before taking a seat on the "Felis Domesticus" side of the waiting room.

Sia, still inside the carrier, made growling noises.

Micah leaned down and whispered to him. "If you don't knock it off," he threatened, "there will be no more treats in your future. It'll all be dry cat food and generic brand at that."

The cat quieted down until the nurse came over and said, "You can bring Sia back for his shots now."

The cat started growling in a very low pitch that continued as they walked down the hallway and into the examination room. When the vet technician pulled Sia out of the carrier, the cat went all fur and claws, spitting and making shrill sounds.

"We got us a live one here," the vet said. "Careful now."

"I'm so embarrassed," Micah said. "He's never acted this bad before and I apologize. I don't know what got into him."

The vet said, "It happens all the time. They don't understand why they're in a strange place with all kinds of strange people and strange smells, different animal smells. They get all nervous and act out in the only way they know how." He stroked Sia's head. "See, he's calmed down a bit. No reason to be so scared. We'll take good care of him. Why don't you have a seat back out in the waiting room and we'll get you when we're finished. Then you can take this big guy back home where he belongs. How does that sound?"

"Are you talking to me or the cat with that last question?"

"Either or."

"I'll just be waiting out there," Micah said as he pointed toward the waiting area.

He stepped out of the room and closed the door behind him. On his way back out to the waiting area, he walked by one of the hospital rooms reserved for severely injured animals, its door open. Stopping to glance inside, he saw a man in a suit standing in the corner of the room. The man looked up. Micah smiled at him, and after a split second the man smiled back.

"I apologize if I'm disturbing you," Micah said, "but I couldn't help it."

"No apology necessary," the man said.

The beeping caught Micah's attention as soon as he stepped into the room. A small dog lay curled up; a monitor as well as other machinery were attached to the poor pup.

"Is it yours?" Micah asked.

"She will be soon," the man replied.

"What happened to her?"

The man hesitated before answering. "Evil happened to her. Someone's idea of fun. Two of them, actually."

Micah turned back to the man. "I'm so sorry."

"Her pain will soon be at an end."

Micah didn't have the opportunity to question the man's statement because the heart monitor stopped beeping and instead emitted a steady droning sound.

When he turned back to the man, Micah was shocked to see the man holding the little dog in his arms. Micah turned back to the table—the dog was still there. He didn't understand.

"How in the world…?" he started to say as he once again turned to the man in the suit. "How is it…?"

"Now she is mine," the man said as the little dog licked his chin. "She suffers no longer and she will never again suffer at the hands of brutality."

Again, Micah didn't have the chance to question the man because a vet tech walked into the room.

"I'm sorry for being here." Micah held up his hands.

"It's okay," the tech said. "There wasn't anyone else to be here at the end. She was brought in by one of the Volunteer Ministers, the group from the Church of Scientology who are in town helping out at the Mission down on Victor Street," he said as he turned of the monitoring equipment. "Found this little lady beside the Dumpster out back."

"So she had no owner?"

"None we could locate. Of course, she's only been here since yesterday and didn't have a collar or tags on her when she was brought in. And she was in such terrible condition, the doctor at first thought it would be a blessing to just put her to sleep and save her any suffering,"

"I understand the doctor's opinion. Such a disgrace, what people will do to innocent creatures," he said. "So is this the Volunteer Minister who brought her in?" Micah pointed to where the man in the suit stood.

"Who are you talking about?" the tech asked, looking where Micah pointed, obviously not seeing the man. "Did someone else come in or was there someone else here, Mr. Graves?"

"No one, my mistake. Would it be okay if I stayed a couple minutes? Maybe to say a prayer or something."

"Of course." And tech left the room, closing the door behind him.

The man in the suit smiled at Micah. "You have questions."

"Yeah, a lot of them."

"I would have questions, as well, were I in your position. I thought it strange you smiled at me," the man said. "But sometimes I forget there are those among you who can see us."

"Us?" Micah held his hands out. "Who are us?"

"There are those among you who have often called us angels," the man explained. "It is we who take you into the Mourning Light when it is your time to go, for lack of a better explanation."

"Yes, I've heard the myths," Micah said. "You're an Angel of the Mourning, as I've heard my grandmother say often enough. So you also come for animals when it's their time, as well?"

"After all, do they not have a soul?"

Nodding, Micah said, "I've always believed so. That's why I don't eat meat or wear anything made from animal skin or fur."

"Most do not believe our animal brethren have souls. *Animal* comes from the Latin word *anima*, meaning *soul*," the man explained as he rubbed the tummy of the little dog he still held in his arms. "In fact, in the Bible you can find a Hebrew term—*nephesh chaya*—that literally means *living soul*. It is my privilege to be there to greet the animals who were unwanted, so they know *I* want them. I am the first face the neglected or abused ones see when they have passed. I take them with me into the Mourning Light. Of course, I am not the only one. There are others who are here for the animals."

Behind Micah, the exam room door opened. The tech stuck his head in and said, "I hope I'm not disturbing a prayer or anything."

Micah turned to face him. "No, you're not."

"I just wanted to let you know Sia is ready whenever you are."

"Thanks, I'll be out in a minute."

The tech shut the door and Micah turned back toward the man in the suit, except the man was no longer there. Both he and the dog had simply vanished.

Micah left the room and made his way back to the examination room where Sia was waiting for him. A lot of questions ran through his mind. The most obvious one being: *Am I completely crazy?*

Once Sia's bill was paid and they were ensconced back in the car, Micah told the cat, "I had the weirdest conversation in there while you were with the doctor."

The cat stared back at him through the mesh of the carrier.

"Didn't someone once say something," Micah wondered, "about things getting curiouser and curiouser?"

PART II

Silent as the Grave

Chapter Nine
In A Dream

Sunlight came through the window, bright and intense, because he'd forgotten to close the drapes when he went to bed shortly before dawn. He closed his eyes as tight as possible to try to block out the sunlight, but it didn't do any good. Instead of blessed darkness there was a pinkish color before his eyes.

No way could he fall asleep with the bright light cascading into the bedroom. Pulling the blanket up over his head only made him feel like he was camping and his tent had collapsed. He resolved to get out of bed and close the drape. But if he actually opened his eyes and got up, then he'd really be awake and wouldn't be able to fall asleep again.

Rolling onto his back, he sighed heavily, eyes still closed.

Sia climbed onto his chest and pressed his cold, cold nose against Micah's lips.

"What do you think you are doing?" Micah raised one eyelid and asked.

Sia purred, pressing his face closer to Micah's.

"Thanks, that makes it easier for me to sleep." He glanced over at the alarm clock on the night stand. Eight-fifteen. "You've got to be kidding me," he moaned. "Way before the crack of noon."

He gently slid the cat off his chest and threw back the covers before getting out of bed. "Close the curtains and get back into bed," he told himself. "Drift back off to sleep. Go nighty-night."

But it wasn't meant to be. As soon as he closed the drapes, his body informed him he urgently had to pee.

"What have I done to deserve this?"

After availing himself of the facilities, Micah stumbled back into the bedroom and collapsed upon the bed; Sia jumped right up alongside him and snuggled in close.

"Don't be waking me up for another two hours," he warned. "Minimum."

Fading to black, Micah began to dream.

He floated through several scenes before coming to rest in the crumbled ruins of a city. Walking along the cracked paving stones of the city streets, Micah took in his surroundings. Huge temples reduced to rubble. Monolithic statues lying in fragmented sections. Dry fountain beds, dead vegetation.

From there he took flight, as if he possessed wings. Landing at the base of a mountain, he looked up. The smell of the trees around him was nearly overwhelming. After taking a few steps toward the base of the mountain, he stopped. His ears clearly picked up the sound of rumbling, like thunder. The surface of the mountain began to crack and then to slide before crashing down in a hail of stones and dirt.

When all had cleared, Micah looked upon what should have been the face of the mountain. Instead, what he saw was a temple, complete with pillars and statues and intricate symbols and details, all carved inside the mountain itself.

Through the rubble he walked, climbing up to the great carved doors of the mysterious temple.

He knew he needed a key to enter. How he knew, he didn't know.

A key.

To fit into the oddly-shaped keyhole.

Just as he knew he needed the key to enter the temple, he knew he would be the one to find the lost key.

Micah reached out to touch the temple. Under his fingertips, the carved stone felt very cold, almost freezing to the touch.

He backed slowly away from the temple.

The sun shone down warm against his back. Around him, birds sang and flew through the air.

He moved closer to the temple to once again caress the carved stone. As his fingers touched it, he swore he heard a whisper. The sunlight seemed to dim and shadows moved in closer to him.

Micah held his breath and waited to hear the whisper again.

Nothing but the bird songs around him.

And then they suddenly became silent.

Everything around him began to shimmer, like wavy images in a carnival mirror. He closed his eyes against the oddity. When he opened them, he was in a chamber. A cavern. Barely lit with flickering lights, Micah squinted to make out more of his surroundings.

Inside the temple. He had to be. But how?

He didn't understand what was happening, so he decided to go with the flow and ride it out to the end.

Carved into the walls, and he more felt them when he reached out than he could see them, were symbols. He traced one with his finger, getting lost in the motion. All he could do was follow the curves of this one symbol.

He stopped only when he suddenly felt he was no longer alone.

Someone was in the cavern with him.

Some thing.

The voice was back. That whispering…barely able to make anything out. Hardly more than a hushed breath forming the words.

An'khyr.

Micah knew that name. He came across it in his research for David Cordone.

He listened intently, trying to make out more of what the voice was saying. Careful not to move lest the sound drown out the whispering, Micah breathed in very shallowly.

Statue.

Statue? Was it talking about the one Cordone asked him to find?

Was it possible?

Find, the voice softly urged.

Bring.

To me.

"Who are you?" Micah asked, finally finding his voice.

No answer.

But whatever was doing the whispering was still there with him. He felt its presence, and he felt it very close to him. So close, in fact, he waited to feel the breath against his face or the back of his neck.

"What do you want with me?"

Statue.

"What about it?"

Find.

"I get it. You want me to find it. So does David Cordone," Micah said. "Why is it so important?"

Bring.

"To you."

To me.

"What is it?"

Key.

"To what?"

Everything.

Micah waited for more, but there was none. Still the presence was near. He waited, certain there was something more it would say. He knew it would say something else, just one more thing.

And he was almost positive the voice was going to call his name.

Chapter Ten

"Micah."

The voice woke him, bringing him back to the darkness of his bedroom. His eyes flew open and he blinked rapidly.

"Holy night," Micah blurted. "You damned near gave me a myocardial infarction. For the love of all that's holy."

"Sorry, didn't mean to spring death upon you. Graves, were you talking in your sleep?" Luc Sterling asked his friend.

Micah sat up in the bed, dislodging Sia from his chest. "I don't think so."

Luc reached out and flipped the switch by the bedroom door and light flooded the room. "Did you know you left your door unlocked? That's an open invitation for someone to come in and rob you blind, or worse."

Rubbing his eyes, Micah just ignored his friend's comment. "What time is it?"

"Too early for you: it's eleven."

Micah laid back and said, "Why me?"

"I heard something on the radio and rushed right over because I knew you'd be interested," his friend explained.

"What's interesting enough to wake me up so early?"

"You should be up and ready for work anyway."

"I don't have to go in today," Micah said. "I was planning on a lazy day."

"Sorry. But since I woke you up," Luc said, "I might as well tell you what I heard. You won't be happy."

"Tell me already."

"One of your favorite movies is being remade."

"Not another one," Micah groaned. "Which one?"

"Maybe your favorite of all time."

"No. You're lying," he said, the shock evident on his face.

"Nope. I heard on the radio there is a remake of *Rosemary's Baby* in the works. Should I call those paramedics now?"

"Why why why why why?" Micah whined. "I hate it when they destroy my favorite movies. Why do they do it?"

"Yeah, I had to see the remakes of *The Fog* and *Halloween* with you," Luc said. "You almost got thrown out of the theatre on that last one."

Micah shuddered. "Don't remind me. Dreadful remakes. I would rather have herpes viral infections of both my retinas than to have to sit through either one of those abortions ever again."

Sia wound himself around Luc's legs and Luc reached down to scratch the cat's head. "He's awful friendly for someone who was dumped off the bed."

"He'll get over it," Micah said.

Sia meowed.

"See, he's pissed at you. For making him get a shot in the ass last week and for throwing him off the bed just now. One of these days you may wake up and find yourself on the wrong side of feline revenge, my friend. Ever hear of a little thing called Cat Scratch Fever?"

"Besides the Ted Nugent song? Blah blah blah." Micah looked at the clock and made a face. "I guess there's no use trying to go back to sleep since you woke me up." He yawned, as if for effect. "Might as well crawl out of my nice, warm bed and face the day."

Luc looked strangely at his friend and said, "You were making weird noises in your sleep. You weren't having some sort of bizarre sex dream, were you?"

"Yeah, I have them all the time," Micah answered. "Now get out of my room so I can get dressed in private."

As Luc turned to leave, Micah said, "I'll tell you about my…not a nightmare because it wasn't at all scary. I'll tell you about my really strange dream after I get dressed. Go wait in the living room and I'll be out in a few minutes. And take Sia with you and give him a treat or something." Micah looked down at the cat and said, "Go on. Go get a treat."

Sia looked up at him and then left the room.

"By the by, don't think for a second I didn't see the tiger-print sheets on the bed," Luc said. "You have serious explaining to do, my friend."

Luc closed the door behind him. Micah climbed out of bed and started getting dressed. Thoughts about the odd dream ricocheted inside his head.

It was truly odd. He'd never dreamed anything like it before. And it was also the first time he'd ever had a dream that involved any of his clients and customers.

"Maybe it's because David Cordone put the bug about the statue in my head," he muttered to himself. "Then I spent hours doing all that research. And then I met that guy at the animal hospital last week—the one who said he was a Mourning Angel; the entire situation messed with my mind. Everything from the last couple weeks got all twisted up inside my head and made me dream weird images."

He felt better after he explained it to himself.

* * * * * * * * * * *

After telling Luc about the bizarre dream, Luc said, "Maybe it was a mausoleum like the one built for King Mausolus, since it sounds so ornate what with all the carvings and such."

"It may have been a pyramid, you know, like the Egyptians or the Aztecs built," Micah said. "I felt the relief carvings on the walls but that doesn't really narrow it down much."

Micah and his friend began talking about the different monuments to death that had been erected the world over.

"What about something else really ornate like the Taj Mahal?" Luc blurted. "For all its wonder and grandeur, it still boils down to a glorified tomb."

"Did you know the vast majority of the images of the Taj Mahal, the ones the people of the world are so used to seeing, are actually taken from the back of the monument?" Micah asked.

"And not from the royal entrance in the front by the river as the Emperor intended," Luc said. "You'll have to try to stump me with something else, my friend. I know too much about the Taj."

"Maybe another great ruler like Shah Jahan, last of the great Mogul warriors, built the temple in my dream. That would be really cool," Micah said. "I mean, if it really did exist. I do have another piece of trivia about the Taj you may not know."

"Yeah?"

"Did you know the present word 'mogul' comes from the Mogul warriors because they liked to, for lack of better phrasing, collect stuff? They went out into the world and pretty much built empires for themselves."

Luc thought about it. "No, I did not," he admitted. "You finally got one over on me. But don't be getting too smug because I bet I can return the favor."

"Try me," Micah taunted. He smiled wide.

Luc leaned back and grinned. "Our tale begins back in the early 1800's in Virginia. Toward the end of July, to be exact."

"You sound like you're trying to be Rod Sterling," Micah pointed out. "And that might get you into trouble for copyright infringement."

"Hush and listen to the story," Luc ordered. "A ship docked at Alexandria, en route from Halifax to the West Indies, which in itself was odd."

"Why was it so odd?"

"Because Alexandria wasn't a port of call for the route, that's why," Luc said. "The captain of the ship explained he'd come into port only because one of his passengers was gravely ill, a woman, and her husband demanded she be taken ashore immediately to seek help."

The air of mystery in the story caught Micah's attention. He stopped fidgeting and began to listen intently.

"Even though it was scorching-hot, the woman wore a heavy black veil which concealed her identity. Her husband made arrangements in the Inn of the Bunch of Grapes for the best suite."

"'Bunch of Grapes.' Is that a real name or are you making it up?" Micah asked. "You can't make up stuff, it's against the rules."

His friend waved him off, saying, "I didn't make it up; you can check it out for yourself when I'm finished telling the tale, if you would shut up long enough for me to tell it."

"Fine. Go on, Aesop."

"Where was I?" Luc thought for a moment before resuming his story. "The woman's husband got the best suite at the Inn for the two of them, and he procured the services of a well-known physician of the time only after having the doctor pledge to keep everything in the strictest of confidence.

"But even in the presence of the doctor," Luc continued, "the face of the woman was kept veiled, which was weird enough. The husband, so intent on keeping his wife's identity a secret, refused to hire a nurse, saying he could attend to his wife and perform any actions a nurse could perform. And that's even weirder."

"What happened next?" Micah demanded when Luc stopped to take a drink.

"I'm not done yet. Can I have a drink?"

"Hurry up. I'm intrigued."

"As the weeks went by, the weather got hotter and hotter; the husband began to feel the strain of constantly waiting on his wife and seeing to her needs. He finally agreed to hire two of the guests staying at the Inn to assist him with the care of his wife, but only after they'd taken what is described as 'a sacred oath' to never divulge anything they may learn.

"For the ten weeks or so following the woman's arrival in Alexandria, her condition grew steadily worse," Luc continued. "At dawn on the fourth of

October, the husband announced his wife had breathed her last and departed her body. Fearing someone may glimpse the face he'd kept hidden, the husband prepared the body for burial, literally sealing the coffin himself. And after he attended the funeral and ordered a headstone with a strange inscription, the husband disappeared. No one knew what had become of him.

"Until the following year, that is. On the fourth of October, the citizens of Alexandria were surprised to see the husband's return, although it was short-lived: he stayed long enough to place flowers upon the grave of his wife and make sure someone was taking care of the plot."

"And he was never seen again," Micah said.

"Not quite," Luc answered. "Every year for twelve years he'd return to visit the grave, always alone, or so it's said."

"And then his visits stopped?"

"Yes. Sadly, the grave was neglected for a number of years," Luc admitted. "Until an older man and woman, who have been described as being quite distinguished, arrived and ordered a more costly headstone for the woman's grave. It was to bear the same inscription as the original, only another verse was added. Then they left and apparently never made another visit, taking with them any knowledge of who the woman may have been."

"Was it the husband, only older, and maybe with a second wife or relative or something?" Micah wanted to know, curiosity gnawing at him. "Maybe he came back to visit once more before he himself died."

"There's no way for us to know. It could have been they were relatives who finally discovered where she was buried. No one, to this day, knows the identity of the husband or the woman buried in St. Paul's Cemetery. Or, if anyone ever did, they never spoke of it. You'll know the grave because the marker is a stone table, complete with six legs and a top, and instead of a name it bears the words '*To The Memory of the Female Stranger.*'"

When he'd finished his tale, Luc said, "Go ahead and ask. I see you're full of questions."

"I see you're full of shit," Micah retorted, shaking his head. "It's a good story, I'll grant you, but I've never heard of that. You embellished the story."

He held his hand over his heart. "I swear the story is true and you can look it up on the internet for yourself if you don't believe me."

"Don't think I won't," Micah said. "And if it is true, we just might have to drive down to Alexandria, Virginia, and visit the Female Stranger." Micah scratched his chin. "Okay, your story is weird enough to be true, so I believe you. But you have to believe the quick story I'm about to tell you about a little girl by the name of Nadine Earles and how all she wanted for Christmas was a dollhouse."

Luc nodded. "I'm interested."

"Back in 1933, little Nadine was four years-old and the apple of her daddy's eye. Like I said, the little darling asked her parents for a dollhouse and her daddy assured her she'd get her wish; he promised she'd have her perfect dollhouse to play with for Christmas morning."

Luc took a drink of soda and then asked, "What happened to her? Something bad or sad or something had to have happened or this wouldn't be a story you'd be so eager to share."

Micah sighed. "Didn't you just yell at me for interrupting you when you were telling your story?"

Holding up both hands, Luc said, "Sorry. Continue on with your great epic, o' master storyteller. You won't hear another word from me until I read my verdict." He made a cross over his heart and said, "I swear."

"Okay then. It is a tragic story, but one that proves out of tremendous grief you can build a monument to everlasting love. Like I said, the year was 1933 and little Nadine told her daddy what she wanted for Christmas," Micah picked up his tale. "She told him she wanted a dollhouse and he promised her she'd have it.

"That autumn, her father started building the dollhouse with his own hands in the backyard. But before he could finish, Nadine came down with diphtheria in November. The family was quarantined; the area around their home was roped off and work on the dollhouse was abandoned. Christmas was coming closer and Nadine's health took a turn for the worse: she developed pneumonia."

Micah continued. "In an attempt to lift her sagging spirits, Nadine's parents gave her two of her Christmas presents early: a life-size doll and a China tea set. She asked about her dollhouse and when her daddy told her she'd get it when she was well, she said, 'Daddy, me want it now.' But it wasn't meant to be, at least not in this life."

"What happened?" Luc demanded. "She died; I knew it."

"On December eighteenth, Nadine died," Micah acknowledged. "And within days her grief-stricken father hired a contractor and work began on the dollhouse, only this time in a different place: on little Nadine's grave in the city cemetery."

"They built it in the cemetery?"

"Not only in the cemetery," Micah explained, "They built it right on top of her grave. A beautiful brick house with awnings, a chimney, sidewalks, and all kinds of stuff. Her grave marker is inside the dollhouse. And if you look through the window you'll see..." he trailed off.

Luc took the bait. "What? A ghost? What?"

"If you look in the window you'll see the life-size doll and the China tea set her parents bought her for Christmas. You can also read the inscription on her grave: 'Our Darling Little Girl, Sweetest in the World, Little Nadine Earles. In Heaven we hope to meet. Me want it now.' And if you look over on the mantel of the miniature fireplace, you'll see a framed photograph of a grinning little girl with bouncy brown curls—a four year-old Nadine Earles. According to the legend, her father never recovered from losing her; he was known to visit at her grave for hours on end, even sitting through rainstorms to be with his little daughter."

Looking at his friend, Micah saw Luc's eyes were watery, like the tears were ready to spill in a waterfall at any moment.

"That one got to me," Luc admitted. "Imagine keeping your promise like that; after your little girl dies, you still build her the only thing she really wanted for Christmas."

"I know. I couldn't believe it."

"Wild. To build the dollhouse right there in the cemetery," Luc said. "To enclose her grave. We have to go."

"Yeah," Micah agreed. "I've wanted to go ever since I read the story in an edition of *The Weekly World News* back in the eighties. It was on my mind for years after I read it. I remember I cut the article out and kept it for a long time. I don't know what happened to it, but it popped back into my head a while back. After doing some research to verify the story was real and not a work of fiction, I decided then and there I had to go to Alabama and visit Nadine's grave. It may sound weird, but I always felt drawn to it, like I really had to pay a visit."

Luc scratched his cheek. "We could always take vacation time and go down to Alabama to see her dollhouse. I have time available, and you're your own boss so you can take whatever time you want."

Micah nodded his agreement.

"Then what about going down later this summer or this fall?"

"As long as it's before Halloween," Micah said, "we should be okay with any week we choose."

"And if we go after school starts," Luc pointed out, "there won't be crowds of families on vacation to contend with."

"True."

Luc grinned like a schoolboy. "You think we'll be able to talk the caretaker into opening the dollhouse door so we can take a sneak inside?"

"Why in the world would you want to go in?"

"Like you don't want to go inside and check it out," Luc said. "You might feel a strange presence, like little Nadine is hanging around to play with her doll and China tea set. I'm serious."

Micah shook his head and said, "I don't want to go because I think she's hanging around. I wanted to go because I thought it would be like witnessing the great love her father had for her. Never once did I ever think about sneaking inside. It takes a mind like yours to come up with that."

"I didn't mean we'd sneak inside and steal anything or hold a séance, if you're implying that's what I meant," Luc defended himself. "I thought maybe we could stick our heads in and maybe get a picture that wasn't taken through the window glass. I never meant we should exhume the body."

"I never thought you meant grave robbing," Micah told his friend. "You're all defensive, acting like I accused you of saying 'Dig her up!' Calm yourself before you have a stroke."

Luc laughed. When he stopped, he said, "I'm not defensive. I just think it's hilarious how sometimes you read the most or the worst into something I say, even if I make the most innocent remark."

"As if any remark you make isn't laden with innuendo or double meaning," Micah said. "You've done it so often it's automatic now; you don't have a clue you're doing it anymore."

"I need more to drink," Luc said and got up from the sofa. "I'm not having this conversation, you paranoid weirdo. You live in a state of delusion and I fear for your sanity, my friend."

"Uh huh," Micah muttered to himself as he got up from his seat. "*I'm* the crazy one around here."

Luc's voice carried from the kitchen. "You have any more of those cracked pepper crackers? And I can't find the mustard."

"What are you doing, preparing an hors d'oeuvre tray?" Micah asked. "The mustard's in the refrigerator and the crackers, if I have any left, are in the cupboard where they always are. Didn't you eat breakfast before you came over here?"

Pulling his head back out of the refrigerator, Luc looked at Micah and said, "I don't think you have any mustard."

"Get out of the way." Micah looked into the fridge and immediately pulled out a bottle of mustard. Handing it to his friend, he said, "Knock yourself out. Did you find the crackers yet?"

"You're out."

"Did you even look?"

"I looked." Luc sounded offended. "Exactly where you told me to look—in the cupboard. I looked twice."

"Did you look in this cupboard?" Micah pointed to the one beside the refrigerator. "This is where I keep the crackers."

Luc answered sheepishly, "I might not have looked in that specific cupboard. Maybe I missed it."

Micah located the elusive crackers, and he and Luc once again picked up their conversation about death.

"Where would you rather go," Luc questioned his friend, "to Nadine's dollhouse in Alabama or to the cathedral—somewhere in Asia, I think—the one constructed out of human bones?"

"I read about the cathedral," Micah said. "And actually there are more than one made out of bones in various places across the globe; the one in Asia is supposed to have a great throne of human skulls. Another monastery or something that has a big chandelier made of skulls and bones."

As he chewed his cracker, Luc poured himself some soda. He took a drink and said, "If you went to that cathedral, do you think you'd be able to sit on a throne made of hundreds, if not thousands, of human skulls? I mean, wouldn't it creep you out in the slightest to be perched atop a pile of human remains?"

Micah helped himself to one of the hors d'oeuvres before answering. "Well, it wouldn't be like the remains were fresh or even those of people I knew personally or would recognize. Those people have been dead for probably hundreds of years, or at least one hundred years."

"Still, I think I'd rather go to Alabama and spend some time with Nadine."

"Me, too. Or, we could pack up and head to India and see if we could tour the Taj Mahal. Take a ton of pictures. Maybe head to Egypt and see the Great Pyramid. Check out the remains of King Mausolus' tomb."

"It could be our World Death Tour. Aaahhh, the scent of salacious suffering and the aggregation of agony does serve to inspire me," Luc intoned. "Maybe that's a little morbid, but you get the general idea. This is something we could really do if we set our minds to it."

Would he be able to find the answer he'd been seeking most of his life? The thought of touring the globe to see first-hand all the monuments to death did intrigue Micah. He didn't know if that meant he'd gone off the deep-end or if he just wanted a trip around the world.

"Earth to Graves. You in there?"

The sound of Luc's voice brought him back. He must have had a blank look on his face because his friend threw a cracker at him.

"You might want to cut down on the out of body experiences in the middle of the day, dude, before you get lost out there in infinity."

"I was just thinking about what you said," Micah explained.

"What did I say?"

Micah bent down to pick the hurled cracker off the floor. "About the World Death Tour," he said. "We could actually go to a couple places in the course of two weeks. It's not so much of a stretch. A good many of the places we want to visit are within hours by plane of each other."

"You were listening," Luc said. "I thought you'd tuned into some far away frequency. Good to know what I say doesn't fall on deaf ears."

But Micah had stopped listening. He was back in his own thoughts, thinking about whether or not it was such a bright idea to go around the world visiting places that were erected as lasting reminders of death.

"…ing to a brick wall."

"What was that?"

"I said, most of the time talking to you is like talking to a brick wall," Luc repeated. "Where is it you go when I talk to you? Is it nice there?"

Micah laughed. "I'm sorry. I keep thinking about actually going to see the Taj and the remnants of Mausolus' tomb and all the other places."

"Dude, do I bore you so much you have to retreat inside your own head to find entertainment worthy of your attention?"

"I'm serious."

"I sure wasn't," Luc admitted. "We'd have a cool time off trekking around the world seeing all those places, but do you think we'll ever be doing it? I sure don't. Maybe we'll have the opportunity to see the Taj Mahal or Nadine Earles' doll house or maybe even a handful more, but there's not a chance we'll go on a whirlwind death tour. Get it in check before I call out the whoopy squad."

Micah nodded his acquiescence. "But it was a rather awesome thought."

"Yeah." Luc handed his friend a cracker with some mustard smeared on it. "But it would sure as shit cost an unholy fortune in airfare alone.

"And we'd be gone for a month at the least."

"So I guess a better idea would be for us to sit on the couch and keep watching that sort of stuff on television."

"Unless we did really get to Alabama to see little Nadine's doll house," Micah said. "That's feasible."

"I agree. We could go see it before Halloween, if you're serious about seeing it this year," Luc said. "Or we could wait until next Spring."

"Why next year?"

"If we wait, we can take more time and drive down instead of flying. That way we can stop in Virginia and see the Female Stranger's grave. Yeah?"

Micah nodded again. "I get what you're saying. We could plan our itinerary and see all kinds of sites."

Luc ate a cracker. "You know," he said around chewing, "there are a ton of sites we don't know anything about. But I bet we could gather the info we need on the internet. I know of a couple websites right offhand we could check out."

"The one about celebrity graves," Micah said. "You never know where a celebrity grave might be."

"We can call it our Partial East Coast Grave Tour," Luc suggested.

"You need to work on that one more," Micah told his friend.

Chapter Eleven

The next day Micah found himself with time on his hands at work so he turned on the television. Finding hilarity in the television show he was watching, he laughed so loud and long he almost didn't hear the phone ring.

"Sacred Scarab."

"You sound like you're touching yourself inappropriately while you're supposed to be working, my boy," Vanessa Archer said instead of a greeting. "You better knock it off or one of your customers might walk in on you and either get offended or aroused."

Micah laughed. "No. I'm watching *Hemann Bartholamieux's Very Very Trim Cooking and Talk Show*. His new single debuts this week; it's called *Poison in the Wine*."

"You know that show's neither a real television talk show nor a real cooking show, right?"

He ignored her. "What do you want, you dirty-minded old woman?"

"To remind you about Johanna Edensburg's estate auction at Lansington's; it's a week from Saturday," she answered. "Do we still have a date or did something better come along for you?"

He looked at his desk calendar before answering. "Nope, nothing better has come along yet, so we're still on."

"You can be such a smartass. I'm your elder, so you better start showing a little respect," Vanessa said.

"Please. You're a dirty-minded old woman and you stole that cockatoo you keep in a big golden cage," Micah sassed.

"I rescued Chiffon," she countered. "It was a mission of mercy."

"It was a misdemeanor."

"They never caught me," she pointed out. "I got away scott-free because what I did was Divine; it was probably pre-ordained."

"Such a drama queen. Why does almost every conversation with you deteriorate into melodramatics?"

"Better than overdramatizing everything."

"You are about as good for my soul as necrotizing fasciitis is for my flesh," he told her.

"Flesh-eating bacteria, eh?"

"It's a wonder our friendship has lasted as long as it has," he said.

"We have too much in common to part, pretty boy," she said. "You gotta have friends, especially in our business."

"Speaking of which, will you be meeting me here, am I picking you up, or what?" he asked.

"I don't believe we ever nailed down the particulars, son. What would be the best? We could meet in the middle and call our date Dutch."

He thought about their previous conversation. "I seem to recall you called me up to ask if I was going to the auction and to see if you could hitch a ride."

"Then quit beating around the bush and tell me if you're picking me up or if I'm thumbing it to Lansington's."

"You are an insufferable wench, you know that?"

"It's called charm," Vanessa said before she laughed. "I'm a dainty lady and don't you forget it."

"Yeah, those exact words come to mind when I think of you."

"Don't get fresh."

Micah bit his tongue to hold back the retort that came to mind—it had something to do with freshness and expiration dates, but he thought it would be prudent not to say it. After all, he didn't want to cross the line and risk offending his friend, although she freely admitted she could take as good as she gave when it came to insults. Her skin was as tough as chainmail.

Instead, he said, "Vanessa, do you think Storm Cassavettes will make it to the Edensburg auction? I know he's a big animal advocate and some of the proceeds from the auction will benefit the Von Daemon Foundation."

"Storm, and I probably shouldn't be telling anyone this because he works so hard to keep it private, donates money to the Foundation on a regular, anonymous basis. He respects the fact they take in all sorts of animals and find homes for them, but what really makes him find favor with the Foundation is the strict no-kill policy," Vanessa said. "He has such a soft spot in his heart for animals, and so he does what he can to help keep them from being killed."

The Foundation was originally created and endowed by the wealthy Von Daemon family who lived on an estate in the middle of a forest area in Grantsville, Maryland; the Von Daemon family took the adage of man's dominion over all animals to mean man should protect the animals as best he could and provide a safe haven for them in their times of need. Within a decade, the family had established satellite organizations in three dozen towns and cities up and down the East Coast, providing sanctuary and medical care as well as finding homes for countless thousands of animals.

Since its inception in the early fifties, the Von Daemon Foundation has worked to save the lives of hundreds of thousands of animals—from cats and dogs, to llamas, reptiles, birds, rodents, and even fish—that people no longer wanted to keep as pets. Some animals lived out their lives at one of the many Foundation centers when a home couldn't be found for them. No animals were ever turned away. And the Foundation even made pick-ups so animals would not face abandonment.

Although the Foundation was financed by the personal wealth of the Von Daemon family, it did accept outside donations and held a celebratory award ceremony each year to honor those people who either performed extraordinary actions to save the lives of animals or those who raised funds for or donated rather large sums to the cause. It was one of the most prominent events of the social season, with the ceremony broadcast live via satellite to every Foundation organization on the planet.

Being honored in a few months for his efforts, Storm Cassavettes was the new face for the Von Daemon Foundation; his image appeared in magazine ads and on billboards all across the planet. The commercial produced by the Foundation's studio featuring Storm Cassavettes and his message—in its first week of release—caused the Foundation's website to have more than two million hits from people wanting to lend their support.

The Shadow Cassavettes Memorial Animal Organization, or the Shadow Sanctuary, as it was nicknamed, was scheduled to open in a mere two months, with Storm Cassavettes himself spearheading the organization.

"And there is even a cemetery for the animals who pass on. A real Rainbow Bridge, tastefully done, connects the Shadow Sanctuary and the cemetery. It is absolutely stunning. Wait until you see it."

"How does he manage to do everything?" Micah asked. "I mean, you know him, how can there be enough hours in the day or enough energy in his body to allow him to do everything?"

"I agree his efforts are tireless," she said. "But he believes so strongly in this cause. It plagues him to think of any animal in pain or fear. His ultimate goal is for no animal to be abused, unwanted, or neglected."

"Admirable qualities, but he has to sleep sometime."

"And he doesn't merely pay it lip service, either. He puts his money where his mouth is, literally. At a show a couple months ago," Vanessa explained, "Storm unveiled his collection: ties and boxer shorts and shirts—all with an animal connection or inspiration and no animal products used at all. The profits have been earmarked for the Shadow Sanctuary. They've already been introduced in stores around the world and online."

"I do believe I knew about the clothes."

"The amount of money being raised is so incredible it restores my faith in mankind," Vanessa said. "He is truly an amazing man, and the best is yet to come as he continues to spread his message to the people of the world."

Micah reached for his pen. "Do you happen to know the website address?"

"For the ties and boxer shorts or for the Shadow Sanctuary?"

"For the shirts. They sell shirts, too," Micah reminded her.

"I know, but I know you." She laughed. "You'll be running around in your designer ties and boxer shorts. Oh, pardon me, and your shirt."

"Funny. Do you know the address?"

"Of course." She gave him the website information. "But if you'd like, I can ask Storm to send you over a sampling, a selection of items for you to have. Tell me your sizes and I bet he'll have them sent over in a couple days."

An intriguing thought, but Micah said, "This is for charity, I wouldn't feel right about getting stuff for free."

"Nonsense, my boy. Storm would be happy to do it because he'd see it as publicity and promotion. You could wear the clothes and tell people about them. Word of mouth is the best form of publicity. You're a business owner, you know that."

He did know that. It was the main reason most small businesses survived. "Of course. You don't think it's gauche for me to cadge freebies from someone I haven't met yet? I don't want him to think I'm a leech or anything."

Vanessa laughed again. "He knows of you. I've brought up your name in several of our conversations."

"I hope you spoke of me in a nice manner."

"Like I would say you're a pervert or something."

It was Micah's turn to laugh. "One never knows about you."

She ignored the remark. Instead of a retort, she said, "We need to digress and finish our discussion about the Edensburg auction."

"The auction, yes. How about I pick you up since you're basically on the way and then we won't be taking two vehicles?"

"Sounds like a plan of epic proportions."

"And we can split the cost of gas."

"I knew there'd be a catch."

"Nothing's free."

"Tell me about it," she said. "Okay, we got a deal."

"And maybe we can grab something to eat either before or after the auction," Micah suggested.

"Let's eat after," Vanessa said. "Watching the bidding go higher and higher always gives me an appetite."

"Don't get too excited and buy something you don't want or can't afford," Micah warned. "Some of those artifacts should go for a pretty penny, and I don't want you to have to mortgage the bird to pay for something."

"I doubt something like that will happen," she said, "because the knives and statues aren't really my taste. But the auction for the jewelry…I might be in some trouble there. I get somewhat carried away when the bright and shiny stuff goes on the block. Johanna's estate, so the rumor goes, may have some treasures from Fabergé; I may have to bid on an egg. Maybe a baker's dozen." She laughed at her joke.

"You better not get caught up in the bidding; an egg, anything from Fabergé, will go for hundreds of thousands of dollars."

She whistled. "I know. Fabergé is a hobby of mine. The hobby is reading about it and looking at pictures of the items, I mean. I know there were only supposed to be so many of the Imperial eggs created by Peter Carl Fabergé for the royal family of Tsar Alexander and later his son Tsar Nicholas, along with a select few created for others." Vanessa paused only to inhale before continuing. "Such a shame only a few of the eggs remain intact; I mean, with their treasure inside them. There were, if memory serves, only 69 known eggs, of which only 60 or 61 have survived to the present day. And there are 54 known Imperial eggs, of which only 45 or 46 have been known to survive today. It's so sad to have such items of beauty and craftsmanship lost to the world."

Impressed, Micah gave a whistle of his own. "I never knew you had this passion for Fabergé. It's simply amazing. We should definitely go see the eggs that are in this country. I know there is a handful at the Virginia Museum of Fine Arts, which makes it the largest collection of the Imperial Easter eggs outside Russia. But that's all I know of in America."

"There are three in the New Orleans Museum of Art. And I know of two even closer to home in Walters Art Museum in Baltimore and two more in the Hillwood Museum in Washington, DC," Vanessa said excitedly. "I've even read there was one in the Cleveland Museum of Art."

"Hey, at least we know we can about nine of the Imperial Easter eggs if we went on a jaunt down to Baltimore, Virginia, and DC," Micah said. "It's not unthinkable, you know. What do you say about thinking about it?"

"I'm giddy over the idea," she said. "I think it's wonderful, Micah. Would you really be willing to go see the eggs with me?"

"I sure am; it'll be fun."

"Maybe I could invite Storm and Nannette and maybe Khris King to go with us," she said. "Would you be offended?"

"It would be my big chance to meet these people you're always talking about," Micah said. "What better way to get to know someone than to drive around in a car with them for hours at a time."

"You'll love spending time with them; they're a likeable crew." She sneezed.

"Bless you," he said.

"Thank you. Must be dust."

"Maybe if you'd clean once in a while," he teased.

"You come in here and clean and then we'll talk about why I don't do it very often," she said.

He knew what her shop looked like: furniture piled high all over the place. "Maybe you could lay out the store better or move to a bigger place if you insist on having such a large inventory," he suggested.

"Why the hell would I move when I own this building free and clear?" she wanted to know. "I wouldn't want to have a mortgage at this juncture in my life. Besides, I do rather well in my current environment. And my customers love my cramped shop; it intrigues them and they love it when they find their treasures."

"Just trying to come up with options."

"And I appreciate the gesture." She sighed. "I am so comfortable with my existence; after all my years, I'm thrilled to be able to admit that. It's something not everyone can say."

He agreed. "Not a lot of people out there in the world are comfortable in their own skin or comfortable with themselves. We're lucky to be able to say we are in a comfortable place in our lives."

The sound she made was almost wistful. "When I was young, I thought my youth would last forever and I believed that was the happiest time of my entire life. But as I got older, I realized the best was truly yet to come. And in my twilight years, I have come to understand, like I just told you, this is the most content time of my life. I am the happiest I have ever been and I think I am experiencing the highlight of all my years, if you want to know the unvarnished truth of the matter."

"Wow. You sure are philosophic today. Maybe you could have a second career as a motivational speaker. You could tour the country talking about everything from the Imperial eggs to growing older and wiser."

"And have a damned fine time of it, too," she said. "I tell you, I would enjoy a trip to Russia, especially now that the remains of the two missing Romanov children, Alexei and Maria, have been uncovered and verified. Of course, there is still much debate over which sister it was buried with the son, but at least they can all be reunited in burial in the imperial crypt at the Saints Peter and Paul Cathedral in St. Petersburg."

"That is a comforting thought," Micah agreed.

"My boy, I need to jump off the phone. My friend Nannette just came in the door and we are off for our lunch date. Tootles to you."

And she hung up the phone.

He laughed and put down his own phone.

* * * * * * * * * * *

Later on, just as Micah was about to call it an early day, the phone rang. It was David Cordone calling to discuss the matter of the statue.

"Have you had any luck on tracking the damned thing down?" he asked. "Or is it still as elusive as ever?"

"It'll probably always remain elusive, David. It may never surface in your lifetime or mine or even ever."

"Nonsense," Cordone rasped. "Like I told you, the signs all point to it coming into sight. And it should be soon."

Micah wanted a straight answer about the signs. "You keep talking about these signs. What signs might they be?"

"Son, you would probably think I was a crazy old man if I tried to explain to you the things I have taken as signs."

I'm close to thinking you're nuts already, Micah thought. "We've had this conversation, David. I won't think you've gone off the deep-end if you tell me what you know or what you suspect."

The sound of Cordone's labored breathing traveled through the phone.

"Unless you can't talk about it right now," Micah said.

"Nonsense. I only think I should tell you in person," Cordone said. "You'd be able to understand better if you were here."

"In Grantsville?"

"Yes." Cordone went into a coughing fit.

Micah heard David Cordone's caretaker in the background suggested the elderly man not over-do it. And he also heard Cordone use some colorful language to tell the caretaker what to do with the unsolicited advice.

"Micah, my boy."

"Yes, sir?"

"What are your plans for the evening?"

He had to think about it.

"Well?"

"Nothing pressing, I suppose," he admitted.

"What say you about a trip up here? I suggest dinner and then we can carry on a face to face conversation. I've grown tired of this phone exchange."

Dinner at Cordone's home was a welcome invitation. In addition to being a loyal customer, the man was a friend and his collection included pieces Micah knew were not only extremely valuable dollar-wise but also historically speaking.

"I'd be more than happy to drive up this evening."

"Good," Cordone said. "And just so it is worth your while, how about bringing me up some of those broken statue bits you keep in the back."

"You don't have to buy something so I'll come for dinner," Micah told him. "I'm happy to drive up."

"I'm not being nice. It's a sound business investment."

Micah knew Cordone had more than enough "broken statue bits" in his collection than he'd ever need. The man was being generous as always.

"Do you think you'll be able to make it by six?" Cordone questioned. "I don't want to rush you or anything."

Only about twenty or twenty-five minutes away, Micah knew he could make it by six and said so. "I look forward to it," he said.

"Anything special you'd care to have for dinner?" Cordone asked. "Just state your preference and I'll make sure the cook prepares it."

After having made his request, Micah said, "I'd better say goodbye for now so I can get some things done before driving up."

"Do you need to push back the time an hour or two, my boy? I don't want to rush you; it's not set in stone."

"Absolutely not, sir. I'll be able to make it by six without a problem."

"If you're certain."

"Yes. Now how about we say goodbye for now?"

"As you like it," Cordone said. "I'll be seeing you by six."

They hung up.

* * * * * * * * * * *

On his way out of Rain Falls, Micah noticed a woman working in the yard. Kathy Silvestri was hard at work in her flower garden, decked out in a wide-brimmed hat, sunglasses, high heels, and a very low-cut blouse.

"Apparently her prize peonies aren't the only thing she has on display," he murmured as he returned her wave.

Thrice married and thrice divorced, she put the world on notice she was on the prowl for husband number four—stalking the potential candidates with a stealth any jaguar would envy. The ink was barely dry on her current divorce papers, and yet she was already pricing another wedding ring.

Micah mused on how everybody seemed to know everybody else's business in a small town. "And she thinks she fools people with her pearls on Sunday act. She's about as transparent as bubble wrap."

He knew Kathy Silvestri had been the hot topic of the Sunday after church crowd on more than a few occasions when they congregated in his shop, more in the mood to swap gossip than to shop for antiquities. And she'd most likely be the subject of discussion again and again.

Laughter escaped him as he thought of her walking down the aisle yet again in a formal white gown. That in itself had been a point of shock and awe amongst the gray-haired ladies of society.

He signaled left and turned onto the on ramp to the interstate. The drive to Grantsville wouldn't take long. He checked the dash clock: a half hour before six. The thought of Kathy Silvestri faded as his mind turned to the subject David Cordone wished to discuss.

He thought about the research he'd conducted so far on the subject, the information in a folder on his desk at home.

"I should've brought it with me," he said aloud. "Too late to turn back and get it now. I bet David has either the same research or access to the internet."

A flash of silver light momentarily distracted him. Moments later, the crack of thunder followed.

"Just great," he said as fat rain drops splashed against the windshield. "The reputation of Rain Falls follows me."

He turned on the headlights and the windshield wipers.

The closer he got to Grantsville, the heavier the rain fell.

"Jesus. Maybe I should take this as a sign," he said to himself as he exited the freeway. "Turn back now or be forever doomed."

He turned on the radio just in time to hear the beginning of Bruce Springsteen's "Pink Cadillac."

David lived just inside the town limits of Grantsville. The Cordone estate was less than sprawling but spectacular in its own right. The four story house sat back from the road on a six acre sea of manicured lawn spotted with islands of flower beds.

But none of this was visible from the road because a wall of trees surrounded the property and lined the driveway; so there was an air of privacy to the place. There probably should have been a wall of stone around the place and armed sentries on guard considering the collection of antiquities Cordone had on display in his house.

Despite the apparent lack of security, Micah knew the estate was equipped with a state of the art system, the best money could buy, to keep everyone and everything safe from theft or harm.

As he traveled down the drive, a canopy of green above gave the ride a storybook quality. Micah almost expected to have to brake for the gnomes and fairies to cross. He did see a deer standing beneath one of the trees on the left; grazing on the grass, it lifted its head and stared at him as he drove by.

Cordone's caretaker/butler stood in the open doorway waiting for Micah when he pulled up. Micah knew at some point he had to have either been monitored on camera or his presence detected in some other manner. Micah thought he remembered the man's name was Adam.

"Good evening," Adam said. "Glad you could make it tonight."

"Thank you. I'm always happy to accept an invitation to visit."

"Mr. Cordone is excited you've agreed to come for dinner," Adam said before stepping back to allow Micah entrance to the house. "He's very anxious to discuss certain matters with someone of a like mind."

Micah couldn't help but think maybe David Cordone was a tad off his rocker. If he, Micah, came to discuss matters and if he, Micah, was of a like mind, did that make him off his rocker, too? "It's too confusing to think about sometimes," Micah said aloud without realizing it.

"Yes, I agree," Adam said. "But it may be for the best if we simply shine him on. After all, if he wants to talk about elusive statues and submerged island paradises, who are we to discourage him?"

Nearly blushing from embarrassment at having his thoughts heard, Micah ducked his head and said, "Is David waiting for me?"

"Of course," Adam answered. "I'll show you to the library. That's the room he prefers to use when discussing An'khyr."

Micah stopped in his tracks. "So you do know all about this?"

"I've worked for Mr. Cordone for some time now," Adam explained. "In that time, I have been privy to much of his eccentricity. And I have heard all about the magic and mystery of that long-forgotten imaginary island."

"So you don't believe in it?"

Adam smirked. "I haven't lost my mental faculties, Mr. Graves. My grasp on reality is quite strong. I don't believe in An'khyr, Aladdin, Atlantis, or Abu J'hurda Ian. I'm sure he enjoys his flights of fancy and it doesn't hurt me in any way to listen to him go on and on about them, and he does go on and on. But don't insult me by asking me to share his belief in them. That is something I cannot and will not do. No disrespect intended, either to you or to Mr. Cordone."

Micah stared at him.

"Shall we?" Adam gestured to the library.

Micah nodded and followed.

Once in the library, David Cordone greeted him and invited him to sit. Micah sat in one of the wingchairs and looked around the book-filled room.

"Have a drink, son," Cordone insisted.

Adam quickly served the two men a very dark red liquid in expensive-looking crystal goblets.

Micah accepted one of proffered glasses and drank.

The alcohol burned going down.

"Good God. What's in this? Battery acid?" Micah gasped

Cordone said, "Of course. I frequently serve battery acid to my guests. I find it amuses me to no end."

Adam snorted before making his exit.

After catching his breath, Micah said. "I've never been able to figure that guy out. What's his deal?"

"Adam? He's a tight-ass, sure," Cordone answered. "But he's loyal and I can count on him."

"You have more faith in him than I ever could."

"Oh, don't let his bravado fool you."

"Bravado?"

"You don't think I know how he talks about my beliefs in An'khyr," he shocked Micah by admitting. "Hell, he might be able to blow smoke up your hole, but he sits in here for hours on end questioning me about the statue and An'khyr."

"Really?"

Cordone chuckled. "He likes to tell everyone how he doesn't believe or want to hear my stories, but he's the one who always asks me to tell him a tale or some facts. I don't force him to hear anything he doesn't want to hear."

Micah took another swallow of the red drink before speaking. "To hear him tell it, you practically handcuff him to the chair and force-feed him the stories against his will. At least that's what I got out of the conversation."

Cordone waved it off. "Let him have it. He's a good lad and I couldn't do without him. If he needs to banter on, then he's free to do so. Besides, I didn't invite you here to debate about Adam."

"No, sir, you did not."

"Shall we begin our discussion over a refill before dining?"

"Sounds good."

"Let me summon Adam."

Micah stopped his friend. "Just let me pour the drinks. You don't have to run Adam back in here."

Cordone allowed it and Micah got up to refill their goblets.

"I know you have a lot of questions, my boy," Cordone said. "Tonight I'll see if I can't provide you with some answers. After all, I certainly can't expect you to conduct all this work on my whim, without any proof."

Thinking before speaking, Micah finally said, "There is one thing I really would like you to explain."

"And it is?"

"These signs to which you keep referring. What are they and how do you know about them?"

Cordone leaned forward and clasped his hands between his knees. "Would it better suit the situation if I said they were emanations and disturbances in the universal lining?" He couldn't keep up the tone for long and dissolved into laughter, which became a coughing fit.

After he took several deep breaths from his oxygen tank, he apologized. "I only meant it as a jest. Because I'm sure you must think me a doddering old fool who meanders around making up these stories."

"I was following along and honestly trying to believe some of it," Micah confessed. "My next questions were going to be about emanations and psychic forces, if I decided you actually believed what you were espousing."

"I couldn't help it. But I assure you, I have laid these very eyes," he gestured to his own, "on the statue, like I explained to you already."

"And I completely believe you believe you saw it."

"Don't patronize me and don't hand me that psychological crap—I never did put any stock in that quackery anyway. I know what I saw and I know it's still out there on this planet somewhere."

"And you know it's going to be making its grand reappearance soon," Micah interjected. "I'd like to know why you think this, David."

Cordone leaned back before he began his explanation. "As you probably already know, I was a bit of a name in the field of archeology."

"Of course. Your collection alone—"

"No interruptions, my boy," Cordone requested. "If you please, allow me to continue. What you may not know, because only a few names are out there in the public eye, is that I was also one of the pioneers of cryptoarcheology. Are you familiar with the term cryptoarcheology?"

"Oh, I'm allowed to speak? Yes, I've come across the term in my research. It means to study old civilizations."

"Not quite. In actuality, it means to study hidden or as yet unknown civilizations," Cordone corrected. "I, myself, wanted to form an official group of academicians to help the new field gain respectability, but the majority of my associates wanted to remain anonymous while we conducted our research, et cetera.

"This is a bit of an introduction to help you better understand what I am about to say next. It may come as a surprise to you, but I still have many connections in this field as well as other more mainstream fields of study. I am privy to a great deal of information before museums and universities and even governments are made aware."

"You make it sound mysterious."

Cordone permitted the interruption. "The field can be mysterious. After all, you must research in secret in case someone tries to steal your finds, and you need to keep any information close to the vest lest you later be proven wrong. The field has its many detractors—those who mock it and its researchers."

"Because people do not understand the basic concept so they spread what they think they know, what they've heard in the media," Micah said.

"Precisely." Cordone pointed at Micah. "The majority of the population would much rather perpetuate the chain of ignorance than to take a few precious minutes to do a bit of research and get the true facts. It sounds unsavory and unfortunately it is. Ignorance is bliss, as the saying goes.

"But I digress. I am still in the loop in the field of cryptoarcheology as well as the field of cryptozoology, the study of hidden or still unknown animals or species." He paused for a few seconds and scratched his nose. "For an old guy, I still have my fingers in a lot of pies, come to think of it." He laughed. He breathed more of the oxygen from the tank. "But I suppose I've earned my share of respect in those fields. And there are a great many favors owed to me, debts I never bothered to collect, and so on."

"And that's how you come across your information?"

"My colleagues make sure any information in which I may be potentially interested is passed on to me, yes."

"So you've been tracking this statue?"

Cordone frowned. "Not the statue. In our field, we are not only interested in civilizations but also smaller groups. We concern ourselves with groups who may possess knowledge of the civilizations we are researching. The information of the statue comes from such a group."

Micah was lost and admitted as much.

"Sometimes we must conduct our research covertly, not unlike governmental groups," Cordone explained. "Members have been known to go undercover to perform the tasks to retrieve the necessary knowledge."

"Like the CIA. You send in your agents."

"You make it sounds like an espionage movie. I assure you, it's not at all that intriguing. Although," Cordone sighed, "we have been known to lose good men and women to the cause."

"The covert operations are dangerous, I presume."

Cordone laughed, but not out of mirth. "Let's just say most of the groups would prefer to keep the knowledge and items they possess for themselves; they are not too happy to discover an imposter among their numbers. Unfortunately, we all know when we volunteer for such a service the possibility exists we may not make it out, but the sacrifice is worth the risk for the times we gain the knowledge we are after."

"Can't make an omelet without breaking some eggs theory."

"It's a cut-throat field, my boy. Even fellow researchers have been known to be less than virtuous with each other. It's all in the name of glory. Can you imagine the infamy involved if you were responsible for bringing to light a creature thought to have been long extinct or to never have existed? The same can be said of civilizations. You would most certainly secure your place in history if you were the researcher who brought evidence of An'khyr to the world."

Rubbing his chin, Micah said, "So glory and riches are probably the goal of more than a couple researchers?"

"As much as I hate to admit it," Cordone said, "the answer is yes. But then again there are more who are serious about bringing knowledge to the world in hopes of bettering existence for all. But that is not at all what we are here to discuss."

"Right."

"You wish to know how I can say the signs point to the statue resurfacing soon. And I shall tell you," Cordone said and breathed more oxygen. "There is a group of people of interest on which some of my colleagues have been keeping close watch, a group with a connection to the fabled land of An'khyr to be precise. And the whereabouts of the statue are germane to the interests of this group."

Micah uncrossed his ankles and leaned forward. "So you're saying you know the statue is about to make an appearance because a certain group under surveillance believes this to be true?"

Cordone shook his head. "When you say it like that, of course it sounds ridiculous. Have some faith in your fellow man."

"How in the world can you expect me to take this on blind faith? The only thing you have to go on are the beliefs of some mysterious group who are under surveillance. What kind of evidence is that?"

"It wouldn't mean a thing under normal circumstances."

"And let me tell you in case you didn't know," Micah said, "these are less than normal circumstances, David."

"I understand your hesitance, I really do. This group we're discussing is not comprised of your average weirdos. They've actually had the statue in their possession. I believe they, in the sense of the group and not specifically any individuals, were responsible for the fire which claimed the life of one of my colleagues after he had the statue in his possession. I told you about him."

Micah acknowledged that he remembered. "But still, how can you take this as gospel? I understand you've seen the statue and know for yourself it exists. I have a problem with the idea of some clandestine group squirreling away this statue. And then losing it."

Cordone snapped his fingers. "It was stolen from them a couple decades back and never seen again. They were unable to track it down, until recently."

"Until recently?"

"Yes. And the story is the statue was sold into a private collection. Somehow or other, the collection is going on the market."

Micah was intrigued. "And how did this group learn about this?"

"There are pieces of the puzzle missing, I admit," Cordone said. "From the people on the inside, the information is sketchy. Only top-ranking individuals know more than a few details. Apparently, the group has decided to move once the statue surfaces, since no one seems to currently know its exact location."

"And this is how you know it's about to resurface. I get it." Micah strummed his fingers on the arm of the chair and thought how the story could be right out of his newest paperback novel. "And as farfetched as your story is, it's crazy enough to almost be the truth, as strange as that statement may be."

"Because how could anyone make up a story like it? I completely agree with you, my boy. It's a story right out of thriller fiction."

"So where do we go from here? And how will we know when this statue makes its grand appearance?"

"The situation is being monitored as closely as possible," Cordone assured him. "When I know more, I will most certainly pass the information along to you."

Adam made his entrance to announce that dinner was ready to be served.

"Shall we adjourn to the dining room, Micah?" Cordone suggested.

"Lead the way."

Cordone patted Micah on the shoulder and said, "Don't let all the information confuse you. I realize it is an almost overabundance. Just sift through it and do your best, that's all I ask of you."

"Not at all. If there is anything to be found, I will find it. After all, I've searched for elusive objects before and I haven't come back empty-handed yet."

"And I have enough faith you'll have it in your hands soon enough," Cordone said and then changed the subject. "Let me show you my latest tremendous find; I believe you'll find it intriguing."

Micah was intrigued. He wondered what ancient treasure the man would parade before him.

"I couldn't believe my good luck when I stumbled across them, and in a plethora of colors," David explained as he placed a cardboard box on the table in front of Micah. "Go ahead," he gestured, "look inside and behold my latest acquisitions."

Micah carefully lifted the top off and peered inside. There were several white boxes arranged inside the larger box. He lifted one out and opened it, then another, and another until all thirteen were revealed.

"What the hell are these?"

"Skull candles." Cordone laughed until he was forced to resort to his oxygen in order to catch his breath. "My boy, these are perhaps my greatest discoveries. I'm hoping to reveal to the rest of the world the existence of these marvels of creativity."

"Uh huh."

"Don't pout. I know you were expecting me to reveal artifacts from a heretofore undiscovered civilization. But sometimes you have to just kick back and enjoy the simple things in life." He took a hit off his oxygen. "And I find great joy in these works of art. I have thirteen of them to represent the legend of the thirteen Crystal Skulls."

"Wow," was all Micah could say as he stared at the candles, picking them up and putting them back down. "May I ask where you found these things? You couldn't have gone into the local novelty shop and picked them up; they had to have been hand-poured. They are quite the creations, aren't they?"

"I found them online at a marvelous store. Stormsong-dot-org, I believe; fantastic store, you must check out. I saw them and had to have them."

"Imagine that: You just having to have something."

"You are the last person I'd ever think would try to imply I waste my money. And I admit I may waste money buying things I want, but after all, it is my money to waste. People seem to forget that."

Micah apologized. "I meant no offense. Of course I have no business passing judgment on what you buy or how much you pay for it. These skull candles strike me as more than a bit odd. But you explaining why you bought them does make me worry less about the state of your mental condition." He laughed.

David laughed as well. "I've been called crazy by more people than I care to remember, and I've always known I'm off-kilter, but I am miles away from complete crazy, my boy. No matter what public opinion proclaims. And don't beat yourself up, because I know what you meant; I just couldn't let an opportunity to needle you pass me by. I hope you don't hold it against me."

"Not at all."

"Good. Now, let's put this discussion away for the night and enjoy this nice dinner before the cook has a fit."

"I am in complete agreement," Micah said.

Interlude

Someone was in the room.

He opened his eyes. The overhead light was so bright it hurt his eyes. His eyes fell upon her. Did he know her?

She stood at the foot of his bed, looking up at him.

Her face was somewhat familiar. He tried to think but the haze covered his thoughts and he couldn't find his way through it.

"Were you watching me sleep?" he asked as he pulled the thin blanket up over his chest. "Do I know you?"

"No," she answered. "We've never met."

He thought hard for a minute. "Are you the new doctor?"

"No."

It was confusing. But he knew he was in the hospital. "Are you a new nurse? Is it time for medication?"

"I'm not your nurse."

"You must work here." He looked hard at her. "Don't you?"

"I do not work here." She smiled at him. "I suppose you could say I am merely visiting tonight."

"Oh, that won't do at all. Not at all."

"Why is that?" she asked.

Why would that not do? His mind was too foggy. He wasn't quite sure. "It's too late for visits," he finally blurted out. "You're not supposed to be here and they will throw you out...right on your ass if they catch you in here. Maybe have you arrested for trespassing. Bothering the old people." He stared at her. "Do I know you? I don't know if I know who you are. Maybe we met and I just can't remember. Sometimes I don't remember things so well."

"No, sir. We've never met before now."

"Who are you?"

She smiled again. "I'm a friend."

"My friend?"

"I am your friend."

"Didn't you just say we never met before? I'm...I don't understand." He looked down at the blanket. His mind was a blur of images and thoughts, like television channels bleeding into each other's frequencies. Some of the images overlapped each other and he couldn't tell one from the other.

"You understand. We're new friends. We only met just now, Ted," she explained to him. "We met tonight."

He looked up when she said his name. "My name *is* Ted."

"I know." She moved up to the side of the bed. "I know your name."

"Did I tell you?"

She took his hand in hers before answering. "You didn't have to tell me. I knew who you were before I arrived."

"How did you know?"

"Ted, it's my job to know who you are."

"But you're not a doctor and you're not a nurse," he said. That much he had clear. "And you're not here to visit."

"Right so far," she admitted.

"Do I know you?"

She patted his hand. "It's almost time to go, Ted."

"You leaving so soon?" he asked. "You just got here."

"I'm leaving," she said, "and guess what?"

"What?" His eyes lit up like a kid playing his favorite game.

She leaned down as if to whisper a secret. "I'm leaving and you're coming with me. I am taking you out of this place."

"Really? I get to leave. I've been here…" he trailed off. His mind wouldn't let him think how long he'd been there. "I can't remember."

"It's okay, Ted. You don't have to remember; I already know."

"What do you know?" he demanded. "What is it you think you know about me? What do you want with me?"

"I'm telling you."

"You're not to be here," he said, reaching for the call button. "I'm getting the nurse. This isn't right."

She took the call button from him. "Calm down. It's all right, Ted. I am supposed to be here."

He stared at her. The fog lifted from his mind and he knew. "I know what you are." He didn't say who.

"You do?"

He thought he had it but it was slowly sinking back into the cloudiness. He concentrated and it almost came back. "Are you Death?"

A smile briefly landed and then was gone. "Not quite. You almost had it, didn't you, Ted? You nearly had it nailed."

"You do remind me of someone I knew a long, long time ago. But you couldn't be her. She's been gone for more years than I care to remember."

"You may have seen me before because I've been around for a while, my friend. I've been watching you closely."

He pulled his hand from hers.

"No need to be frightened. I wasn't teasing; I was giving you credit. That old disease has you in its grasp but sometimes you fight through. I see the sparks here and there in your eyes still."

"You're an angel." He said it with pride and great dignity. Tears danced in his eyes. "You've come to take me home."

"Very good, Ted. It won't hurt, I promise."

"I'm not scared. I'm ready. I've been ready." He raised his hand and touched his temple. "They all said I was gone but I'm still in here. Sometimes I feel so far away is all. I'm still in here, but I feel like I'm starting to fade away."

"Everything will be okay, I promise."

"It won't hurt any worse than what I've been through. I'm tired and I just want it to be over."

She took his hand in hers again and began to speak softly. "Take my hand and come with me; from this body you'll be free…."

"Is that a poem?" he asked. "I can't quite catch what you're saying."

She didn't answer him. She continued on. "…and into the Mourning Light.

His eyes felt so heavy. All he wanted to do was lean back against the pillows and close his eyes for a few minutes.

So he did. His breathing grew shallow; in seconds he was gone.

And so was she.

Chapter Twelve

The next day, Micah's head pounded from his lack of sleep.

He rolled out of bed at eight, after getting home and going to bed at five in the morning. And Sia was no help. The cat kept following him around and meowing every two seconds, each cry like a spike piercing Micah's temples.

"Why can't I say no to people?" he asked himself. "And why must you torture me like this, cat? What have I done to deserve this? "

He spent hours with David Cordone after they'd finished eating discussing various things from ancient Egypt to the state of the world until the wee hours of the morning.

And although he was used to staying up until early morning, Micah was not used to crawling out of bed after only three or four hours of sleep. He wanted to pull the blankets up over his head and go back to dreamland for a longer visit.

Crawling into the shower, he hoped the freezing cold water would wake him up in a dramatic fashion. It was a good thing the windows were closed so the neighbors couldn't hear the string of expletives that exploded out of his mouth as the Arctic temperature water hit his naked flesh.

It woke him up, all right. His teeth were chattering by the time he turned off the water and reached for a towel.

If he hadn't promised his assistant Leslie Abrahms he'd be in early so she could take the day off, he would have called in dead and stayed in bed most of the day to catch up on his sleep. But it wasn't meant to be.

Sia kept crying as he followed Micah from the bathroom back to the bedroom.

"Is there anything I can do to shut you up?" Micah asked. It seemed like the cat knew when Micah was tired beyond belief and at those times the cat incessantly cried the distinct meow that grated Micah's nerves.

"I love you. Please stop. I'll give you a whole bag of treats if you cease. I'll give you fifty bucks to go buy whatever treats suit you best if you shut up."

The bribery attempt failed.

Micah knew if he could keep from strangling Sia the cat would eventually stop. It didn't really matter because he had to be at the shop by nine to open anyway. So the cat could keep at it all day and he wouldn't be there to be annoyed by it.

He got dressed and went to the kitchen for a drink. Sia followed like a devout disciple, and got rewarded when Micah fed him some treats.

"At least that shut you up for a couple minutes." He drank his glass of soda before making some toast.

Sia sat with his tail curled around his bottom staring straight at Micah.

"You're not getting any of my toast; I gave you treats."

Micah knew the cat loved to lick butter off the bits of toast he gave him, but he didn't feel like sharing.

Micah sat down at the table to eat.

Sia kept crying for some toast until Micah relented and fed him bits.

"You are so damned spoiled. I don't know why I put up with you."

At this, the cat jumped up on his lap and reached up to put his paw on Micah's face, a gesture he used to show his affection.

"To love an animal and to be loved by that animal in return is to know the greatest love of all," he said.

Sia rubbed the top of his head against Micah's chin.

"I like you a lot, too," Micah said. "It's just sometimes I'd like to flush you down the toilet, especially the nights you keep jumping up on and down off the bed every time I'm falling asleep."

Micah usually threatened to take the cat to the pound, but he knew he would never be able to do so. And he suspected the cat knew it was an idle threat, too. No matter how many times he'd threatened to cart him off to the pound, it never happened because he could never bear to part with the black cat.

The phone rang. Micah got up and reached for it.

"Just making sure you were awake and you didn't forget," Leslie said. "I didn't want to go on about my business without calling."

"Nope, I am wide awake and ready to step out the door any minute. I am bright-eyed and bushytailed."

"I seriously doubt that, but I can't thank you enough for taking my shift. It really helps me out."

"No problem," he assured her. "It's for a good cause."

"I'll make it up to you, I promise."

They said goodbye and Micah hung up the phone.

"I guess I better get going before I say screw it and go back to bed." He reached down to stroke Sia on the back of the head and then left to go to work.

* * * * * * * * * * *

On every continent, in every country, there is a highly caffeinated or stimulating drink used to perk up the people who are feeling sluggish. Micah stopped for one of them on his way to the shop.

Normally, the only caffeinated drink he consumed was soda, but sometimes he found he needed the heavy kick of coffee. He only used it as a last defense against total shutdown because he really disliked the taste; no matter what kind of flavoring was added to the concoction, he found it still tasted nasty and bitter to him.

After stopping for his drink, Micah headed straight to his shop. With cup in hand, he unlocked the door and walked inside in time to hear the phone start ringing.

"And so it begins," he said to the surrounding air.

Still before the official opening time, he decided to let the machine answer.

"Micah, my boy." It was David Cordone. "I know you're not normally in this early and I wanted to leave you a message before I head out of town for a few days. Thank you for coming over and keeping an old man company last night. If I had known you had to be up and at it so early this day I would have sent you home earlier than the crack of dawn."

Micah groaned, thinking of the sleep he'd lost.

"But then you're young enough to miss a few hours of sleep without falling over halfway through the day. I'll be in touch when I get back in town. Hopefully, you'll have some news for me or vice versa." And he hung up.

Micah reached down to delete the message. The phone rang again. He hesitated, deciding not to answer.

"Hey there. It's Vanessa Archer. I just wanted to leave a quick message about the Edensburg auction: it turns out Storm Cassavettes will indeed be making an appearance. So you'll get to meet him, Micah. Finally, right? Anyway, I have to run; I have a lovely customer who wants some knickknacks for her parlor and she's on her way here as we speak. Talk to you soon."

"Must be my day to be popular," he told himself as the grandfather clocked chimed the hour. "Time to open; I don't think I'm going to make it through the day. May the gods take pity on my soul."

But he didn't have time to sit because as soon as he unlocked the front door a group of older women came entered, chattering about picking up some "lovely things" to take home with them.

"Young man." One of the women beckoned. She didn't bother to wait for him to walk over to her. "Yoohoo. Will you help me? I'd like to have more information on this little doggie man." She held up a statuette of Anubis in one hand and pointed to it with the other.

"I'd be more than happy to assist you," he said. "What would you care to know about Anubis?"

"What a funny name. Is it Jewish?" another of the ladies asked. "Ethnic for sure. Maybe Eastern European."

"No," Micah answered patiently. "Anubis is an Egyptian god."

"I thought they worshipped cats," yet another of the ladies said. "Somewhere I remember reading about how they worshipped cats."

The lady holding the statuette turned back to Micah. "Then why on earth would they have a statue of a doggie man? I don't understand."

Micah wished a lightning bolt would strike him down. "The Egyptians had many gods upon whom were bestowed animal characteristics—a complete hierarchy of them, in fact."

"Are you sure?" the one lady demanded. "Because I'm relatively certain I know what I'm talking about when I say they worshipped cats."

"While it is true the ancient Egyptians held cats in high regard," Micah attempted to explain, "they did not literally bow down and worship the cats. That is an inaccurate rumor."

"I don't think I could worship a cat. I like them well enough," one of the ladies said, "but I sincerely doubt I could worship one. Maybe a Siamese, because they are regal and graceful, but that would be the only cat I think I could worship. Of course, those Rag Doll cats are sweet as anything."

This is going to evolve into a discussion on cat worship, Micah thought. *Save me from this.*

"What about this man?" the lady who held Anubis asked. "He's obviously a dog, but I can't tell which breed. Not an Alsatian, that's for certain." She looked to Micah before asking her next question, her face all serious. "Would he have been like their devil since dogs chase cats?"

And here we go. "Not quite. Anubis was in charge of the dead. He has the head of a jackal, not quite a dog, and he is most often associated with mummification and he presided over funerary rites. He's depicted as having the head of a jackal most of the time, but there is a famous depiction of him with a human head in the Temple of Abydos of Rameses II. And there is a statue of him represented as a full jackal in the tomb of Tutankhamen," Micah explained to the group of women. "Anubis is a very ancient god, the original god of the dead before Osiris was named as such. After Osiris was named god of the dead, Anubis was relegated to be the conductor of souls in the Underworld, or the psychopomp."

"You mean he made mummies?" one of the ladies asked. "Pulling the brains out through the nose and taking out the internal organs? I saw that on a special on one of the history channels. Gross. Gave me nightmares for a week, all that talk of mummies and the underworld."

"Oh, Zelda, he was like a mortician," the lady holding the statuette, Hortie, said. "Nothing gross about it. Someone has to take care of the dead. Should they be left in the streets to rot?" She looked back to Micah and said, "What else can you tell us about him? Why the head of a jackal?"

"Probably because jackals hunted around the edges of the necropolises of Egypt," Micah answered. "And a fun fact is Anubis is represented as having a totally black head, unlike a real jackal."

"I'll take it," the lady said without asking the price. "Wrap him up; I must have him for on my mantel. He'll be the perfect conversation piece. I'll steer the conversation to him if he doesn't attract attention. But I believe he's something people will notice as soon as they walk into the room."

"As you wish, Madame." Micah smiled.

He took the statuette away to securely wrap it in bubble-wrap; he knew the woman would regale her friends, probably over a game of gin and a glass of the same, with the tale of Anubis. She'd probably forget most of what he'd told her and fill it in with the first things that came to mind when she retold the tale.

"Young man," the woman called. "Could you come and take this one, too?" She gestured with the statuette of a woman with the head of a cat. "I'd like both statues. Could you take this?"

The woman who kept insisting the Egyptians worshipped cats came over quickly and said, "See? I told you I knew what I was talking about, Hortie."

"Hush now. It's another of the gods, and it will look lovely with the other on my mantel. I'll put some candles on there and it will be simply beautiful, stunning. Won't Sherrijean be so envious?" She giggled naughtily. "Oh, she'll be greener than a spring pea with jealousy."

Micah returned to take the statuette. "This is a lovely lady by the name of Bast, or Bastet, depending on which name you'd prefer to use. She is the keeper of cats. And of secrets." He whispered the part about the secrets and the ladies giggled like teens. "Bast is probably the best known goddess after Isis. She was known to give great blessings and rewards to those who were in her favor; to those who were not in favor, let's just say her wrath was legendary and very frightening. She is one of the avenging deities whose duty it was to punish the sinful and the enemies of Egypt. No evil-doer escaped her attention and she meted out justice as she saw fit. Judge, jury, and oftentimes executioner. Sounds grisly and bloody, but a necessity."

"Ohhhhhhh," the lady whose name Micah never caught drawled. "She sounds like a lady you didn't want to mess with unless you were looking for trouble. I needed her on my side for my third and seventh divorces."

"Cats were held sacred by Bast," Micah continued, "and this is probably why many people believe the ancient Egyptians worshiped cats. The truth, as I said, is the Egyptians did not worship the cats. Cats were held in high regard. And it is possible Bast's importance in the pantheon was due to her association with cats since the Egyptians placed such a high value on the cats. To harm a cat was not only a major transgression, it was a guarantee that Bast's vengeance would fall upon you and, as I said, her wrath was indeed frightening."

"I love them both," Hortie said referring to the statuettes. "I'll purchase both, please. And I'll continue to look around to see if anything else strikes my fancy. I bet there are all kinds of lovely things hiding in here, waiting for me to find them and take them to their new home."

"Please feel free to browse," Micah said. "I'm certain there a many items here which may 'strike your fancy.'"

He took the statuette of Bast to be wrapped and placed in a box beside Anubis for the transport to Hortie's house.

The ladies took their time browsing through the Sacred Scarab. Micah was grateful for the distraction from his sleep deprivation. Their questions had him on the border of madness after the first hundred, but still he smiled and answered as best he could because they were paying customers; the pair of statuettes Hortie picked out was worth opening the shop for the day. He could rest easy knowing he had money in his pocket because of the older lady, to make the annoyance more palatable. Not that they were annoying, just the inexplicable sweetness they exuded.

Still, his patience began to wear thin because of the constant attention the ladies craved and he was glad to see the door close behind them when they left. He was never so happy to treasure the peace and quiet in his life. It was as if he'd been trapped underwater and just broke to the surface for air.

He sat down and said, "Thank God."

The door opened and Micah looked up.

Hortie stuck her head back into the shop and smiled, her eyes sparkling beneath the brim of her hat.

"Thank you again, young man," she said. "You certainly were worth stopping for, and you made my day."

Micah smiled back at her and she was gone, shutting the door behind her, the little bell above the door tinkling.

"Higher power, deliver me from this," he looked to the ceiling and begged. "I can't take anymore of it today."

* * * * * * * * * * *

The remainder of the afternoon was deader than dead. No other customers ventured into the shop. Micah spent his time doing the dusting Leslie was famous for doing. He poked through the shop discovering smaller items he'd nearly forgotten tucked into nooks and crannies. It was like a whole new world he was seeing: he'd never quite realized all the various items he'd brought into the shop. Of course he knew his inventory, but it was really something to slowly walk about and look intently at the items—an oddly spiritual moment.

And he cursed himself for not bringing the disk with the manuscript for *One-Eyed Esmeralda and the Bowtie Thief* on it; he could have spent the down time writing a few more chapters and fleshing out the story. But he was forced to meander around the shop or search the internet for more information on An'khyr, and he was up to his fill on that subject for a while.

Bad enough images of An'khyr were filling his waking moments, but they'd been leaking into his sleeping ones as well. He was dreaming about a place he was pretty certain existed only in the realm of mythology, contrary to the belief held by David Cordone and his friends.

He'd poured over innumerable pages of information, surfed countless dozens of websites, and came to the conclusion the statue, if it truly existed, was unknown in its whereabouts. He'd been suspicious of Cordone's mental faculties even before having dinner with him and listening to his wild tales. After that, he was more than positive Cordone and his fellow cryptoarchaeologists were more than a tad touched in the head, what with the stories of infiltrating secretive sects and funneling information back to their fellow researchers.

"If the damned statue is more than a myth," he muttered to himself, "I'll kiss my own ass."

Then he remembered the envelope on his desk from the auction house—Lansington's—which had been messengered over the night before. Inside the envelope were photographs of the lots up for auction from the Edensburg estate.

Micah had connections and he wanted to have a look at which items were going to put before the public before the rest of the public was able to have a look.

He knew somewhere in the collection was an item or three for which he could find a home or homes, and at a marvelous profit. David Cordone, for all his kooky talk of winged ankh statues, knew a wonderful piece of antiquity when he laid eyes on it, and Micah knew Johanna Edensburg had a similar sight when she was putting her own collection together.

He spread the three dozen or so photographs out on his desk and perused them. The knives were amazing in the pictures; he could only imagine how glorious they would appear in person. Of course there were the simplistic daggers carved from stone, but others were works of art with gemstones and inlaid gold and silver details. Absolutely amazing, it was. And to think Johanna had collected most of the sacrificial knives in secret, because as a society lady it simply would not do to be in possession of such a bloodthirsty assortment.

Micah knew the woman personally and he knew she took great delight in hiding her knives and statues away from the ladies who lunched. She often joked about how they would all become light-headed and positively pass out should they ever lay eyes on her objets d'arts.

He laughed in spite of himself. Sad to know she was gone. Ladies such as Johanna Edensburg were few and far between.

Chapter Thirteen

The last thing he ever thought he'd have was a pseudo-career as the author of paperback bodice-rippers. Micah laughed every time he received a royalty check in the mail for his work as his alter-ego Iamma Trampp.

But the money wasn't half bad; he'd lucked into the market and immediately found a niche. The readers seemed to go into a feeding frenzy each time a new Trampp novel was published. Although none of his books ever made it onto a bestseller list, each title managed to sell several thousand copies—generating enough money to keep him happy, and his publisher, too.

Micah managed to keep his secret identity just that for years. He enjoyed the extra income and the outlet for his creativity. Once upon a lifetime, he dreamed of writing period mysteries a la his literary idol Elizabeth Peters, but it was not meant to be. He couldn't get the plots to be cohesive and the characters were weak imitations of the worst of the worst. Stereotypical crap.

Then as a lark, he began to pen a romance for a contest being held by one of the small-time presses. What began as a joke became his semi-career; it turned out he had a flare for the world of romance…the hokier the better and the readers ate it up like sugar to a candy-addicted child.

The publishing house snapped up his manuscript and contacted him— actually, they believed they were contacting the lady who had crafted such a fiery tale filled with lust and historical intrigue: Ms. Iamma Trampp.

His being a man didn't even make them break their stride as they wooed him to sign a publishing deal with their house.

It was then Micah learned some of the biggest selling names in the romance industry were really men writing under pseudonyms, and many of their readers were none the wiser. In fact, some of the readers knew their favorite writers were men, but they much preferred to keep the illusions alive. And some of the publishing houses and the men writers actually went as far as signing actresses to contracts to appear as the "lady" writers. It happened far more than people realized.

When his first title for the publisher—the manuscript which won the contest—was released as an actual paperback book it miraculously sold—to the wonder of Micah. The royalties on that book were still coming in since it never went out of print because new readers come to the genre everyday. And Micah did enjoy getting those royalty checks in the mail.

Of course, Micah's publisher didn't schedule public appearances because to do so would shatter the image Iamma Trampp's readers had of her. When asked to describe their favorite author, they usually said she wore red high-heels and feather boas as well as a lot of animal print.

The description always made Micah laugh.

But as farfetched and out of this world as his readers may seem, Micah knew they were loyal to the core and would often camp outside bookstores all night to ensure they would be the first through the door at opening time to secure their copy of the newest Trampp masterpiece.

And he never breathed a word of his romance writing to anyone, not even friends and associates like Leslie Abrahms, Vanessa Archer, or Lucian Sterling. None of them would care, but Micah preferred to keep his writing close to the vest. He'd rather not share it with anyone.

Vanessa would have a field day with it. Micah knew she'd read several Trampp novels while toiling away the hours in her shop because she'd find one way or another to weasel a synopsis of the plot into their conversation. Vanessa loved to read anything that may possibly have a dirty scene or six in it. "Because if it's in a book," she'd claim, "it's not porn, it's literature."

And he had to admit, some of his plots were as convoluted and bawdy as Vanessa Archer, herself. The woman could cuss a blue streak and tell a dirty joke without cracking a smile.

She was as one of a kind in her own way as Johanna Edensburg had been in hers, he thought.

* * * * * * * * * * *

Luc called around seven and asked Micah if he had any plans for the evening. Micah admitted he didn't and before he could say he wanted to turn in early because he'd lost too much sleep the night before, Luc had already invited himself over. Micah resigned himself to the fact he probably wouldn't be catching up on his sleep just yet.

"I'll even stop and get pizza or Chinese," Luc offered. "My treat and you pick. Go ahead and tell me."

Micah didn't care and said as much.

"C'mon, you have to care," Luc prodded. "Just pick one."

"How about you pick and I'll be surprised? That way I don't have to concentrate and make a decision."

"Okay, but don't complain all night if you don't like what I bring over," Luc said. "You're so picky I don't know how you survive. You can't live off cereal, you know. I know you have boxes of the extra sugary stuff in the cupboards. I know you have an unholy attachment to white pizzas with sweet peppers, but you need to take chances on new dishes. There's a whole buffet of food out there for you to experience, man; order something new."

"Maybe you'd better get me some of the mixed vegetables in garlic sauce and some lo mein to go with it," Micah said. "I love their garlic sauce and they're the only place around that doesn't cook the broccoli to mush. That's gross. Get me some of that and—"

"And make sure there's no meat in it," Luc put in. "I know the drill. You want some of those crunchy noodles, too?"

"Yes, and some of those mozzarella sticks they make. And get some of those onion rings, too. I like those. Make sure you get extra garlic sauce so we can dip. Maybe a couple pieces of the chocolate cake, the kind with all the almonds on top. Don't get the white, it's dry and tastes like chalk dust."

Micah heard Luc laughing and asked, "What's so funny? Did I miss the joke or am I the joke?"

"For a guy who said he didn't care what we had for dinner, you're awfully specific with your order. You think you want to call it in yourself so I don't forget anything?"

"Just make sure you grab a couple sets of chopsticks."

"What'll we watch?" Luc asked. "Anything good on TV tonight or do you want to get a movie?"

"Let's watch that special on the Seven Wonders of the Ancient World," Micah suggested. "Sounds like it should be good. They're supposed to do computer reconstructions of each Wonder."

"Recreating all seven, eh? They're shooting for the stars. Imagine the research they must have put in."

"Yep. And not only are they showing the recreations, they're supposed to explain how each Wonder was built. I saw a couple previews of the program this week and it looks interesting. It's two hours long and they're gonna have to pack a lot of information into those two hours considering entire books have written about the subject. The temple of Artemis in all its white marble glory should be a sight to behold. The temple was supposed to have been built twice and between the two stood for more than a total of 800 years: two centuries the first time and six centuries the second."

"I didn't know it was built twice. Learn something new every day, don't you? Sounds like a plan then. Hey," Luc said quickly, "I never asked how your dinner with David Cordone went last night. He talk your ears off with all his weird nonsense? And how did you manage to feign interest?"

Micah rolled his eyes. "Sometimes you can be an ass," he said. "I didn't have to feign anything. David's good company and full of very interesting information, I'll have you know."

"He's full of something," Luc said, "and it's called crazy."

"Find your manners. Go get the food. The show starts at eight," Micah said and hung up the phone.

* * * * * * * * * * *

Luc arrived about fifteen minutes before the start of the program.

He walked in, bags of take-out Chinese food in each hand, and instead of a greeting said, "Is it true there's a crystal skull up for auction in the Edensburg estate? I thought they were extremely rare."

Micah answered, "No, the skull is not part of Johanna's estate; it's part of another lot up for auction the same day. And I do believe it is one of the real, rare crystal skulls. Who told you about it?"

Luc had put the bags down in the kitchen and was portioning out the food. "Juanita down at the convenience store. I stopped for gas on the way to pick up the food and she was blabbing it to everybody who came through the doors. Talking about how the skull was here because it wanted to impart ancient wisdom to us and cure us of all our ailments."

"That's a belief some people have about the skulls, that they are something like computers in which the wisdom of either the ancients or an advanced civilization is stored and we need to crack the code or figure out how to access the computers," Micah explained while plating his own food. "There are a million different beliefs and myths surrounding the skulls or dealing with who or what created them. I'm not one for wild theories, but imagine if it's true and they can unlock the mystery of how to save the world. That's worth more than any amount of money. It's a provocative thought. People have built their entire belief systems around it."

"How do you know so much about this stuff?" Luc asked between bites. "You know more weird stuff than I do."

Micah ate a forkful of lo mein noodles before answering. "Because I make it my business to know all sorts of stuff in case my customers are interested in any of them; you never know what catches someone's fancy," he said, remembering Hortie and her fascination with the statuettes of Anubis and Bast. "Being knowledgeable is one of the ways you establish a good reputation. People respect education and experience, and Cordone has plenty of both."

"Maybe David Cordone would be interested in adding a crystal skull to his collection. You should ask him."

"David Cordone already owns one." Micah smiled. "I know a great deal about my customers, including but not limited to their tastes and their possessions. You could say I make it my business to know such things."

"Seriously, the man has a genuine crystal skull?"

"Seriously."

"That is wicked cool," Luc said. "How does he know it's real?"

"A man like David Cordone has his methods," Micah answered. "I've learned to never question him. He has more experience and better connections than I could ever hope to have."

Luc reached for a mozzarella stick and dipped it in the marinara sauce before taking a bite. "He has a wide sphere of influence," he said around the cheese and breading, "that's for sure."

Micah used his chopsticks to swirl noodles. "The experience the man possesses is amazing; imagine the things he's seen and done over the course of his career. And he's still out there, traveling to these awesome places and investigating. Granted, in his condition it takes him longer and is more of an effort, but the point is he's still out there doing it. He's a damned good role model."

"He's climbed pyramids and trekked through jungles and deserts," Luc said in agreement. "I envy him that. To walk among the ruins of antiquity. You experience some of the same feelings, don't you?"

Micah looked at him and said, "How so?"

"Well, you handle pieces from ancient civilizations on a daily basis. I've seen you uncrate statues and such, and the look on your face leads me to believe you'd love to be out there excavating the pieces yourself, uncovering the treasures and bringing them back to display."

Micah nodded. "I understand where you're coming from, and it would be an experience to be out in the field, but I'm built more for this end than the actual trekking and excavating." He took a drink and continued. "I enjoy what I do and I don't discount the idea of someday traveling to Egypt or Peru or somewhere equally as fantastic, but for the moment I'm content to work in my shop and bring these treasures to people who otherwise might never have the opportunity to see or touch them."

They ate in silence for several minutes before Luc said, "You've said you'd enjoy traveling to see the Taj and the ruins of Mausolus' tomb, why not visit Egypt to see the Valley of the Kings? It's along the same lines."

"No, it's not."

"How is it not? It all deals with death in one form or another. Death of a person or a people, death of a civilization."

"Visiting is just that, visiting; it means I'm not out digging in the dirt or sand to discover something I want to see."

"You're arguing semantics at this point," Luc said. "I don't think you'd be allowed to dig in the Valley of the Kings unless you had a government permit anyway, Graves. All I'm saying is you should broaden your horizons. If the two are different animals, try to combine them. Take one of those archeological vacations, the ones where you go on a dig so you can experience what it's like. You get the best of both worlds. You might get a surprise."

After thinking about it, Micah said, "Might be something I'll look into in the future. I think I have an aversion to digging. That might be why I don't garden, not even a potted plant."

"Twisted as twisted can be, you are."

"Thanks a lot."

"Your logic can be difficult to follow at times," Luc said.

"Tell me about it," Micah mumbled. "My mind is mixed up more than normal these days. More questions than answers. I need answers."

Luc paused before taking another bite and asked, "What was that?"

"Nothing," Micah answered. "Nothing at all." He silently vowed to search for answers to his questions.

PART III

Grave Secrets

Chapter Fourteen
In A Dream

Darkness all around.

The only lights were the dancing flames of candles placed here and there, flames that caused shadows to seemingly sway in time to silent music. Peaceful.

"Where am I?" Micah asked out loud.

Here with me, came the answer.

"Where is here? And who are you?"

No answer.

Micah turned in a circle. He couldn't see very far in the dim light but there was nothing out there as best as he could tell.

The stones under his bare feet were smooth and cool against his soles. He began to walk, following the stone street. A feeling in his gut urged him on whenever he'd stop and think about turning back. The need to continue grew inside him; he needed to follow this part of the journey to its end.

Someone had gone to all the trouble of placing candles along the street. Along each street, as far as he could tell.

To guide him?

To light his way?

He thought it was a possibility.

But who?

Maybe the person who has been speaking to him through his dreams. The same person he must be seeking now.

A cool breeze eased through the night air, causing the candle flames to dance even more, but not enough to blow any of them out.

Micah stopped again.

Find me, the voice came again.

"Where am I supposed to go? Where are you?"

Find me, the voice urged.

"How am I supposed to find you? I don't know where you are," Micah yelled, his voice shattering the calm and echoing away. "Give me something. Some clue. You have to help me here."

Nothing.

Not a single response.

Still he continued walking, following the candle-lined street. He walked for what felt like an eternity.

Eventually he came upon a huge pile of stones.

Rubble and ruin.

And then it changed. Stones and shards shifted. A temple rose from the ruins; it rose high into the sky. Carved into its walls were a multitude of symbols; Micah felt he should understand what they meant but he didn't. He reached out to touch the symbols and remembered doing the same once before in a different place.

"What do you mean?"

Divine inspiration did not overwhelm him. As hard as he tried, he could not find in his mind the key to unlocking the secret of the symbols.

All in time, the voice whispered, sounding so very close to Micah.

He turned, thinking whoever spoke must surely be standing behind him. No one in sight.

All will be revealed when the time is right, the voice assured him. *And the time is drawing near.*

Micah felt at ease. He didn't understand everything yet, but deep down inside he knew he would because he believed the voice.

You must find me.

"I will. I promise," Micah said.

Bring the key to me.

Micah thought he understood part of what the voice asked of him. He believed he knew a piece of what he must do.

Release me and I shall reward you.

And the scene changed in the blink of an eye.

Micah found himself standing in a valley, standing before a mountain. The ultra-bright sunshine made him shield his eyes with his hand as he looked upon the mountain before him.

The scene felt familiar to him.

"I know this place," he concluded. "I know I know this place."

Looking around him was no help because everything was blurry, severely out of focus. He couldn't make out anything no matter how hard he squinted.

But he couldn't shake the feeling he knew the place.

Here.

Micah wasn't certain he heard the voice the first time.

Here.

"Here?"

I am here.

Somewhere, Micah knew, somewhere near. He felt it: a tingling like electricity spinning up his spine and along his skeleton. There was a great power located somewhere nearby. He trusted the specifics would be made known to him.

A rumble in the ground—subtle at first, and then becoming stronger.

Everything began to shake.

A sound like harsh thunder filled the air.

Darkness descended.

Fear didn't touch him; Micah knew although he was experiencing this no harm could come to him. He was protected.

Voices.

Loud voices.

Men yelling and the sound of machinery.

He didn't know exactly what it meant, but he knew he was experiencing something yet to come. A premonition, but a vision given to him by the power behind the voice which spoke to him.

Without being able to see what was happening in the darkness, Micah couldn't be sure, but it sounded like a horrible accident had occurred, a gigantic explosion or something.

It was followed by an even louder rumble and the earth trembled.

More yelling. This time it was drowned by the increased rumbling noise.

Micah felt the air close in on him. Dust and grime filled his eyes and they immediately began to tear up.

And then it was all gone.

He awoke to Sia sitting on his chest and kneading the blanket and sunshine streaming in through the window because he'd forgotten to close the drapes when he went to bed the night before.

The cat stopped pawing the blanket and peered closely at Micah's face, almost as if he was checking to make sure Micah was okay.

"I'm fine, buddy," Micah assured him. "Just a dream"

But he knew it wasn't.

Chapter Fifteen

Eight-twenty-six Ashwood Avenue was a quiet tree-lined neighborhood. The Victorian house, set back from the street in the middle of a lawn enclosed by a wrought-iron fence, appeared to be more of a private residence than a place of business. He double-checked to make sure it was the correct address before finding a parking spot and getting out of the car.

A tasteful plaque on the right brick column announced quietly **T and A Psychic Investigation and Paranormal Research Facility**.

He'd phoned ahead and spoke to a secretary, he assumed, and made an appointment, so he knew he was expected. Still he was nervous about meeting the psychics. The only psychics he knew of were the telephone psychics he saw on those television commercials late at night.

But these people wouldn't be distant voices on the other end of the phone line; he'd be face-to-face with them. And he hoped they'd know what the hell they were doing, what with a name like "T and A" conjuring up all sorts of imagery, because they were the only ones listed in the phone book—with the exception of Madame Rita's Palm Reading and Vegetarian Hot Dog Stand. Somehow Micah didn't think Rita was a viable option for him.

Summoning his courage, he walked up to the front door and rang the bell; actually, he pulled the chain to ring the bell inside the house because it was an old-fashioned door bell.

The woman who opened the door looked like a cross between Bea Arthur and Wayland Flowers' Madame, not that there exists much difference between the two. Once she opened her mouth to say hello, he definitely heard the resemblance. Her beyond-blood-red lipstick distracted him for a few seconds.

"Hello, I'm Micah Graves," he said, "and I have an appointment."

"Of course you do." She smiled and opened the door wider. "Come on in."

He followed her through the foyer and into a sitting room, where she spoke to the back of a high-back chair. She spoke to the woman seated in the chair, but the chair was so big it consumed the woman until she stood up: a Doppelganger.

"Then we better put on our professional faces," the double said. And then she said, "Close your mouth; we're twins."

He recovered his composure and apologized. "Just a surprise I wasn't expecting." The pile of fur on the love seat caught his attention for a moment.

"We do tend to get that reaction," the first said. "Introductions are in order. I'm Tangerine."

After the fruit, he thought. *Hope you don't live up to your name.*

"And I'm Angina," the second said.

Angina? he thought. *You were named after chest pains?*

"And we are T and A Psychic Investigation and Paranormal Research Facility," they said together. "Welcome."

"Uh huh," Micah responded. "Okay, I'm here to get your help." His eyes traveled back to the fur on the love seat.

The two ladies noticed Micah noticing the pile of gray, black, and white fur and exchanged glances.

"We have cats," Tangerine explained.

"Two of them," Angina volunteered.

At that point, the fur undulated and separated. What was black and white fur became a skunk; what was gray fur became a possum.

"Purry Mason is on the right," Tangerine said.

"And Raymond Purr is on the left," Angina added.

Micah stared at the two ladies and said, "Uh, you know those aren't cats, right?" *Could it get any weirder? A skunk and a possum they treat like cats.*

"Shhhh," the ladies whispered, "don't tell them."

"Okay," he said. "I don't mean to interrupt, but I called earlier and I do have an appointment."

"Yes, you do." Angina gestured to the coffee table. "We were just reading to pass the time.

He looked at the two hardbacks on the table: *The Witches of Lipstick* and *The Wizard of Gauze*, both by the same author.

"No interruption at all," Tangerine told him. "After all, we were expecting you. Now, we prefer to conduct all of our business transactions in the part of the house we set aside for that purpose."

"If you would follow us, please." Angina led the way out of the sitting room to the corridor; she stopped in front of a door with a rather large mirror on it. "Through here is our research facility."

Nice, down in a damp, dark basement with two crazy ladies, he thought. *Perfect. This is a serial killer moment if I ever saw one.*

Once he followed them through the door and down the stairs he realized his initial assumption was incorrect. It was a basement, but a fully finished basement.

"We converted the rooms to house our facility several years ago when we realized our hobby was fast becoming our calling in life," Tangerine explained. "It was a common sense decision."

"After all, why pay rent on office space when we had all this space down here we weren't using for anything?" Angina continued. "As my sister said, what started out as a hobby grew into a full-time occupation and we find it simpler for us if we work from home."

"Except for when we go into the field to research or investigate," Tangerine said.

Micah closed his eyes against a vision of the twins outfitted like the *Ghostbusters* and stifled a laugh behind his hand. "Do you get out into the field very often? To investigate paranormal activity or sightings, I mean?"

"Very much so," Tangerine answered. "Most of the time it's because we are asked to look into manifestations of those who have gone beyond the veil and need assistance realizing their time here is done and the like. Spiritual beings who have no corporeal state."

"Ghosts," Angina simplified for him.

"Ah." He nodded. "I'm not being haunted; at least, I don't believe I am. Unless there is something I'm missing."

"Why don't we sit in the conference room and begin our discussion?" Angina asked. "We can make a record of the conversation there."

"Absolutely," Tangerine agreed. "We can give you the nickel tour after we talk about what has brought you to us."

They escorted him, one on each side, to the conference room: a twelve by twelve carpeted room complete with a circular table.

"Have a seat," Angina offered as she picked up a remote control and pushed several buttons. "You do have to agree on camera that we can record this conversation, of course."

"Yes, I give my consent," he said, "but we haven't discussed price or anything yet. How much is this going to cost, if I may be blunt?"

Tangerine waved him off. "My dear, we do not believe in charging those who are legitimately in need of our gifts."

"Avarice is alien to us," Angina said. "We are able to live as we wish, so there is no need to take advantage of the people who come to us for help."

Tangerine looked at him for a moment before speaking. "What brings you to us? Why are you here today?"

He smiled, not quite sure he knew how to explain why he sought them out. "There have been several—well, two—incidents recently that could have resulted in my death. I was saved, snatched from the jaws of death, by the same person each time, a person who should have been elsewhere both times." Micah looked down at his hands before continuing. "I'm here to find out the reason behind what's been happening. I get the weird feeling I'm missing something that should be so obvious, but I can't put my finger on it."

"It's not always easy to discover answers, but I believe you already know that. Sometimes there are forces which cover up the answers, cloud the circumstances," Tangerine said cryptically.

"What does that mean?" Micah asked.

"Ask the folks who live in Kecksburg, Pennsylvania," Angina answered. "The truth is out there, but it may be buried under layer upon layer of deceit. You may have to excavate before you can discover what you seek."

He stared blankly at the twins. "Thanks for clearing that up."

Smiling, Tangerine patted her hair. "Take, for example, a woman by the name of Beth Ann, by all accounts a very nice lady to be around. She always had a kind word and a smile for everyone who crossed her path. What did she have to smile about? That's what most people asked themselves. After all, she'd had two husbands die on her, leaving her nothing but a stack of unpaid bills each time. Her teenage daughter ran off one night never to be heard from again. All this tragedy in her life and yet Beth Ann still managed to have such a sweet disposition. For years she was a shining example to the community, a pillar of strength overcoming misfortune."

Micah shook his head. "I'm not sure I follow."

"It falls along the lines of the layers of deceit," Angina said. "For all the smiles and kind words floating on her surface, a maelstrom of conniving evil boiled inside Beth Ann. Some years later the truth came out, as it usually tends to do. It was discovered, when her third husband took ill and passed on, that Beth Ann had poisoned him. Well, speculation just ran wild. After further investigation, the woman was indicted on three counts of murder."

"Three?" Micah said.

"All her husbands had been poisoned," Tangerine explained. "She did away with them because she wanted out of the marriages and she didn't believe in divorce; she thought it was a disgrace to be divorced. She was a wicked pistol of a woman, Beth Ann was. A real piece of work."

"Did anyone bother to track down the daughter?"

"No one could find her," Angina said. "That is, not until the new owners of the house wanted to put in a pool. They found her then. She had been planted in a bed of roses; she'd never run away at all."

"And Beth Ann found herself charged with another count of murder," Tangerine said. "So you see, the truth can be found, it just may take awhile to dig through the layers of deceit to get to the right answers."

Micah nodded and smiled, understanding what they were saying but not quite sure why he shouldn't get up slowly and exit the house. But he stayed seated because he'd come asking for help and that's what he wanted.

"What we're trying to say is sometimes things are not always what they seem." Angina reached over and placed her hand on his. "And the answers we find aren't always the ones we want."

This is getting freaky, he thought. *Like they know what's inside my head.*

"Oh, we're not really psychic," Tangerine said and then blushed. "I mean, we rely on good old-fashioned investigation and research to come to our conclusions. We wish to prove our beliefs by finding concrete evidence."

"And we know that when people come to see us it's usually because we are a last resort," Angina said. "When they've tried other methods and have had no results; when their questions remain unanswered."

"Don't be nervous or feel out of sorts," Tangerine assured him. "You are among friends and we may be able to provide comfort."

Micah shivered and goosebumps broke out on his flesh. For all his misgivings about the two women, he suddenly felt like they would be able to help him find some answers. "I'm glad I came."

"Tell us more about the person who saved you both times, this person who shouldn't have been there," Tangerine said.

"Is he a stranger or is he known to you?" Angina asked.

Clearing his throat as subtly as possible, Micah explained. "My friend's name is Luc Sterling and we've known each other for about a year now. He's the managing editor for our local magazine."

"Ah, yes." Tangerine nodded. "I thought I recognized the name. Go on."

"We met at a funeral. It turned out we both had a penchant for going to them, although for different reasons. Since then we've discovered a lot of things we have in common and we usually go to funerals together now. It was the initial basis for our relationship."

"Understandable. But why did you say he shouldn't have been there when these incidents took place?" Angina questioned.

"Neither time should he have been there because we'd just gone our separate ways. Both times he was due back at his office. The first time was after an interment ceremony in Rose Hill Cemetery, and Sterling had to hurry back for a staff meeting. He made a big deal about some honcho from corporate being there and he had to be on time so he didn't get his butt chewed out. He dropped me off at home so I could get my car and go to work and then he hit the road. It was about a half hour later when the incident took place."

"Tell us about that."

"I had to go to the post office, which is a couple blocks down from my shop. I was in a hurry and wasn't paying as much attention as I should have been, I guess. I came to the corner of the Gephardt building and started to cross the street. I'd just stepped down off the curb when a horn sounded loudly. My head jerked up and I saw a bus coming right up on me. For those seconds I stood there frozen, and then somebody grabbed my arm and dragged me back up onto the curb. I turned around and it was Luc, much to my surprise."

Angina put a glass in front of him and poured water into it. He lifted the glass to his lips and allowed the cold water to soothe his dry tongue.

"It was Luc Sterling who pulled you back to safety, yes?" Angina asked.

"Yes."

"Could there be another explanation for why he was there?" she asked.

"None I can think of," Micah said. "The magazine building is further away than the post office. Luc should have been in his meeting instead of there to pull me out of the way of the bus."

"Did he explain why he was there?" Tangerine questioned.

Micah nodded.

"And what was his explanation?"

"He said the meeting had been canceled at the last minute because the corporate guy was held up in Baltimore and didn't make it in time."

"Is that explanation farfetched?"

"No, except for the time factor," Micah explained. "The incident took place, like I said earlier, about a half hour after he dropped me off at my house. He didn't have enough time to get to work, have any kind of staff meeting, and be there in time to pull me out of harm's way."

"Go on," they said together. "We're listening. Explain it further."

"We may need a little bit more information," Angina said. "You lack some descriptive skills. Part of our method is to go at this from several different angles, which is why we ask you to repeat your story three or four times. The devil is in the details, as the saying goes."

"Your bare-bones story leaves too much to the imagination," Tangerine chimed in. "Flesh it out some more so we can get a bigger picture of the incident.

You know, fill in some of the details. The more you tell us, the more we'll have with which to work, understand?"

"At the same time I was walking to the post office, Luc was supposed to be in a meeting at his work. Instead, he was there to pull me back up onto the curb so I wouldn't get creamed by an oncoming bus that ran a light. He magically reappeared when he was supposed to be across town at a meeting at the magazine. It's something, to me at least, that doesn't have an explanation."

"Did you ask him about this?" Tangerine asked.

"Of course I did. I wanted to know how he could be there."

"And what did he say," Angina queried.

"He said it had been canceled at the last minute because the bigwig didn't make it into town in time for the meeting."

"So you have an explanation."

"Not at all," Micah said. "Even if the meeting had been canceled, there wouldn't have been enough time for Luc to drive to my shop, find out where I had gone, and catch up to me. There just isn't." He thought for a second and then said, "I should have measured the distance and timed how long it took me to go from one place to the next. You'd see it's not possible."

The sisters shared a look and then looked to Micah. "We'll have to do a timetable on that. Time how long it takes to run the course, calculate the distance, et cetera," Angina explained.

"Only then will we be able to rule out his explanation," Tangerine said. "Until such a time, we'll have to say this is less than conclusive. When you rule out all the possibilities and then what you're left with and all that from the old quote, I'm sure you are more than familiar with it."

"There is a concept in the world you may wish to consider before doubting your friend," Angina offered. "Consider it a coincidence."

"All the times? Suspension of disbelief only goes so far," Micah said. He scratched his cheek. "Coincidence isn't an explanation. I would have written it off as that the first time, but since it's happened more than once…" His voice faded away to nothing.

"There are times when one thing appears to be something else," Tangerine explained. "When all evidence and experience points to one conclusion. But one must remember there can almost always be more than one answer, even if the other answers aren't quite correct."

"Case in point," Angina picked up the conversation, "the Ghost Children of San Antonio, Texas; the infamous haunted railroad crossing which is visited by thousands of people every year."

The twins exchanged a glance before continuing. Micah sat captivated.

"The story is that a long time ago—and there is no specific date or time period, because the date changes with the versions of the story—a group of children were killed—the number of children varies just like the time period—because either their school bus stalled or the wagon broke down on the tracks," Tangerine told him. "As for what occurs when one's car either stalls or is turned off and put in neutral, allegedly the ghosts of the poor children, not wanting anyone to come to harm as they did, push the vehicle up the incline and across the train tracks."

Angina picked up the tail. "If one were to put talcum or baby powder all over the back of the vehicle, one would see the evidence of the ghost children: their handprints will be seen in the powder."

"And to lend credence to this story," Tangerine said, "the streets of the town were named after the children lost in the tragedy. Multitudes of people have experienced this phenomenon time and time again. So it appears the legend is true, right?"

Micah nodded. But before he spoke, Angina did.

"Until you look closer at the story," she said. "There is no definitive date of the accident, either for a wagon or a school bus reported. So who were the children these streets were named after? The truth behind that is simple: the streets were named after either the children or the grandchildren, the exact answer escapes me at this time, of the developer. He and his family have verified this."

"But what about the vehicles being pushed uphill and across the tracks?" Micah asked. The answer hit him because he had recently experienced the same phenomenon. "A Gravity Hill."

They both smiled at him.

"The question of the handprints in the baby powder still remains," he pointed out. "How do you explain that one away?"

"There are different views on the matter," Angina answered. "Some believe the powder simply absorbed the oils left behind from people who had touched the car at an earlier time, and some believe people are reading too much into spilled powder. There are explanations galore, if you'd care to research the matter further."

"Of course there are people who claim to have experienced sightings, sounds, smells, tastes, touches," Tangerine said, "you name it. But you have the basic facts of the matter. Does it help you understand what we meant when we said sometimes something can, for all intents and purposes, appear to be something else?"

"Absolutely," he said.

The sisters assured him they would do their best to assist him. His mood perked up when they offered to explain more how they went about their investigations.

"Camcorders are used so we have a video log of our investigations to review and archive. We use voice recorders, hand-held recorders like this," she showed him the device, "to pick up EVPs."

"Electronic Voice Phenomenon," Angina explained.

"DVRs," Tangerine said, "digital voice recorders."

It looked to Micah like a mini-tape recorder. Nothing fancy.

"Because often on playback we hear voices and sounds that were not audible while we were recording," Tangerine went on. "Usually we ask a question out loud and wait about ten or fifteen seconds before moving on to the next question. You never know what you'll get."

"You would be surprised," Angina said, "if you heard the things we've been able to pick up on investigations. Sometimes it's a name, and sometimes it's a direct answer to the question we've just asked; we call those 'question and answer' EVPs. The results can be astounding."

"Have you seen or recorded anything on video?" Micah asked. "Anything like a wispy figure or lights moving?"

"It's not unusual for us to visually record our investigations," Angina said. "We try to gather as much information, both visual and audio, as we can to bring back and study—because you never know what you'll see or hear later that you missed during the actual investigation, as we said."

"We've heard names and words repeated over and over," Tangerine told him. "We've also heard sentences and many different sounds."

Intrigued by this, Micah asked, "Give me examples of things you've heard. Can you tell me something more specific?"

"As long as we don't tell you the names of our clients we aren't breaking any confidence," Angina explained to him. "We once heard on playback a voice calling 'Mathilda' over and over in a plaintive voice. Plain as day we could hear it on the recording, but when we were taking the recording we didn't hear a thing. We were rather stunned on playback, as you can imagine."

"It was utterly heartbreaking and disturbing at the same time," Tangerine said. "The voice belonged to a child, preteen because we could not discern whether it was a boy or a girl calling, and it literally gave me the chills listening to it." She shivered at the memory.

Her sister said, "Creepy. Never could stand children like that in movies or books, much less on an audio playback."

"I bet," he said, remembering the character of Gage Creed from *Pet Sematary*. "I can appreciate what you mean."

"There have been occasions when we have captured what we believe to be imagery of entities on video," Tangerine informed him. "Once upon a time we had video of something we saw through a thermal imaging camera; we believe it to be a woman in a long dress and cape walking through the dining room of a century-old home here in Western Maryland."

"We also use EMF meters," Angina continued and showed him a meter. "Electro Magnetic Fields—EMF. A spike in levels may indicate possible activity; it could be an entity putting in an appearance."

Tangerine pointed to goggles. "Night vision. Usually used as an accessory to the camcorders, but we do don them when walking around at night. Something people tend to forget: flashlights are simple but important investigation equipment. Especially when you're alone. At night."

"In the dark," Angina said. "Digital cameras, motion sensors, and even a Geiger counter." She held out the piece of equipment to him.

He accepted the Geiger counter she offered him and looked closely. "Radiation can indicate ghosts?"

"Radiation being evident is not always a sign an entity is near, but it is part of what we measure." She took back the Geiger counter when he was finished looking at it and placed it where it belonged. "Thermometers are very important. We must monitor the temperature because an increase or decrease of any significance could mean an entity is nearby, but only when the change cannot be explained by ordinary means. Like a draft when no window is open. That doesn't mean there is an entity because there could be other explanations."

"Such as a crack in the wall," he said.

"Correct," Tangerine said and smiled. "More conventional necessities include duct tape, extension cords, and items such as dolls or balls. These latter items, playthings, may be used to lure activity, especially if the suspected entity is a child or children. Interaction with an entity is very desirable."

"Of course," Angina continued, "there are people who utilize such things as dowsing rods, pendulums, talismans, protection stones, et cetera. These we term metaphysical enthusiasts."

Micah had difficulty coming to terms with the fact people devoted such time and money to what amounted to ghost hunting, but he enjoyed the banter of the sisters.

"But many ancient civilizations believed in such things as spirits and the afterlife," the women said in unison, as if reading his thoughts. "It's not such an extraordinary thing."

"I understand that on an intellectual level," he said. "I'm having a bit of difficulty coming to terms with the fact I may be experiencing it myself."

The women exchanged a glance.

"Quite a few people deny the possibility of anything super- or preternatural," Tangerine said to him, "especially if it happens to them. Because it challenges their beliefs."

"It's far easier to vehemently deny the existence of something one does not understand," Angina told him, "or something which is outside the realm of one's belief system."

Comprehension was not his problem; fear better described his feeling. "I ride the fence between wanting to believe and not wanting to believe, if you can understand what I mean."

"We've mentioned the incident at Kecksburg earlier," Tangerine reminded him. "Talk to a sample of people still living who remember the time to which we are referring and you will ultimately get two firm stances: one maintains the incident is absolutely real and the other maintains it never happened at all. In these extreme cases, there doesn't appear to ever be a middle ground."

Micah took his time looking around the room, from ceiling to floor, all the while turning thoughts around in his mind. And then he spoke. "Maybe I'm struggling because it seems like it would be so much easier to simply deny any existence and go on with my life. It's more difficult to attempt to grasp a situation so far out of my comfort zone. And you'd think, given my profession, I'd be more open to the possibility of otherworldly subjects." He stopped and swallowed; his mouth was dry. "May I trouble you for some more water?"

"No trouble at all," they said together. Angina poured water from the pitcher.

He lifted his glass and drank deeply. "Thank you. I needed that. My mouth got so dry, like salt."

"The first step is always the hardest." Tangerine reached over to place her hand over his. "And you're not alone in your journey. There are others who share the path you are about to travel and many who would be willing to exchange their experiences and knowledge with you."

Angina added her hand. "We're always here should you have any questions or just feel the need to talk."

"Feel free to call us and you're more than welcome to visit," Tangerine assured him. "If this is to be your journey, we expect you'll need some advice and guidance along the way."

"This is a lot to take in at one time," he admitted. "I originally came here because I thought I'd tell you what's been going on and you'd give me your interpretation or tell me what was what. You've given me more to cogitate than I anticipated."

They laughed. "We tend to do that."

Micah thanked them again for seeing him and the women led him upstairs to the front door. At the door, they both gave him a hug and wished him the best. He left with a sense of accomplishment.

"At least I know there exists the possibility I'm not completely crazy," he told himself.

Chapter Sixteen

Feeling more than slightly disturbed instead of relieved after his visit with Tangerine and Angina, Micah decided to take the rest of the day off and relax. Try to relax anyway. Still early in the day for him, just after two in the afternoon, and he found himself hungry. He stopped for some take-out Chinese food, broccoli in garlic sauce and vegetable fried rice, and took it with him to the cemetery to eat. For some reason, a picnic in the graveyard sounded like a solid idea.

Seated on the crumbly stone bench under the shade of the tall tree, his favorite spot, he started feeling better, calmer. The old graveyard, a good many of the markers dated back more than two hundred years and some of the markers were much older but the dates had long been worn away by the elements, had managed to soothe his nerves on numerous occasions in the past. He figured why not see if the magic worked this time around.

In the shade of the tree, Micah ate his lunch and thought. His thoughts wouldn't gel in the fog in his head. Failing to work things out, he resorted to speaking aloud to the occupant of the grave nearest him, Mr. Donald Oswald Andrews, who was born on 14 February 1809 and died on 17 March 1872. Micah looked closer, out of morbid curiosity, to see if a description of what killed the man was carved on his marker. No such luck.

"What would you advise, Don?" he said to the gravestone. He waited but no answer came. "Guess you never had to deal with anything close to this situation. Probably spent your days in the fields or in the mines." He leaned closer to inspect the carving on the marker. "Great, I'm talking to a guy whose initials are D-O-A. You're not going to be much help, are you?"

Micah finished the last of his rice, put the container and fork back into the brown bag, and opened his fortune cookie. It broke almost evenly in half; the slip of paper on which the fortune was printed stuck out from the smaller half.

"Terrific. 'When seeking answers be certain to ask the correct questions.' Exactly what I've been trying to do," Micah said. To the man in the grave, he asked, "Can you believe this fortune, Don? It's like Fate is having a big laugh at my expense." He threw the halves of the cookie to the two chipmunks scampering around the gravestone to his left and watched as each one grabbed a piece and ran away with it; they stopped several yards away and greedily stuffed their cheeks with the sweet treat. The sight tickled Micah and he stifled a laugh so as not to scare them away.

"Bon appetit, boys," he said. "I never could stand the taste of the things." He collected his trash and stood. "Thanks for listening, Don. We'll have to do this again sometime. You take care now."

After he left the cemetery, Micah thought about going to the Sacred Scarab and then decided against it. He figured Leslie was scheduled to work until close so he didn't have any reason to put in an appearance. Next, he considered going home to spend some quality time with Sia and work for a few hours on his new book. The cat would be happy to see him; Sia always greeted Micah as if he'd been gone for days instead of a few hours. Micah thought maybe the cat sitting on his lap while he wrote would help calm his nerves.

So he headed for home.

* * * * * * * * * * *

Back home, Sia greeted Micah by meowing loudly. He leaned down to scratch between the cat's ears.

"Found the good spot, huh?" he asked as the cat began purring rapidly. "How about we work on our book? You like writing with me."

He may not have gotten the answers he went to T and A expecting to find, but he came home feeling better for going. The ladies were not complete crackpots and seemed to know their stuff; they introduced him to concepts he'd known nothing about. And he made two friends whom he could feel free to contact when and if he needed them. He felt more comfortable in his world.

Johanna Edensburg's estate would be on the auction block in a few days and Micah knew among the items listed were several his clients wished to obtain for their own collections; he also knew a handful of surprise items—ones not listed in the official brochure—would be up for grabs, going to the most aggressive, highest bidder. The items listed in the brochure were enough to ensure a tremendous turnout, but the surprise items would guarantee the big guns would be in the crowd, waiting their chance to secure one or more of the sought after items to make their own. Treasures were treasures and anything could be a treasure as long as there was someone who wanted it for him- or herself. Bidding wars were common; Micah had seen many and experienced his fair share of them, only rarely losing the desired item.

Sia drew his attention by reaching up and placing his paw on Micah's cheek.

The cat demanded attention and Micah responded by scratching under Sia's chin.

"You disrupt my thinking process too often," he said. "What if I was coming up with the solution to global warming or the perfect plan to restore peace in the Middle East? You'd like to visit home, wouldn't you? Me and you staring up at the Sphinx. Think about it."

Sia responded by staring at him for a second or two before jumping down off his lap and sauntering away.

"Such respect, dude," Micah called after him, "such respect."

He laughed when Sia looked over his shoulder without breaking stride as he walked out of the room.

The phone rang and he reached to answer it.

"My friend Micah," the voice with the lilting accent said.

"Mohinder," he said. His Indian friend. "To what do I owe the honor of you calling from halfway around the world?"

"The Edensburg auction," his friend answered. "It has caused quite the stir among those in our circle. Many are anxious to bid upon the collection."

"She did amass a major collection," Micah agreed. He'd had the occasion to view Johanna's daggers and statues a few times. "I figured the auction would draw a lot of attention, yours included."

Mohinder laughed. "Not mine, per se. More like the attention of some of my clients. But I have yet to decide whether or not I will be in attendance."

Micah knew, in spite of the soothing voice and seemingly laid back demeanor, his friend was a shrewd businessman.

"You better come to a decision before too much longer," Micah told his friend. "Or you'll run into a time constraint."

Laughter. "Have no worries. I will be there if I feel the need."

They spoke for a half hour before hanging up. Micah had a feeling his friend was either on his way to Rain Falls or he was already there. The number came up "Private Caller" on the phone's ID so he couldn't be sure.

Sia peeked around the doorway.

"I see you," Micah said. "You coming in to write with me or not?"

The cat crept into the room, keeping low to the floor. Micah pretended he didn't see anything. Slowly, Sia inched closer and closer, uttering his war cry mere seconds before attacking Micah's ankle.

"That hurts," he said, reaching down to gently pry Sia's jaws open.

Puncture holes were evident but no blood oozed out. Micah watched in simple amazement, half expecting the bleeding to start at any second. He rubbed his hand over the damaged skin.

"You little terrorist. One of these days you're going to slice a major artery or something and I'll be laying on the floor bleeding to death,"

Sia stared up at him, and then jumped onto Micah's lap.

"You better knock off the covert attacks, boy, or I just might drop you off at the Chinese buffet," he threatened. "Are you going to help me write or continue to wage war? I have to get busy or I'm never going to finish the new book."

The black cat acted as though sugar wouldn't melt in his mouth. He rubbed against Micah's chin, perhaps to make amends or perhaps to lure him into a false sense of security so he could launch another assault.

"I'm not falling for it," he said. "If you're not going to help write you can go into the other room and let me work in peace."

Sia snuggled down in place and Micah set to work.

Nearly a half hour and three pages later Micah paused typing and stretched. As was his custom, he read aloud the pages for Sia's approval. The cat yawned and proceeded to perform ablutions on his front paws and face.

"I can see my words have piqued your interest. Either that or you're feigning disinterest." Micah scratched one of Sia's ears and the cat purred loudly. "That's better. Sometimes I swear getting a tiny compliment from you is like pulling a claw."

As a wordless retort, Sia stretched and sank the claws of one paw into Micah's thigh before slithering to the floor and leaving the room.

"A simple goodbye would have sufficed," Micah called after him as he rubbed the punctured area. "I'm an abused pet parent. Where's the government agency to protect me?" He laughed at his own words and then decided to make note of the sentence so he could use it in one of his books.

The phone rang. He contemplated answering it but decided it would interrupt his creative process too much, so he let the answering machine serve its purpose.

Iamma Trampp's website needed updating; it had been a few weeks since "she" had posted "her" last blog entry. Micah spent a few minutes writing an entry so his eager fans would have access to all the latest and greatest news in the Trampp world. And then he spent the better part of the next hour responding to a few dozen emails, most of the emails were sycophantic and the rest were requests for autographed books and/or photographs.

He decided one of these days he'd either have to hire a stand-in or begin dressing in drag to make public appearances at book signings. If the books continued to grow in popularity, he'd have to make that decision sooner rather than later.

The thought of revealing himself to his growing number of readers creeped him out. On one hand, they could embrace him, since they knew a good number of romance authors were in fact men writing under female pseudonyms. On the other, they could get all riled up over having been deceived and hunt him down in order to draw and quarter him. The last thought did bring a smile to his face: the image of elderly ladies in support hose brandishing torches descending upon his house in the middle of the night screaming for vengeance.

But the storm in his mind came whirling back with a vengeance.

An'khyr.

Iamma.

Lucian Sterling.

The Dreams.

It all swirled around in his head and mixed together, making him dizzy enough to have to rest his head in his hands. Too much information, too many questions, and not near enough answers.

* * * * * * * * * * *

Vanessa Archer called to once more confirm their plans for the auction. Micah was happy for the distraction from thinking, even though he couldn't help but wonder if she thought he'd leave her high and dry on the day of the auction.

"Are you as excited as I am?" she asked.

"That depends," he ventured. "How excited are you? The goosebumps excited or the wet your panties excited?"

Her schoolgirl giggle made him laugh. "You can be naughty, Micah. That's why I like you so much; we connect on many levels. You may be an older soul than you think. I bet we knew each other in previous existences."

"You never answered me. How excited are you?"

"I'm extraordinarily excited," she gushed, "because I'm going to buy me something very nice from one of the lots."

She didn't have a clue what she was buying but she knew she was buying something. He wanted to roll his eyes. "You are the most ridiculous woman I've ever known. Planning on throwing your money at the auctioneer and you haven't seen a single piece from any of the estates yet. You might not find anything that strikes your fancy," he pointed out. "Don't be disappointed."

"Never you fear," she assured him. "I will be spending my money on something and bringing home a treasure. I heard," she whispered as if confiding a secret, "there will be a crystal skull up for grabs."

This time Micah did roll his eyes. "I've heard the same rumor, but I understand it's part of another estate, not Johanna's."

"Doesn't matter," she purred. "I might have to have it for myself. Imagine, my very own crystal skull."

He didn't know her intimate financial details and he wanted to advise her in the nicest manner possible how expensive buying a skull could be without insulting her. "Vanessa, a crystal skull sells for many thousands of dollars—if it's a genuine one and not one of the knock-offs."

"It would be more of an investment," she countered, "instead of an extravagant piece of art. Just think how much more it would be worth in another fifty years. I could retire if I sell it later in life."

"You could retire now. Any later in life and you'll be well on your way into the next one."

"They're ancient computers, you know. Repositories of wisdom. Information in there that has been thought lost for millennia." She barely took enough time to breathe before gushing on. Vanessa Archer was famous for her diatribes. "After I get my crystal skull, I'll have access to the data of the ages stored inside," she said, "and I won't share a single tidbit with you. Not a solitary one."

"Have I told you lately how much you disturb me?" While he genuinely liked her and enjoyed spending time with her, sometimes she flummoxed him, especially when she went off on one of her transcendental, mystical tangents. "Seriously, Vanessa. You weird me out like nobody I've ever met."

"There's nothing weird about wanting one of those skulls," she said. "Didn't you tell me you know people who own one or more of them?"

He sighed. "I told you I know *one* person who has a skull," he clarified.

"Semantics." She coughed.

He waited for what came next.

Not a long wait.

"Do you think you could maybe find a way for me to take an up close and personal look at the skull? Perhaps I could hold it in my hands?" she said in a sing-song voice. "Pretty please?"

He rubbed his temple and phrased his response carefully. "What makes you think I have the type of relationship with David Cordone that would allow me to come and finger his possessions as I please? He's a serious collector and is known for keeping the items in his collection under lock and key. Away from prying eyes. It's an extra measure to keep them safe."

"A safety precaution, I see," she said.

But something in her voice made Micah believe she was about to swoop in from another angle.

"Surely he wouldn't have any qualms about showing a fellow antiques enthusiast his skull—the crystal one, I mean." She sounded completely sure. "Why don't you ask him when a good time would be for me to see some of his collection? You and I will drive up together; maybe he'll invite us to dinner. What a fantastic way to spend an evening. Perfect."

Once the woman made up her mind, you couldn't derail her no matter how hard you tried. Might as well play along. "I make absolutely no promises," Micah told her. "Do you hear me?"

"I hear you. I haven't lost all my senses yet."

"I'll say this: I will ask David if he would be willing to allow you to see the skull. *See*," he stressed. "Not fondle or hold or toss. *See*. And I will not persist if he says flat-out no. Deal?"

"I can live with that," she said. "Give it your best shot and I know you'll convince him to let me experience the skull. It's my destiny."

Micah allowed Vanessa's comments to roll over him; he tried not to ponder them too much lest she confuse him any further. And then he said, "Destiny or not, I'll see what he has to say about the matter."

She changed the subject abruptly, as was her trademark. "How's the kitty? Has he learned any more of the King's English or do you still have to say the words in Farsi and then repeat them in English?"

They both laughed. Micah recalled telling her the story for the first time about how the black cat didn't understand English and so the Middle Eastern doctor who adopted him spoke to Sia in a language the cat could understand. Only until Micah adopted him did he have to learn English.

"Not at all. Sometimes he reverts to his native tongue when he meows," Micah said, "but he's all naturalized now."

Sia, sensing he was the topic of conversation, graced Micah with his presence, rubbing against Micah's shin and purring loudly.

"The Pharaoh is making himself known," Micah told her, wincing as the cat bit his ankle. He gently pushed the nipping feline away.

"Oh, good. Hold the phone up to his ear so I can tell him hello," she said. "He doesn't get to hear from me often enough."

Micah did as he was bade. Sia sniffed the phone and gave it an odd look as Vanessa rambled on to him. He backed away before spinning and running from the room. Micah stifled his laughter.

"He says hello back," he told Vanessa. "And sends his love."

"Such a good boy. Chiffon just adores him," she said, referring to her cockatoo. "I know she misses little Shadow. You should bring Sia over for a visit. Chiffon would love that."

Micah didn't have the heart to tell her Sia was a lone feline and probably wouldn't want to visit a big white bird that screeched like a murder victim when the mood struck her. But he mumbled something about it being a good idea and he'd talk it over with the cat.

Vanessa suddenly said, "I just noticed the time and I need to close up the shop and get ready for my dinner out with Nannette. I hate to rush off so abruptly, but I don't know what happened to the time today."

"No apologies. You go right ahead and get on with what you need to do," Micah assured her. "We can catch up on the ride to Lansington's."

After saying goodbye, Micah hung up the phone and reached over to turn on the stereo. One of the six Lita Ford CDs began to play, her self-titled *Lita*, which contained one of his favorite songs from the Queen of Metal: "Broken Dreams." Closing his eyes, he listened to the opening chords for a couple seconds.

He brought up the document file for his manuscript in progress and began to write, inspired by the music playing. Normally, he did his best work while listening to music—the theory about one form of art inspiring another.

The phone rang.

"Dude, I have something very cool to tell you," Luc said before Micah could even say hello.

"What?"

"Do you know who write 'Frosty the Snowman'?" Luc asked. "I bet you don't know his name much less where he's buried."

Intrigued, Micah admitted he didn't know the man's name.

"Walter Rollins co-wrote the song. He also wrote or co-wrote 'Here Comes Peter Cottontail,' 'Smokey the Bear,' and a bunch of other songs. And guess what? He was born in Keyser, WV. That's so cool." Luc kept talking. "I want to do a story on him for the holiday issue of the magazine. There are so many people who don't know who wrote those songs much less know he was born in Mineral County."

"That would be a great cover story."

"And I haven't even told you the best part yet," Luc said.

"What's the best part?"

"Scuttle has it Rollins admitted in an interview a year or so before his death in 1973," Luc continued, "'Frosty' was originally meant to be a cautionary tale and not a frolicky Christmas tune. I have to dig up the issue of *Life* magazine to be sure," Luc barely paused for a breath, "but Rollins allegedly stated the song was a warning about nuclear winter."

"Heavy subject matter for a children's song."

"And he's buried in Queens Point Memorial Cemetery in Keyser. We gotta go visit his grave," Luc said. "What do you think for the cover: Frosty standing in front of Rollins' grave? Like Warner Brothers did when Mel Blanc died."

"I think it's kinda macabre for a holiday issue," Micah reluctantly said. "Warner Brothers had the characters standing in a semi-circle with a spotlight shining down on a microphone."

Luc thought about it. "My idea is similar."

"Your idea will probably scare the hell out of any kids who see the magazine," Micah said. "I appreciate your thought, but maybe you should scale it down a few notches, man."

"I'll...I'll work out all the kinks with the art department," Luc said. "And I think I'll write the story myself because it's too good to pass on." He cleared his throat. "I just can't believe a celebrity like Rollins is from near here and buried near here and so many people don't have any idea. This whole area is so gangbuster over tourism, you'd think they'd make a big deal out of this guy."

"Scandal," Micah said. "So shameful."

"It's the truth. This guy is in a grave all but forgotten. It's not right," Luc said. "I want to bring him to the attention of the public."

"It's a noble gesture. But don't be too judgmental in the article; I didn't know about the guy, but I couldn't hazard a guess as to how many people know about him being buried near here. It would behoove you to hedge your bets and not condemn the tri-state area for their lack of attention on the matter."

After discussing Rollins and Frosty for several more minutes, they ended the conversation and Micah got back to working on the latest Trampp manuscript.

Chapter Seventeen

When Micah and Vanessa arrived in Cumberland at Lansington's, they were pleasantly surprised to see the number of vehicles parked in the two lots.

"A shame Storm couldn't make it. I knew there would be a full house," Vanessa said. "And I bet you there are cars parked on the other streets and in the parking garage."

Micah nodded. "But you have to remember there is another auction today, not just the Edensburg estate. And there are always smaller lots up for grabs, too."

He drove slowly through both designated parking areas before finding an empty spot. Pulling in, he took a deep breath, as he did before every estate sale he attended, to cleanse his system.

Vanessa poked him in the shoulder. "Are you hyperventilating or having an asthma attack or something?"

He ignored her.

She placed her hand on his shoulder and spoke louder, directly into his ear. "Do you need an ambulance?"

Jerking away from her voice, he said, "I'll need a hearing aid if you keep screaming in my ear."

"I was only offering assistance." She pouted before another personality took over. "Can you feel the vibes?" She smiled broadly. "I feel like a school girl at her first prom. Aren't you excited?"

The ringing in his ear subsided and he caught the last portion of her comments. "I'm not giddy like a school girl," he said, "but I am excited."

Vanessa continued to yammer; Micah blocked out as much as he could and still pretend he was listening. All he heard was "Blah blah blah Tink."

He came to the surface and knew he'd missed some sort of question. "Say that again, please."

"I said: it's going to be fun, don't you think?" she repeated.

After parking, the pair exited the vehicle and meandered their way to the entrance of Lansington's. They stopped to stare up at the great black iron chandelier before entering through the white double doors of the auction house. Socializing in the lobby were the potential clients and onlookers, most with a glass of wine or a highball glass in their hand.

Micah recognized a score of others who also trafficked in antiquities. Johanna Edensburg's collection had indeed attracted people interested in the knives and other pieces of her collection.

Vanessa grabbed his elbow and said, "Look over there."

He tried to follow her chin nod but couldn't. "Where?"

"I can't point," she said. "That's inappropriate. There." She again nodded her chin in the direction she meant.

"For chrissakes," he muttered. "Describe who we're talking about if you refuse to point him out."

"Can't you understand who I mean?" She glared at him. "The man over there. *Over there*," she emphasized.

"There encompasses a big area, doll. Can you narrow it down?" he asked. "Just walk us by him."

"He's the man in the dark red shirt," she whispered as if it was a state secret. "Red shirt at two o'clock."

"Red shirt, okay. My two o'clock or yours?"

"Mine," she said. "See him now? We should know him."

"I don't even see him; how would I know if I know him?" Micah said. He kept searching for the man in the dark red shirt. "Will you just walk us by him, please? I don't see the guy."

She sighed heavily. "If I must." She took him by the elbow and steered him across the crowded lobby. They strolled by the man in the red shirt and Vanessa whispered out of the corner of her mouth, "See him now?"

Micah nodded discretely.

"We should know him," she reiterated.

"You keep telling me," he said as they walked by the man, "but I don't have a clue; doesn't even ring a slight bell."

Vanessa stopped and turned to him. "Am I crazy? I swear I recognize him from somewhere."

"Yes, you are crazy," he said, "but it is entirely possible you recognize him because you know so many damned people. Now, can we move on before he realizes we're discussing him?"

"Of course." She took his arm again and looked over her shoulder. "You don't think he heard us, do you?"

"Probably not, but if we stand within earshot and talk about him he might hear us," Micah said. "Would you care for a drink?"

She smiled. "Why, yes, I would."

They made their way to the bar area and soon they each had a glass of their preferred drink. Into the first auction room they walked.

"This is part of one of the other estates listed today," Micah said.

Vanessa looked around. "People do collect the oddest items sometimes. These look like ancient sex toys," she said with a touch of disdain in her voice. "Do you think people actually used them?"

"I don't want to think about it," Micah said dryly. "However, I doubt the auction house would have century-old dildos for sale."

She wrinkled her nose before suggesting they leave the room. On the way out, she suddenly said, "Oh, I know who he is." She grabbed his hand. "He's Patrik Saint-Siere. You know the family name, I'm sure."

Micah knew the name and admitted as much. Several members of the family were clients. And he knew the family had many holdings, including a massive law firm.

"You don't think he's here for the skull?" she asked. She put her hands on her hips. "Well, that's very awesome. I do hope he'll allow me visitation."

He turned his head slightly so she wouldn't see him rolling his eyes. "What is this bizarre fetish you have with crystal skulls all of a sudden? I've never heard you talk about them before these last few weeks."

"Don't think for a minute I don't know you roll your eyes when we're on the phone and I know you just did it again." Then she changed and said, "Crystal skulls are unique—watch out for the fakes—for the reasons I explained to you, and so much more. Many, and I don't know if I include myself in that number, believe the skulls could be the salvation for the people and the planet."

He decided the woman was indeed a raving lunatic; he tried not to let the thought show on his face. "Interesting."

She nodded, a big grin plastered on her face. "I have dozens of books on the subject and hours of documentaries I recorded off one of the educational channels. You'd be as fascinated as I am if not more."

A diversion presented itself and Micah, never happier for an interruption, seized upon it. "Excuse me, my dear. I see Marjorie Beckman and I owe her a phone call; I'd better say hello before she spies me and accuses me of avoiding her."

Micah took his leave and Vanessa perused various lots up for grabs.

* * * * * * * * * * *

After saying hello and discussing a few minor things with Marjorie Beckman, Micah set out to find Vanessa since the first auction was to begin in minutes. On his way into the first venue, he spotted a man in a white shirt—sleeves rolled up to the man's elbows, exposing several tattoos including a couple spiders—and a black cowboy hat. The man acknowledged Micah by nodding once and touching his hat.

Seated beside Vanessa, Micah had the perfect view of the cowboy who was directly across the room, seated beside Patrik Saint-Siere. No matter how much he tried to pay attention to the auctioneer, Micah kept looking out of the corner of his eye at the tattooed cowboy.

Vanessa noticed it. "What the hell is up with you?" she leaned close and whispered. "You're like a chicken sitting on a grenade."

"The guy in the white shirt and black hat," he said, "sitting beside Mr. Saint-Siere. Light sandy brown/blond hair. Do you know him?"

Casually glancing in the direction Micah indicated, she said, "Can't help you, dear. Don't know the face."

As the auction continued, Micah watched item after item from the Edensburg estate sell to the highest bidder. By his side, Vanessa cooed over the amounts people paid for what they wanted.

"It's tacky to say," she admitted, "I can't help but think this is a big fuss over what amounts to old cutlery."

He closed his eyes and tried not to laugh. Leave it to Vanessa to boil it down to bare bones. "Ceremonial daggers are more than 'old cutlery.' People spend years searching for additions to their collections."

"I know. I have my eccentricities."

During a break in presentation and bidding, the pair decided to check out the other auctions. They made their way to a smaller room next door to the Edensburg room. Barely a dozen people had taken seats.

"Obviously not one of the more popular venues," Vanessa said.

Micah agreed and was about to say so when the cowboy walked into the room and took a seat. He looked straight at Micah and stroked his goatee before turning his attention to the auctioneer.

Not coincidence. "Let's take a seat," Micah told his friend.

"Why?" she asked. "Do you have an inside scoop?"

"No. Call it a hunch."

She gestured to a pair of seats and said, "Then by all means. I cannot in good conscience ignore a hunch." After they had taken their seats, she added, "It may very well be the hands of Fate at work."

He frowned and then shrugged. "I just want to see what transpires because I'm intrigued for some reason."

"Some reason or someone?" She winked.

"Pay attention."

"I am paying attention to the auctioneer. To whom are you paying attention?" she coyly asked.

Micah ignored her question and watched the man out of the corner of his eye. Every so often, the tattooed cowboy would nonchalantly glance in Micah's direction. Each time the two locked eyes the man would smile and nod.

Fidgeting in his seat, Micah was not comfortable at all.

"What's wrong?" Vanessa whispered.

He leaned closer to her and said softly, "I think it's too warm in here."

She reached over and felt his forehead. "You don't feel clammy nor do you look flushed. Are you nauseous?"

"No. I'm not sick; I'm not light-headed."

Concerned for her friend, she said, "Should we leave? I don't want you to stay if you're not well." She placed her hand on his shoulder. "I won't be disappointed. You might need some water. I'll be back in a minute."

Micah smiled at her and she left. Not long after, someone sat down beside him. He looked over. The cowboy had seated himself in Vanessa's chair. Micah waited to see if he'd speak.

The man didn't look at him. He stared straight ahead and said, "It's not just you, you know."

"Not just me what?"

"How you're feeling. Not only you."

Micah looked around the room. People were rubbing the backs of their necks and squirming in their chairs.

"See?" the man said. "Not just you."

Looking down at the man's tattooed arms, Micah saw the spiders on his forearm, the red triangles on them. Black widows.

"Okay. If you know so much, tell me what's happening."

The man laughed and scratched his chin. "Did you think you were here by sheer coincidence?" He still hadn't turned to look at Micah.

"I'm here to find items for my clients."

The cowboy smiled again, a slightly crooked smile. "If you say so, bud."

"Back to my original question: What's happening?" Up close, the man appeared to be in his mid-twenties.

"Not to sound conceited, but it's me." With this said, the cowboy finally turned to Micah and smiled again. "I seem to have that effect on people sometimes. Not really my fault; I guess it's almost like a side-effect to being around me. I can usually control it and sometimes I don't want to."

Not sure if the man was a lunatic or not, Micah said, "Okay. If you'll excuse me." He started to stand; the cowboy's hand fell onto his thigh. "If you'll excuse me," he said again.

"Just hold on a second, bud. Let me tell you this before the lady gets back with your water."

"How the hell did you know what she went to get?" he asked, surprised their conversation hadn't interrupted the auction. But no one seemed to notice they were talking to each other.

"Not important. What's important is that which you are about to see." He nodded toward the stage.

And Micah sucked in a breath. The statue took what breath he had left away. He did not believe he was seeing it. He never believed it existed. On stage, the auctioneer's assistant held the winged ankh statue. Light danced off it, reflecting arcs of color that dazzled through the air.

"Holy shit," Micah uttered in astonishment. He blinked, thinking the statue might be a figment of his imagination. *How the hell is it possible?*

As if reading his mind, the cowboy said, "A beauty, huh? Never thought you'd see it, did you, bud? Thought the old man was off his rocker. Just goes to show you there are more things out there than you know."

Unable to speak, his mouth suddenly too dry, Micah shook his head. He took in every inch of the statue. It was more elegant than the sketches he'd seen online led him to believe, a symbol of both beauty and power. The intricate detail of the down-turned wings; the inlaid gems of the ankh itself. Roughly the twelve or so inches described in the articles he'd read. It blew his mind to know David Cordone had actually touched the statue those many decades ago, because now he knew it was real and not a piece of legend, and he knew this was an object worth the years Cordone spent pursuing it. He felt more than knew its importance.

"Go on," the man urged Micah. "You know you want it. Bid on it. Nobody else is. You could win."

It was true. The auctioneer stated the starting bid, a surprisingly low bid, and no one acted on it. The people around him sat as if they were mesmerized by nothing, like they weren't paying attention to the item up for bid.

"Nobody here knows what it is, except for you and maybe me."

Finding his voice, Micah asked, "Why don't you bid on it if you think it's so special?"

"It's not here for me and, more importantly, I'm not here for it," was the answer. "Don't let it slip through your fingers, not when you're so close. It hasn't seen the light of day in so long."

Micah's hand, the one holding the paddle with the number emblazoned on it, twitched. He almost raised it.

"Looks downright real. For something you don't believe exists, I mean," the man said. "You're seeing it, do you believe it now?"

"Yes. I can't believe it though."

"Go on," the man urged. "He's about to call it quits. Who knows where it will end up if you don't grab it. Some vault somewhere. Never to be seen again. Would be such a damned shame if it got away." He scratched his goatee again. "What's stopping you? Go for it, bud."

Micah raised his paddle just as the auctioneer began to call the close of the item, barely beating the gavel.

"Sold," the auctioneer said, "to number 1-4-8-0-6."

Micah jerked when someone said, "What did you buy, dear."

Vanessa stood behind his left shoulder holding a bottle of water. She handed it to him before sitting down.

The cowboy was gone. Looking around, Micah couldn't see him anywhere in the room. No white shirt, no black hat, not one tattoo.

"Something grab your attention?" She watched him twist off the bottle cap and take a drink. "Feel better?"

"Yes and yes," he answered. "I do feel better and something caught my attention, indeed." He smiled wide at her. "I bought a statue."

"And here I was hoping for a crystal skull."

They laughed. Micah did feel better. In fact, the mood in the entire room had shifted. People stopped squirming in their chairs. It was warm but not nearly as warm as before. Something had shifted and everything had returned to normal. The entire atmosphere was altered.

Suddenly it sunk in: he'd found the statue David Cordone told him about. Not only that, he now owned the damned thing. His mind spun the proverbial mile a minute; thoughts spiraled and crashed into each other. He almost felt dizzy from the overload in his head. Too easy. Too weird.

If the statue exists, he thought, *does that mean An'khyr does, or did, as well? And what else does this mean?*

"David Cordone will be in ecstasy," he said.

"Oh, and why should he be in ecstasy?" Vanessa sweetly inquired.

Grasping her hand, he brought it to his lips. "Because I have a surprise for him, something he's dreamt of holding again."

"Sounds so romantic."

"In a strange way, yes." He laughed and then realized they shouldn't be talking. Whatever spell had been cast while the cowboy was speaking with him had been broken and they'd be disturbing the auction if they continued to chat. "Let's go see what else we can discover."

"I'm game." She followed him out of the room. Back in the lobby, she said, "How about we check out the furniture. I still want a bed, a big canopy bed. That would set off my bedroom perfectly."

He put an arm around her shoulder. "Not too big I hope; your apartment is nice but I'd like to see you try to squeeze a great big canopy bed in there. You'd walk into your room and immediately have to crawl into the bed."

As they perused the auction gallery, where many of the larger furniture pieces were displayed, they discussed the merits of a bureau with a bullet hole in the accompanying mirror, a pair of carved peacock columns—which Vanessa assured him Storm Cassavettes would love to own for his dining room, and a marble-top vanity. Vanessa wanted to bid on the peacock columns for her friend Storm. Micah tried his best to talk her out of it, but once she made up her mind, he couldn't change it. Stubborn was one of her more endearing qualities.

"He'll just love them," she said. "You don't understand."

"Uh huh. And what if you paid a ludicrous amount for them and he doesn't want them? They really are a custom order. To whom will you sell them if he politely declines?"

Her laugh echoed. "Storm will love them, and even if he didn't, he'd buy them anyway and store them someplace in his big house so he wouldn't hurt my feelings. No, he'll absolutely have to have them."

It was difficult for Micah to stay and make small talk when all he wanted to do was wrap up the statue and make a break for it. Even though he saw it, he honestly couldn't believe it was the real thing until he held it in his hands. Of course, there existed the possibility it was a great fake, but he doubted it. Not with all the odd events that had happened over the course of the afternoon: the tattooed cowboy in the black hat, the weird feeling and behavior, the winged ankh being on the auction block, and all the rest. No, it had to be real.

No way in hell is the statue a fake, he told himself. *If it is, I'll eat it piece by piece.*

He kept an eye out for the cowboy but he was nowhere to be seen. Even the man Vanessa recognized, Patrik Saint-Siere, was missing in action. He remembered seeing them together at various points and wondered what the connection was between the two; were they at Lansington's to guide him to the statue?

I can't believe I walked in here today and the damned statue came up for grabs, he thought. *This is weirding me out.*

"…and then we could put it in my shop." Vanessa said.

When he didn't answer, she poked him in the ribs.

"Ouch. Do you have a fetish for inflicting pain on me, woman?"

"Only when you fade out and ignore the world around you," she said. "What on earth is the matter? You said you were feeling better."

"I am," he insisted. "Just lost in thought."

The comment was enough to make her switch gears. "Oh, I know how that goes. I get lost in thought and sometimes it takes days before I'm back on track, to find my way. Why, there was this one time…"

And he tuned her out.

* * * * * * * * * * *

By the end of the auction, Micah had picked up several items for his clients, as had Vanessa, who was quite bitter the rumor about a crystal skull being in one of the lots turned out to be false.

"Figures," she kept muttering to herself. "Get all excited for nothing. How do these rumors get started?"

"Buck up," Micah encouraged her. "You may run across one yet. I know for a fact there is a convention held annually down in DC."

She smiled. "Thank you for trying to cheer me up. I do want to go to the convention. And," she stole a sideways glance at him, "there's always your friend Mr. Cordone's skull."

He laughed at her trying to be coy. "I said I would ask him, and I can't promise anything more."

Their purchases were in the process of being crated so they could take them home. Lansington's offered delivery for the large items, such as the big wood columns Vanessa bought for her friend Storm. But the other items, especially the statue, they wanted to take home with them.

Micah picked at his fingernails, anxious about the statue and eager to get it home where he could investigate every detail. He couldn't decide whether to call Cordone right away or wait and surprise him by delivering the statue out of the blue. David Cordone would be most appreciative.

The hour wasn't late, mid-afternoon, and the drive to Grantsville from

Cumberland wouldn't take much more than twenty minutes. Dropping off Vanessa at her house would only add fifteen minutes to the drive. He decided to surprise Cordone with the statue.

Vanessa hinted she wanted to accompany him to Grantsville. When he pretended not to notice her hints, she flat-out said she was going along.

"You don't know the man and it wouldn't be polite for me to bring a guest," Micah explained. "He's a polite man and I'm breaking the rules, if you will, by showing up unannounced and uninvited."

She pursed her lips. "But it's a special occasion. You obtained the statue he's wanted for so long." Her mind shifted gears. "I could explain to him that I came along as security, to protect his investment."

A ninety-year-old ninja. "Nope. I'm dropping you off at your house and continuing without you."

"Party pooper."

"Be that as it may," Micah said, "I will ask him, but not tonight, about you planning a pilgrimage to his crystal skull."

"Can't blame me for trying," she said.

"You are so obsessed with the damned skulls. I think I may have to get a court order to have your cable disconnected so you can't watch anymore of those shows," he said. "I'm serious."

"Listen to you," she said. "The way you talk, people might think I need a twelve step program or something. It's fascinating to me. That's all. I want a closer look and there's nothing wrong with that. Being so close to one of the skulls, like with the Faberge eggs, makes me want to visit."

He gripped the steering wheel tighter. "You're all but planning to show up in the dead of night and break into Cordone's house so you can get your mitts on the skull and yet you don't see anything wrong with that."

"I don't think it will speak to me or grant me superpowers or anything like that. Honestly." She started looking for gold in her purse and changed the subject. "I think I'll make homemade macaroni and cheese for me and Chiffon tonight; she does love her pasta," Vanessa said, referring to her cockatoo.

"Salt's not good for birds," Micah pointed out.

"I couldn't take away her treats," Vanessa said. "A bit here and there won't hurt her, and she gets so excited when I give her noodles."

Vanessa extolled the virtues of her cockatoo and recounted the story for the umpteenth time of how Chiffon came to live with her. Micah had heard the story a million times before, but he didn't have the heart to interrupt her because she so enjoyed sharing the tale.

"I could live without all the teeny tiny white feathers that get everywhere. She sheds," Vanessa explained. "They don't call it shedding when they lose those little feathers; it's called mulching."

Micah thought about it before he responded. "Molting, dear. Birds molt; gardeners mulch."

Chapter Eighteen

After dropping Vanessa off at her house, Micah drove to Grantsville on his mission to surprise David Cordone. The weather cooperated, no rain like last time, and he enjoyed the scenic drive up the mountain.

Every so often, he would see deer grazing by the side of the road, and he hoped they'd stay out of the way of traffic. He stopped and watched a group of four deer, what he thought were a mother and three fawns, nonchalantly stroll across the road. One of the fawns paused long enough to stare at him through the windshield before hurrying to catch up to the rest of the family.

Once at Cordone's house, where he almost expected to be denied entry because of his breech of etiquette, he felt light-headed again. He leaned his head against the steering wheel and breathed evenly in an effort to stop the world from spinning. Cordone, a stickler for the rules of etiquette, would forgive the unannounced visit once he had the statue in his hands once again. The sin of Micah's unexpected intrusion would be happily forgiven.

Panic struck.

What if it's not the statue? It was way too easy, just popping up like that at the auction.

But then what about the weirdness at the auction?

I'm over-thinking the situation, he told himself. *There can be no over-thinking when it's all so damned strange. Do it. Just go in and find out if it's the real thing or not. David'll know as soon as he lays either eyes or hands on it. There will be no fooling him. Present it to him.*

He turned off the engine and got out, pocketing the keys. Cradling the wrapped statue in his arms like a long lost child, Micah walked slowly toward the doors of the big house. The sound of the doorbell echoed through the great doors.

Micah waited.

No one answered.

There were definitely lights on inside the house; he could see them through the windows. Was he being ignored? After several minutes, he summoned the courage to ring the doorbell again.

And Micah waited.

Finally, he heard the sound of the deadbolt being drawn. The viewing panel swung open and from behind the security screen, David Cordone smiled.

"My boy, what a magnificent surprise. Just a moment and I'll wrestle this monstrosity open to admit you," he said, referring to the big door.

Unable to hear the bolts being thrown through the heavy wood, Micah waited patiently outside. He squeezed the statue, as if reassuring himself of its solidity; it was solid, all right. The weight in his arms felt good; it made his heart race to know he held the statue in his arms.

Cordone opened the door and beckoned Micah inside. "To what do I owe the honor?"

Micah smiled. "David, I believe I have something you've been waiting to lay eyes on for over half a century."

Cordone paled, his skin even whiter than normal. "Don't tease me, son." He saw the look on Micah's face and knew it was no joke. "Is it…?" he couldn't catch his breath. "I need…to sit….oxygen."

Sitting the statue in the foyer, Micah helped Cordone into the library where the old man could make use of the oxygen tank. It didn't take long for a bit of color to return to his face.

"Where is it?" he asked.

"Out by the front doors."

"By gods, man, go fetch it," Cordone said. "I've waited over half my life for this moment in time. To be this close and not see it or touch it is utter torture. Go get it; I don't want to wait any longer."

Micah turned to retrieve the statue, pretending not to notice the watery look in the man's eyes. *Were they tears of joy or madness?* he asked himself. Not wanting to prolong the moment for his friend, he hurried back to the library with the statue.

He placed it on the floor before David Cordone, who reached out a shaky hand to caress lovingly the fabric wrapping.

"I'm almost terrified to look," Cordone admitted.

Micah didn't respond.

Cordone looked up at him; Micah could see the man didn't want to tear his eyes away from that which stood before him, but he managed to do it.

"How is this possible? So quickly?"

He couldn't do anything but shrug his shoulders. "I don't have a clue, David." After explaining quickly what transpired at Lansington's, Micah said, "And there it was, on the auction block. That's all I can tell you, because how or why it was there is beyond me."

Cordone had stopped listening; he was busy pulling the fabric from around the statue. Layer by layer he revealed the carved details.

"Can you tell if it's the real thing?" Micah asked. "I'd hate to think I disrupted your evening like this for a fake."

When Cordone looked up at him again, Micah could tell it was genuine. The smile on Cordone's lips and the twinkles in his eyes verified it.

"Whether by your hand or Deus Ex Machina, I don't care. It doesn't matter. The signs were correct; although I never expected it to find its way so quickly," Cordone said. "All that matters is it's here once more; I have it. And this time I will never let it out of my sight. It's too precious."

"Like I said, I don't have a clue," Micah confessed, "but you told me all along it would make itself known when the time was right. I can only hazard a guess and say this is the right time."

By this time, Cordone had the fabric in a pile on the floor. The statue stood for all to see, it's colors even more vibrant than Micah remembered from a few hours earlier—like it was freshly retouched by the artist or something.

"Only this piece could complete my life's work. It's concrete evidence of the existence of An'khyr," Cordone explained, his hand never stopped caressing the object. "We can prove beyond a shadow of a doubt An'khyr and its people not only existed but their legacy still exists in every great civilization that came after."

Micah watched Cordone come more and more alive in the presence of the winged ankh. The old man removed the clear tube that carried the pure oxygen from under his nose and laid it aside. Micah witnessed the man take deeper and deeper breaths, a feat David Cordone had not been able to accomplish in all the years Micah had known him. It seemed the statue was feeding Cordone a new life essence and helping to restore his deteriorating health.

Standing up, Cordone stretched and smiled. "I'm feeling better, more energetic, like the years have fallen away." His laughter reached his eyes. "I feel as if I'm a youngster again. Truly amazing."

The difference was both amazing and frightening. Micah watched his friend breathe and move easier than ever in all the years of their friendship. Upon closer inspection, the lines and wrinkles, once so prominent on Cordone's face, had begun to fade; the thin, white skin had taken on a more flesh-like tone. And even his hair appeared to take on more pigment, more salt and pepper than blatant silver. Perhaps the most flagrant portion of Cordone's transformation was his hands: normally arthritic and somewhat twisted, they were straight and strong when Cordone grasped both of Micah's hands in his.

"H-How?" Micah stammered, at almost a complete loss for words.

"Most religions would proclaim it a miracle," Cordone exclaimed. "But in actuality, it's a power source untapped since the time of An'khyr."

Micah looked from Cordone to the statue and back. He recovered his vocabulary. "It's healing you. Is it turning back the clock? This is not at all possible. What is going on, David?"

Cordone let out a bellowing laugh. "What I've long suspected, from my experience—which I will explain in a moment—is the statue helps the body harness its natural healing elements and agents and somewhat kicks them into high gear. A simpler explanation: my body is regenerating."

"How?" Micah repeated his question.

Shrugging, Cordone thrust his hands in the air. "Who knows? Who cares? It's working."

Coming to his senses, Micah took a seat and said, "You said you long suspected it had this capability. What do you mean?"

"I told you my story, about how as a youth I laid eyes on the statue. What I may have left out of the story was the fact that I was a cripple, a young victim of the polio epidemic, my boy."

"But the vaccine?"

Cordone shook his head slowly and took a seat. "Dr. Salk's solution came years too late for me. It wasn't until quite a few years later the first vaccines were tested successfully." The man stopped to taste the sherry in his glass. "I was considered by many to be lucky…because I was still alive. Crippled, but alive. Considered lucky, but pitied because I lost the use of my legs. Nothing worse than the stares of strangers, unless it's the stares of people close to you."

"Obviously something happened because you've been able to walk since I've known you."

"I suspected the healing properties of the statue mainly because after touching it my useless legs started to become useful."

Micah leaned back against the chair and let out a breath. "And you were able to walk once again. How did your parents explain it?"

"How else?" Cordone smiled and gestured toward the ceiling. "Heavenly intervention. A divine miracle. Of course."

"Of course," Micah repeated. "No other explanation necessary."

"Not at that time; not with those who possessed such faith. Even though my family dabbled in ancient artifacts, they were upstanding members of the church and viewed the beliefs of those ancient civilizations as heathen and barbaric."

"But they weren't too opposed to the money selling the artifacts brought them," Micah mused. "Interesting. Off point, but interesting."

Cordone laughed again and patted his chest with a hand. "I'm still getting used to having lungs which function so well. How will I ever be able to repay you for recovering the statue? For helping me restore my body?"

"More importantly, how will the world repay you for curing all ails of its people?" Micah asked.

The question caught his friend by surprise. The shock registered on Cordone's face. "There is no question of repayment."

"A great humanitarian gesture, David."

"Because the world can never know about the power of the statue."

The revelation caught Micah off-guard. He'd expected the generous nature of his friend to shine; he'd thought Cordone would use the power of the statue to better the world and its people.

"You want to know why," Cordone said, as if reading Micah's thoughts. "If you'd think about, you'd eventually come to the same conclusion. Who would be the first people to benefit from the statue's capability? Children, the elderly, those in the last stages of cancer or AIDS?" He leaned closer to Micah, their eyes level with each other. "How could you possibly pick and choose? What makes one person more important than another?

"And are you naïve enough to believe someone wouldn't want to profit from this?" He lifted the statue and placed it on the coffee table. "Nations go to war over oil, land, and more. Something of this magnitude would throw us into another global conflict. More people would be killed than could ever benefit from the statue. Slaughter for the sake of salvation."

Unable to speak, Micah merely sat in shock.

"Not to mention the pharmaceutical companies," Cordone continued, his voice rising. "Those companies that make billions of dollars from governmental grants and billions more in profit from their drugs, how would they react? Do you think they would allow such a loss to their pockets? Would they be happy to lose the millions of people they've addicted to their drugs? No, my boy; they would not.

"Revealing the statue and its power would throw the world into a chasm of chaos from which it would never recover. It could spell the end of humanity as we know it; it would spell the end of everything."

Micah felt the need to extricate himself from the conversation, from the house, and go home. The entire range of events was too much for him. Cordone was becoming irate over the concept of someone else knowing about or using the statue. The power of the winged ankh may have partially restored his body, but it seemed like his mental state was deteriorating rapidly. Cordone's wide eyes were fixed on Micah, as if expecting a response to his tirade.

Finding his voice, Micah explained that while the conversation was fascinating, he hadn't planned on the trip to Grantsville and truly needed to excuse himself to go home. "I'm happy to reunite you with the statue, but if you'll pardon me."

He stood and walked as normally from the library, from the house, as he possibly could in case Cordone followed him or was watching. Once he was off the estate, he felt better. Even though he understood some of the concerns David Cordone addressed, he still thought Cordone had caught a case of the crazies as an after-effect of the healing he'd received.

On the drive home to Rain Falls, Micah had a barrage of thoughts.

Age regression.

He'd witnessed David Cordone actually rejuvenating. The ailing old man's body healing right before his eyes. The signs of age being erased like chalk from a blackboard. Vitality returned to a broken body.

Again.

The price.

Micah should have been happy for the man; a return to youth has been sought by scholars and religious men and women alike. But what Cordone gained in his body, he seemed to have lost in his mind.

His ranting and raving about keeping the statue secret from the world terrified Micah in a way he'd never know before.

A fucking lunatic.

No one would believe a word of it, even if he gathered the courage to tell anyone about it. Who'd believe a wild tale about a mythological statue showing up out of the blue at an auction; a tattooed stranger conversing with him about it? The whole chain of events was out of this world.

Par for the course, he thought. *Lately my life has been nothing but a chain of strange events.*

Darkness had fallen. The weather was clear; stars glittered in the black velvet of the night sky. He rolled down the window to get some fresh air flowing around him. The cold helped snap him back to himself.

He nearly regretted buying the statue. He definitely regretted bringing the damned thing to Cordone. And above all else, he felt responsible for the mental deterioration of his friend. If he hadn't brought the statue to Cordone, the old man would have remained in a broken body but at least he would have kept possession of his sharp mind. The mental break was the hardest part, the most difficult thing to watch. Knowing the intelligence David Cordone lost, sacrificed in order to regain youth and health, was the hardest part to accept.

Micah questioned Cordone's choice. *Did he realize the toll the he would pay? How could he have known? He didn't show any obvious negative signs from the encounter with the winged ankh in his childhood.*

Or did he and Micah just never noticed?

Would he have noticed?

Busy navigating through his thoughts, Micah didn't see the possum in the middle of the road until it was too late.

He swerved to avoid the nocturnal animal, slamming the brakes. The tires shrieked their defiance. Micah barely maintained control of the vehicle as it went off the road. Gravel crunched beneath the tires. Finally coming to a stop, Micah looked over his shoulder and found the possum, not having moved an inch, staring at him.

"Yeah, it's my fault," Micah said aloud.

The possum turned and walked off into the night.

Micah steered back onto the pavement and continued on his way home, his heart still beating a mile a minute. He put one hand on his chest; it felt like there was no barrier of ribs and muscle between his palm and heart—it felt like he held his heart in his hand. And in a way, it soothed his nerves.

* * * * * * * * * *

By the time Micah returned home, his heart was no longer thundering in his chest. The bizarre events of the day still bothered him, but he had to push them out of his mind or he feared he'd end up in an institution, drugged out of his gourd for the rest of his life. Who'd believe a single word if he attempted to explain? He'd be carted away in a nice white coat, the one with the straps that buckled in the back.

Magic winged statues.

Rejuvenation of a diseased body.

Antiquities from a mystical ancient civilization.

Holy shit.

Not a damned thing he could do about any of it. So he might as well seek sanctuary and wait to see of the storm hit. And no better place than his house, with a stockpile of both books and food…and Sia.

The black cat met him at the door, like a living shadow, rubbing against his legs and nearly knocking Micah off his feet before he could walk into the house. In the midst of the great show of affection, Sia reached up and sunk his front claws into Micah's inner thigh, causing not a small amount of discomfort.

"What the hell?" Micah bent over and delicately removed the claws from his sensitive flesh. "Is this how you tell me you missed me?"

Uttering his signature, plaintive war cry once his claws were disengaged, Sia took off like a smoking vampire running from sunlight. Micah laughed as he rubbed his wounded thigh.

"Don't be ripping at the mattress," Micah called after the cat, "you demon-possessed beast."

In spite of the warning, Micah heard the sound of claws shredding fabric. By the time he got to the bedroom, Sia had headed to the safety of higher ground—the cat was perched like an Egyptian statue on top of the antique armoire.

Sia stared at him while Micah inspected the damage to the side of the mattress. A couple shreds. The comforter sustained most of the damage. Strips of black velvet hung by threads, more strips were piled on the floor; enough destroyed black velvet to make Alannah Myles moan.

"Dude," Micah looked at the cat, held up a handful of the shreds, and said, "no one else would ever put up with you. You insist on this aberrant behavior. Why must you terrorize me?"

Sia sat stoically on the armoire.

Gathering up the shreds of velvet, Micah alternately chuckled and cursed under his breath.

Sia lost interest in lording over the destruction and began grooming himself. Micah, disgusted and somewhat amused, left the room before bothering to threaten dropping the cat off at the animal shelter or the nearest Chinese restaurant.

He tried hard to push the bizarre events out of his head so he could at least enjoy a meal in relative normalcy.

He threw the shredded comforter and all the renegade pieces in the trash before searching through the kitchen for something quick he could make for dinner. In the freezer, he discovered a cache of spaghetti sauce he'd made for situations like the one he found himself in. It would thaw and heat up in the microwave in a flash, and then taste like he'd freshly made it.

Pasta only took ten or fifteen minutes to boil and garlic bread would heat in the toaster oven in less than five. Dinner could theoretically be plated and served in under thirty minutes. And in his stomach ten minutes after that.

Micah felt like he was starring in his own show on one of the food channels. Water boiled. Timers were set.

And not long after, timers dinged and dinner was ready.

Sia jumped down from the armoire and came into the kitchen to investigate. He played with the spaghetti noodles Micah put on a plate for him, flipping them across the floor and chasing after them.

He kept pushing the events of the last few days into the back of his mind. Try as he might to keep them there, they slowly crept to the forefront.

Micah ate while he watched the cat sprint from one end of the kitchen to the other, from corner to corner, acting like a kitten with a piece of yarn. Every so often, Sia stopped to "whoa" in his native tongue at the pasta before returning to the chase. The pasta fell victim to his relentless attack; he assassinated every noodle until barely anything remained.

Each time Micah started laughing uproariously and said, "Speak English, you little terrorist."

By the time Micah finished eating, Sia was tired and done playing with the mashed pieces of pasta. Micah tried to clean the mess off the floor; it stuck like dried glue. He ended up getting a metal spatula and scraping it up. Then he had to scrub it off the spatula.

Vacating the kitchen in favor of the plush sofa, Micah reached for one of the albums containing his In Memorial card collection. With the TV on for background noise, he started to look through the cards. Sia jumped onto the sofa and curled up beside him. He scratched behind Sia's ears and the cat purred; Micah felt the purrs vibrating through the fur.

Remembering the names and services served to soothe his nerves, as did the sound of the cat purring. He immediately began to relax.

Only the ringing of the phone shattered his peace and quiet. The shrill noise startled him.

"What did he say?" Vanessa demanded as soon as he answered. "Tell me everything he said."

"About the statue?" Micah asked. "He thanked me and said he knew if anyone could find it for him it would be me. That's pretty much it in a nutshell." *Except for David transforming before my eyes into a younger, healthier version of himself.*

She sighed heavily. "I was eagerly anticipating more of a reaction from him; I thought for certain he'd be overwhelmed, maybe give you a big hug or something. Are you sure you're telling me everything? You're not leaving out anything that might intrigue me?"

"I'm positive."

"Did you ask him about granting me visitation with the crystal skull?" Her obsession reasserted itself and Micah was happy to hear it for once; it would keep his mind occupied.

"He was so fascinated by the statue, I just kind of excused myself so he could do whatever it was he needed to do," Micah explained. "I didn't want to keep him from whatever business he had with the statue, and he would have felt obligated to entertain me. You know?"

"I suppose I can understand that," she said. "You men, always playing whenever you get a new toy."

He heard her breathing and waited for her to continue. He didn't have to wait for long.

"However, he should be used to having all sorts of artifacts," she said. "What's the grand importance of this statue?" She paused. "Are you certain you couldn't have slipped in my request?"

Annoying as she could be at times, as much as her multi-tracked mind could irritate, Micah was so grateful Vanessa called to distract him from his thoughts. Once the call was over, maybe he could segue back into his beloved In Memorial cards and find the tranquility he sought.

Vanessa chatted on and on again about how grand the wood columns she bought for her friend Storm looked and how much he was going to adore them in his dining room. Micah responded with the appropriate "I'm sures" and "I bets" so she didn't pick up his odd mood.

True to form, Vanessa went off on a variety of tangents during the conversations, always eventually returning to the crystal skull. If he never heard her mention it again, he wouldn't miss the topic. But anything to take his mind off David Cordone and the winged ankh statue.

"Unfortunately I promised Chiffon I'd roast some peanuts for her tonight," Vanessa said, "or we could chat the night away."

They said their goodbyes and hung up.

Micah turned on the TV and tried to watch a documentary on the discovery of a fourth pyramid at Giza. The "lost" pyramid was not a new discovery; Egyptologists had known of its existence for over a century. And it wasn't located at Giza, but miles away at Abu Roash. Reputed to have been constructed on the orders of a renegade pharaoh, it was to have been bigger and grander than any of the other pyramids—quite possibly the crowning glory of Ancient Egypt.

Normally it would not have been so confusing, he would have sat mesmerized by such a show, but he found he couldn't concentrate enough to follow along. He figured he'd record the show and watch later when his mind wasn't so jumbled, when he could better appreciate it.

So he hit the record button, turned off the television, and picked up the first of his albums.

Page after page, he recognized the names of the departed—for the most part—and recalled the services in detail. Here and there were names he couldn't recall offhand, even after careful deliberation. But he felt compelled to peruse through the albums again; he felt like there was a piece of the greater puzzle somewhere in one of the albums and he wanted to find it.

Sia continued to purr contentedly by his side.

After looking through the first album, Micah reached for the second. Reviewing years and years worth of funerals brought back memories of his mother's service: the dark skies, the pouring rain, the questions.

Years and years spent on a quest to find the answers to his questions, and he'd found none.

"Sterling's probably right," he said to the cat.

Sia raised his head and meowed.

"It'd be for the best if I stop obsessing over these. Or I'll end up like Vanessa and the crystal skulls."

But he didn't close the album. There was a nagging at the back of his mind. Something he needed to find. Something that had been tickling his memory for weeks. He felt it was close to his fingertips.

And with one turn of the page, there it was.

A memorial card from four years earlier, similar to the thousands of others in his albums. Only this one was very different. For he knew the name; he knew it well. Still the shock permeated his bones.

Lucian Sterling.

"Holy shit." Micah dropped the album like it had seared his flesh. He jumped off the sofa so fast it scared Sia, who raced from the room.

He took the card from the album and looked closely at it.

Customary white card stock with gold and silver accents. A dove, the universal symbol for peace. Lucian Sterling written in black calligraphy on the front. No poetry quote or Bible verse.

Opening the card, Micah read the inscription. Not only was Luc's name on the front of the card, his birth date and the date of death corresponded to Luc's birthday and the date of the car accident.

No way could it be a coincidence. Luc told him the first day they met about the accident, the date, everything. There couldn't be another person with the same name who died at the same time. Lucian Sterling, not a common name like John Smith or Jane Doe, couldn't be someone else.

His friend died four years before.

Did that mean he was friends with a ghost?

Impossible.

When it rains, it pours, he thought. One bizarre revelation followed by an even more bizarre one.

Reeling from the newest disclosure, Micah tried to stand. His knees refused to cooperate and he collapsed back onto the sofa. With shaking hands he held the card up to take another look. Seeing was believing and it was definitely Luc's name emblazoned on the front of the card.

What the hell is going on? Micah asked himself. "How could he be dead? I see him; I hear him." He laughed bitterly. "But that would mean I'm completely fucked in the head. What are the options? I'm insane or he's dead. People have seen him; I'm not the only one."

But what if, by bizarre circumstances, it was true? Would it explain some of the strange events involving Luc?

Possibly it could.

And maybe it's all merely a figment of my freaking imagination.

Wouldn't it be nice?

No such luck.

The cumulative effect of the day's events, coupled with the discovery that the man he called his best friend kept the secret of his death from Micah, physically and emotionally drained him. Exhaustion wore him down. Too wiped out to do anything but lay on the sofa, his eyes soon closed.

Sleep came quickly.

He didn't feel Sia jump onto the sofa and curl up on his chest.

In his sleep, he lost his grasp on the card; it fell to the floor.

Chapter Nineteen

Asleep for roughly three hours, he wasn't ready to surface from the realm of dreams. The ringing of the phone probably wouldn't have disturbed his deep slumber, but the sound scared the sleeping Sia, who launched off Micah's chest, rocking him enough to wake him.

He fumbled for the phone.

"Hello?" he mumbled, still not fully awake. He listened and the asked, "What are you talking about?"

He listened again, focusing as best he could.

Sitting up, he said, "Say it again."

The voice repeated itself.

"Fire?" The news jerked him wide awake. He sat up. "Do they know what the hell happened?"

Vanessa's voice was shrill. "I've called the police and fire departments several times. If they know, no one is saying. I saw it on the news. The fire broke out and spread so quickly. At this point, they are suspecting arson. Two people, motorists driving by, called in the fire. It must have been burning big."

Micah moved to the edge of the sofa, tension gripping his body. "Where's David? Is he in the hospital?"

"Poor man. He hasn't been found. The fire engulfed the house so quickly, darling; the speculation is he wasn't able to get out. How could he if the flames became an inferno so quickly?"

Having spent some time with Cordone earlier in the evening, Micah couldn't believe the man was dead, that he had been burned alive. The memory of David Cordone telling him how ravaged the homes of people who were in possession of the winged ankh statue came rushing back.

Rubbing the back of his neck, he asked Vanessa, "What time is it now? Around ten or eleven?"

"Yes, eleven-fifteen. I just saw the breaking story on the news and called you immediately," she answered. "I can't believe it. This is a horrible tragedy. I never really knew the man, but the loss is so great. The loss of Mr. Cordone as well as all the artifacts he'd amassed through the years."

Micah stood. "I need to drive to Grantsville."

"What? Why?" she gasped. "Honey, there's nothing you can do. The news story said there are several fire companies on the scene; they can't get into the house because the flames spread so quickly. You might be in the way. Let them do their jobs. You can go up tomorrow."

"But they suspect arson?" *Could it really be the revenge or whatever of the statue?* he asked himself. *The lure must have been great if David had dared to possess it in spite of the curse.*

"No way to tell for sure, of course. Not until an investigation can take place," she said. "They'll need to put out the fire before anything else can be done."

Fire ravaging David's home. The picture filled his mind. Flames eating through the treasure-filled rooms. "And the official word on the house is a complete loss? That means his collection is ash, a complete ruin."

"Tragic."

Sia jumped up onto the sofa and crawled on Micah's lap. He scratched behind the cat's ear. Sia purred.

Vanessa kept talking about how the newscaster called it one of the worst fires reported in local history.

"Should be recapped by midnight, Micah," she said, "if you want to see the footage they have. I don't know how those reporters and camera people get to the scene so fast."

"I don't know if I can sit through it," he admitted. "Remember, I was there just a few short hours ago. Do you think I should call the police and tell them? What if they want to question me?"

"What would you tell them? You visited a friend, came home, and hours later his home was ablaze. There's no information pertinent to the fire," Vanessa assured him, "but I know you, and I know you'll call anyway, so who am I to try to dissuade you? Call them and tell them everything you don't know."

The reasoning behind her argument was sound but he knew he'd feel better speaking with the authorities and he told her so.

"Call them in the morning," she advised. "You need rest. And really, there's nothing you can do for Mr. Cordone now, honey. Go back to bed and sleep."

Like I'm going to be able to fall asleep again.

* * * * * * * * * * *

Micah greeted the dawn.

True to his prediction, he hadn't been able to fall asleep after learning of the fire. Lying on the sofa, he was wide awake when the sun peaked over the horizon; he watched the rays spread, making the sky lighter and lighter, the day brighter and brighter.

Demanding attention as soon as he noticed Micah was awake, Sia rubbed his face against Micah's. Kneading Micah's chest with his paws, he licked Micah's chin and kept purring loudly.

His mind full of thoughts and questions and confusion, he couldn't give the cat the attention Sia wanted. Tired beyond reason, he couldn't go back to sleep. He felt he owed it to David Cordone as well as himself to see the remains of the great house with his own eyes.

"I need to get in the shower and then drive to Grantsville," he told the cat. "I can't wrap my mind around the destruction until I see it in person."

Sia looked up at him.

* * * * * * * * * * *

On the early morning drive to Garrett County, Micah remembered his revelation of Luc. Remembered holding his friend's memorial card and staring at the name printed on it. He instantly revisited the moment of cold shock.

He also remembered Tangerine and Angina and their words of wisdom about how the answers to his questions may not necessarily be the ones he wanted.

"What am I supposed to do with the answers once I get them?"

They didn't tell him that.

Wait until I go back and show them the memorial card and tell them about being friends with a guy who's been dead for four years. He imagined the looks on their faces and wondered if they would offer coincidence as the catch-all answer the second time around.

He wished he had a smoke.

Craving one more than he had in a long time, he could taste the smoke, feel the slim cylinder in his fingers.

Digging around the glove compartment, he found the treasure for which he searched: almost a half a pack of cigarettes. He lit one and inhaled deeply, dragging the luxurious smoke down into his lungs.

And almost drove off the road because he'd immediately launched into a coughing fit.

"Too much too soon," he said between coughs.

After the hacking was over, he took another, shorter drag. This time the smoke flowed smoothly into his lungs. Exhaling a stream, he looked at himself in the rearview mirror. He'd missed having an affair with his long lost friend nicotine.

When he got to David's house, his mouth dropped open in disbelief. Fire had reduced the massive house to ruin. The great doors were beyond cinders, a gaping hole where they used to be. Many of the stone walls had collapsed and now lay as debris, stones broken and blackened, scattered across the ruined lawn. Remnants of the slate roof that had collapsed lay everywhere, much like shrapnel from a mortar shell. Glass shards from the broken windows reflected the morning light, turning the muddy ground into a glittery graveyard. Rivulets of black water trickled from the destroyed house.

Several firefighters remained on the scene to make sure there were no flames hiding in the house or sparks smoldering, waiting to spring to life. Already the fire marshal from the Bureau of Fire and Arson was in the house, investigating what would surely be suspected arson.

The breeze shifted directions, bringing the smoky smell to Micah's nostrils. Fighting the urge to gag, he put his hand over his mouth.

He stood his ground, gazing upon the house to which he'd been a visitor the previous afternoon. Whether from tears or a bit of dust, his eyes watered. He wiped it away and turned from the sight before him.

Back in his car, he reached for the pack of cigarette, put one between his lips, and lit it. It felt like a malediction, smoking within sniffing distance of the ashes of his friend's house.

No way Cordone could have made it out of the house, that was the general consensus. Not an old man in his physical state; not as crippled up and dependent on his oxygen tank as Cordone was.

But Micah knew a different man. He'd witnessed the transformation himself; with his own eyes he saw David Cordone remove the oxygen tube, stand up, and reach out with no-longer-crippled hands.

But people wouldn't know about that. They'd only remember him as being partially crippled, never without his oxygen. And they'd believe he perished in the inferno, not a chance in hell of escaping.

"And maybe he didn't get out. If it spread so fast, how could he have gotten out?" Micah said to himself, exhaling a stream of smoke out the window. "Who's to say he wasn't cremated, his ashes mixed with those of the house, and then washed away. Bits and pieces of him could be all over the lawn. "

Feeling melancholia creeping up on him Micah tried to shake it off as he started the car. No use shedding tears. Wouldn't help anyway.

Quiet on the drive back to Rain Falls, Micah tried not to dwell on David

Cordone. There was no way he could have known the fire would occur, not even after Cordone spoke of the fires that had destroyed the men who'd possessed the statue in the past. The thought never entered his mind; he'd been so thrilled to have found the statue, he never stopped to consider the consequences.

Stop thinking about it, he warned himself. *It's not your fault; you didn't cause a damned thing to happen.*

Another cigarette.

The quiet wasn't working, so he turned on the CD player and cranked the volume. Maybe the lovely Lita Ford could blast the thoughts from his mind. "Shot of Poison" blew out of the speakers and filled the car. Micah sang along, losing himself in the song, forgetting Cordone and statues and Luc and death.

The CD shuffled and "Holy Man" began to play.

Again he sang along.

Singing with Lita worked until he arrived back in Rain Falls, back to his house. It all came thundering back to mind, a cyclone of confusion wreaking havoc, as soon as he shut off the music. Resting his head on the steering wheel, he wondered briefly what it would be like to drive, get Sia and just drive away and not look back for any reason. Leave all the bizarre questions and even more bizarre answers in the past, in the dust, and never think about them again.

It all snowballed, one flake at a time, into one hell of a storm—one incident after another until a blizzard blighted out his normal existence. He wanted nothing more than to make tracks for sunnier vacation spots.

He thought about where he'd go. Starr traveled back and forth across the country on a regular basis; he could call her and get her opinion on the matter. Hell, he could keep her company on her runs; she'd enjoy having him around more. Or he could stay in her house in Texas while she was on the road. She only made it home for a few days a month anyway. They could be roommates.

Pondering, he finished his cigarette and lit yet another one.

"Jesus, I can't believe I smoked so many in so little time," he said, crumpling the empty pack and putting it in the trash bag.

Sell the store and get a house in the Hollywood Hills. One of the ones that used to belong to an old time movie star from the silent screen era. Secluded. Far away from anyone he knew.

Or a house on the coast of Maine. In a small town. He could start over, be anybody he wanted to be, make new friends. And he could still write the Trampp books in peace and quiet.

Drive to the airport and get on a plane out of the country. He decided against that because of the difficulty he'd have getting Sia through customs in a foreign country. The cat would have to be in quarantine and he knew he couldn't be away from his buddy for that long.

The idea about running away appealed to him.

But instead of packing it in and running away, because it wouldn't solve anything, he turned off the engine and got out of the car.

Rain Falls lived up to its name: large droplets of water began to fall from the gray clouds. He was soaked through his clothes in the amount of time it took to get from his car to the front door.

Dripping, he reached to insert his key in the lock.

The explosive flash of lightning, immediately followed by the roar of thunder, took him by surprise.

Chapter Twenty

Slamming the door against the torrential onslaught, Micah was grateful for the dry warmth of his house. A hot shower called his name. Before he could turn and take a step, someone spoke.

"I told you, you should get rid of these albums, Graves. I told you over and over again," Luc, seated on the sofa and looking through one of the albums, said. "You didn't listen and now it's too late. Everything is ruined."

Turning, Micah said, "What are you doing here?"

Luc held up one of the memorial cards. Micah didn't have to guess which one of the thousands it was.

"Okay," Micah said.

"I knew you were at my funeral. Because I was there and saw you." Luc shook his head. "No one could see me."

"How can this be possible, Sterling?"

He ignored the question. Throwing the card back to the floor, Luc said, "You hadn't looked at them in months; you were so damned close to tossing them in the garbage. Everything would have been fine."

Micah didn't know what to say.

"Why didn't you just throw them away like I wanted?" Luc looked into his eyes and asked.

Micah held his friend's gaze; he could do nothing but shrug his shoulders. "So many times I was this close," he held up his hand, thumb and forefinger a millimeter apart, "to tossing them, but I couldn't quite bring myself to do it. On the other hand, if you were so concerned about me discovering the truth, why the hell didn't you tell me yourself? You had opportunities to explain."

Luc didn't break the stare. "Because you are so judgmental and you wouldn't have understood the bigger picture."

"Since I've stumbled onto the path to the bigger picture, tell me what the hell is going on. How can you be dead and be here? And you are dead, Luc; I went to your funeral four years ago. Or is there another even odder explanation? Given my luck, there will be more strange shit coming my way."

Luc looked down at the floor. "As I'm sure you surmised, I didn't survive the car crash; everything else was the truth."

"That doesn't explain why you're here. How are you here?" Micah demanded. "I think I deserve the truth. I cannot tell you how messed up it is to find out one of your closest, if not best, friends is in reality dead. In case you don't know, let me tell you: it's a mind fuck. But I could have handled the truth; you obviously didn't trust me enough to tell it to me. And I want to know why. Damn, Sterling, I want to know why the hell you never told me."

"The truth? You want the truth?" Luc said, an edge to his voice. "I'll give it to you, Graves. Say the word. I'm tired of hiding in shadows and careful wording."

"Yes. Tell me."

Luc scratched his cheek. "Unbridled truth, my friend?

"Spit it out."

"Here it is: You propagate the myth that you are so open-minded," Luc said softly, almost in a loud whisper, "but you know that's not the true you. Your mind is not nearly as liberal thinking as you believe. There is much you don't see, you can't see, Graves. You're blind to what you desire so much to see."

It cut quick and it cut deep. Micah looked away, knowing the truth when he heard it. Harsh to hear.

"Your vision is two-tone: you view everything in black and white," Luc continued. "The only problem is there are so many shades of gray in the world, from deep to so light they're hazy, and you can't see any of it. You see one extreme or the other, and you miss everything in between. And in between is where you'll discover all the answers for which you've been searching."

The description was accurate, but Micah said, "You make it sound like I'm blind; I'm not completely oblivious to what goes on around me. I see and know a lot. I've learned so much in the years since my mother's death. Granted, not everything I wanted to learn, but I learned many things."

Luc stood and walked to the window. He looked at the rain fall. "That's not what I mean. Like I said, you are blind in a sense. There's so much more you could see if you'd allow your mind to be more open; your sight would develop and you'd see everything clearer."

He turned from the window before continuing. "Answers will not fall into your lap. Gaze into the sky for years, knowledge will not fall into your lap. You seek the answer to what awaits each of us after this existence, but after all these years you're no closer to discovering it."

"Now I know. Now I know there's something after death. Obviously," Micah said, gesturing to his friend.

"But my point is you knew that before me," Luc said. "But knowing there's something and knowing what it is," he drew closer to Micah until they were face to face, "are two entirely different concepts. Understand what I mean?"

Micah didn't say anything.

Luc put his hands in his pockets and chuckled. "You're mad. You asked me for the unvarnished truth and I told you. Now you're pissed."

"No, I'm not," Micah refuted. But he was. Because deep down he knew he wasn't nearly as open minded as he wanted to be. For years, he asked himself if that's what was keeping him from finding the answers he'd longed to know. Deciding to be completely honest with his friend, he admitted it. "Yeah, I'm pissed. Not at you, though. I'm mad because I know what you said is the truth; I'm mad at myself. I've thought it about myself. But to hear it voiced by someone else is difficult. Makes me wonder if I'm as transparent as plastic wrap, if I'm as deep as veneer."

"Feeling sorry for yourself always has been one of your faults." Luc put his hand on Micah's shoulder. "You feel sorry for yourself whether or not you understand that's what you're doing. You don't think 'Oh, poor me,' but underneath it all there is a part of you that does feel sorry for yourself and it holds you back. Break the bond keeping you from your full potential. I have faith in you; you can do it, my friend. Give yourself more credit because you deserve it."

Micah exhaled the breath he'd been holding since Luc touched him. A hand on his shoulder. Simple friendly gesture. But this hand belonged to a man who died four years earlier. He couldn't shake that thought and to have Luc touch him unnerved him more than words could say. His skin didn't crawl nor did his stomach churn, but he felt very uncomfortable.

If Luc sensed Micah's discomfort, he said nothing about it nor did he move his hand. "When you uncover the part holding you back, when you release it and get rid of it, you'll be on your way to being the person you want to be," Luc told him. "Then and only then will your mind be as open and as free as you desire, as you deserve. Do you remember the old phrase that goes something along the lines of free your mind and the rest follows?"

"Like what doesn't kill you hurts a hell of a lot," Micah said.

"Makes you stronger," Luc corrected. "Clarity is a wonderful achievement. And once your mind is clear, there's nothing you cannot do."

Micah knew what Luc said made perfect sense, but he was still off the rails about the whole supposed to be dead thing. "Perky little pep talk. But we still have to address the monstrous pink elephant in the room: You're dead. I can't pussyfoot around the major issue, dude. You. Are. Dead."

Holding his arms wide, Luc said, "I cannot believe you are still whipping that corpse. Get over it. I'm here telling you what you've always wanted to know. There is something after this existence. What more could you possibly need to know?" His arms fell to his sides. "I've given you the answer you've been searching for, my friend. After how many years and countless funerals?"

"Too long." Micah rubbed his eyes. "So damned many years. Thousands of funerals. A never-ending quest."

"Then be happy with the knowledge you've been given. Most people don't get to know this, Graves," Luc said. He sat back down and picked up the memorial card from his funeral service. "You're riding a roller coaster of emotion and I understand how difficult this is for you. I admit it's an overload of information to take in and process. It has to sink in. I'm here for you."

It was unsettling for Micah to see his friend holding his own funeral card. "What was our friendship?"

Luc shook his head. "I don't understand."

"Was it real or not?"

"How can you ask me such a question, even consider it? Didn't we have a ton of good times? All the stuff we have in common," Luc said. "Remember and then rethink your question."

"Quit twisting my words." Anger rising, Micah slammed his fist on the end table, jarring the lamp. "That's not what I'm asking and you know what I mean. Tell me what I was to you."

"You're my friend. We became close friends. Why can't you just accept our friendship and continue on?"

"Because you're dead," Micah yelled, "and I'm not. That's not the way it's supposed to be. That's one hell of a hurdle to jump. How am I supposed to get past it?"

"Let it go," Luc said.

"You're asking a lot of me."

Luc spoke calmly, in a modest tone. "You don't have to get past it. All I ask is for you accept it so we can move on. There are reasons for everything I've done, if you would allow me to explain."

"Our relationship is based on a lie. You lied to me," Micah accused his friend. His head started to thump and he pressed his palms against his temples. "How can I trust anything you ever say or do?"

"Graves, you trusted me so far, before any of this. Why should things change now? Just because you know? Come on."

"I..." Micah trailed off and stared past Luc, into the other room. "I don't think I can get over this, or trust you, Sterling. Not ever. It's betrayal. You betrayed our friendship, you betrayed the trust I placed in you. There is nothing you can say or do to make me change my mind."

"Let me explain. There are more things you need to know, things you need to understand before you can come to a conclusion," Luc said. "Will you let me explain? I'll help you understand. There is a bigger picture for you; you were meant for something. You're here for a reason. You can gain so much knowledge from this, from our relationship. Don't you want to learn?"

Micah shook his head. "I don't want to hear anymore. And I think our relationship has come to an end."

"No."

"Leave me alone, please."

He closed his eyes and put his palms over them. When he opened them, Luc was no longer there.

Chapter Twenty-One
One Month Later

Standing in Piazzo Cappuccini—a brief walk from Palazzo Reale—at the entrance to the Capuchin Catacombs, Micah looked at the non-descript building. In keeping with their vows of poverty, the monks did not build an elaborate monastic building, but rather a plain and ordinary one; he may very well have missed it if he hadn't been told to pay attention to the signs. The catacombs dated back to 1599, over 400 years. He anticipated his journey into antiquity.

Inside waited the infamous mummies of Palermo, Sicily, and for some reason, even after traveling so far, Micah felt almost reticent about entering. Not that he believed an antiquated contagion would infect him or the ghosts of the dead would haunt him to his own death and beyond if he dared intrude upon their place of eternal rest. Something bothered him.

A tiny wiggle, nearly a tickle, in his brain warned him he should avoid entering the catacombs; it warned him something waited for him down there below the ground. He nearly turned and left.

But he shook it off. After all, he did travel all the way across the ocean and Europe to see her, arguably the most famous resident of the burial chambers: Rosalia Lombardo, one of the last—or as some sources argue *the* last—mummy admitted to the catacombs.

The first and oldest resident: a monk from the Order, shortly after the Order arrived in Palermo, by the name of Brother Silvestro from Gubbio who died in 1599. The last monk to be interred was Brother Riccardo of Palermo, who passed away and was embalmed in 1871.

Visiting hours were 9 am to 12 noon and 3:30 pm to 5:30 pm. Not as open to the public as he'd thought they'd be, but then again, an awful lot of people could traffic through the catacombs in a few hours. Strange there was no one else to accompany him down into the earth.

An elderly monk smiled in greeting and gestured towards the dark stairway, inviting Micah to enter the catacombs. Micah smiled back and didn't move an inch. A bit of trivia came to mind: the Capuchin monks took their names from the distinct hood they wore on their robes. Another tidbit of trivia floated to the front of his mind: the foam of the coffee drink cappuccino allegedly resembles the hood of the monks. Micah didn't see it himself.

The monk bade Micah to walk down the stairs. He still felt the pull of the warning and nearly backed away again.

Shake it off, he ordered himself. *You're a big boy.*

Warm from the rays of the sun, Micah refused to lend credence to the chill spiraling its way up his spine. He assured himself if he ignored it, it would go away. He breathed deeply and took a step forward. Then another. And soon found himself in the cool stairway.

No damp smell, like that of a basement, at all. Of course, he didn't expect the putrid aroma of decaying corpses to waft up the steps, but he'd expected some sort of smell like a mildewy concrete basement or a wet dog. Approximately eight thousand mummified corpses were entombed below and, damn it, he'd expected some kind of terrible smell but there was none, not even like that of a hospital.

Weird to be in a tomb and not smell the flesh. Perhaps the smells one experienced in funeral homes were not those of the corpses but those of the building and the living, the chemicals used in the processes and such.

Making his way down the steps, he attempted to mentally prepare himself for the macabre spectacle that lay before him. He'd seen pictures on the internet when he'd done the research for the place, but he doubted that would equip him for the sight he was about to witness. Five thousand funerals, all of which featured a single body, might not be enough to lay the groundwork for what awaited below.

No amount of preparation could have prepared him for it.

He stopped and stared as the first section, the monks of the Order, came into view. The remains of Brother Silvestro from Gubbio welcomed Micah into the catacombs. Despite having been to those thousands of funerals, Micah was jarred by the remains of the monk; a disturbing image to see upon first entering. But then again, that was why so many people came to call upon the catacombs.

So many people.

Odd for him to be the only person taking the tour.

He didn't care to dwell on the fact he was alone underground with thousands upon thousands of mummified corpses. He knew the dead couldn't hurt him; he also knew the dead weren't supposed to walk and talk and be your friend, but that apparently didn't always ring true.

Second came the men's section; corpses dressed in the clothes of their time. The women's section, including a sub-section for virgins—who were distinguished by a metal band worn around the skull—was next.

Corpses, corpses everywhere. Reclining in coffins, seated in chairs, lying on shelves, hanging from places. Micah stared in complete astonishment; and many stared back at him with their own still-there eyes. Dull, dead eyes and empty eye sockets stared at him from multiple directions.

His skin crawled and not from the chilly air. It was chilly, but not a wet cold; it was a dry, cool air. Probably helped to preserve the mummies; little or no moisture in the underground caverns helped stave off the onslaught of rot. The sickly sweet stench of decay didn't assault his sense of smell.

The professor's section—the designated final resting place for professional men—included doctors, lawyers, professors, and other vocations that were designated as professionals; also included were soldiers and officers, the colors of their parade uniforms still just as vibrant as the day they were interred—as if the passage of time had not touched them but instead past them by.

The section for priests was much smaller than Micah had anticipated, but a multitude of corpses were available for viewing. The sight of the holy men adorned in their tattered cassocks and vestments unnerved him more than seeing the remains of the children. Most of the corpses throughout the catacombs were close enough to touch, if one were so inclined.

Micah was tempted, just to see what a century- or centuries-old corpse felt like. Would any remaining skin feel like sandpaper? Would it disintegrate into dust when he touched it?

As fascinated by the spectacle of thousands of corpses as he was, his reason for visiting beckoned. Rosalia Lombardo. She slept, the young "Sleeping Beauty," in a small chapel at the end of the tour, tucked under a blanket in a glass-topped coffin, which rested on a marble pedestal. Quiet; so quiet in her chapel. Felt like a place of reverence. He almost got down on one knee.

Micah stole into her chamber, nearly on tiptoe. Closer and closer and closer he crept, all the while expecting a monk or a security guard to jump out and order him away from the child.

Such a sight to behold.

The pictures he'd seen on the internet didn't do her justice. Although the descriptions he'd read said she looked as if she were sleeping and could wake up at any moment, he thought there at least had to be some decay. Only one site had said she no longer looked as if time had ceased and stood still; it said her skin tone was no longer flesh-like.

But it was wrong.

Rosalia truly looked as if she were asleep; an angelic-looking two year-old girl taking a nap. He looked at her through the glass. Not a trace of the passage of time. Not a single blemish on the child's face.

Micah knew the story: she was born in 1918 and died in 1920; embalmed by an allegedly secret, lost method. Speculation was the man who completed the process on her might have taught the people who would later embalm the body of Vladimir Lenin. It was also speculated the man might have refined his technique before embalming the little girl, using his medical knowledge and skills to advance the technique he'd learned from the leading morticians of his time.

Lombardo Rosalia

Nata il 1918

Morta il 1920

A shadow passed over Micah, startling him out of his concentration, as someone joined him in the small chapel.

He looked up.

"Graves."

A voice he recognized and never expected to hear ever again. "What are you doing here? Come to finish me off? Leave me among the other corpses; who would notice one more body, right?" Micah demanded in a low voice, never taking his eyes off the man who was supposed to be his friend. "Will you kill me and leave me among the dead here?"

Lucian Sterling shook his head and then spoke. "I wanted to try to explain to you again—"

Micah cut him off. "I'm not sure if you being here is profane or appropriate. After all, what's one more corpse here, right?"

"No need to be mean. I may not fit your definition of alive," Luc said, "but I've looked out for you since day one and saved your life on more than one occasion, in case you've forgotten. That should at least buy me enough time to have my say."

Micah couldn't argue with him on that point. No matter what he was, Luc Sterling had never given him reason to fear for his life. "Go on."

Luc held his hands out, palms up, and said, "I apologize once more for deceiving you. My purpose wasn't only deception; it was never deception at all. My ultimate goal was—"

"Was to divert the path of Destiny, Fate, whatever you call it," Micah interrupted again. "I understand that. You liked me too much and didn't want to see my life cut short. I get it. Why the lies?"

Rubbing the back of his neck, Luc looked down at the floor. "Would you really have believed a word I said if I walked up to you and said I was an emissary of Death sent to accompany you into the Mourning Light?" He looked up at Micah. "Can you honestly look me in the eyes and swear you would have believed me? You wouldn't have run screaming and called out the whoopee squad? You know, in the core of your being, you would have thought I was nuts."

Micah knew he would have reacted exactly as Luc thought, but he didn't think that should have stopped Luc from telling him the truth after they'd gotten to know each other better and told him so.

"I agree. Completely. There were countless dozens of times, maybe a hundred, when it was on the tip of my tongue."

"And you swallowed the truth and spoke lie after lie to keep me around," Micah said. He didn't mean it as harsh as it sounded and felt like an ass when he saw Luc wince at the accusation. "My turn to say I'm sorry. I didn't mean it the way it sounded. It was harsh and mean to say it like that and I apologize."

"It's okay, because it's kinda the truth," Luc admitted. "Don't beat yourself up over it."

"So, I understand why you kept trying to get me to pitch my albums of memorial cards. Wouldn't it have been simpler to just take out your card and throw it away?" Micah asked.

Luc didn't answer right away. He looked everywhere, at everything—the walls, the floor, the ceiling, the child—but Micah.

"What?" Micah asked.

"The truth?"

"No, lie to me some more because I like it," Micah groused. "Of course I'm asking for the truth."

"I could give you a long song and dance routine, but the fact is I never thought about taking my card and throwing it away," he said. "Never occurred to me. The simplest thing imaginable and it never occurred to me."

He'd caught the man with his guard down. It made Micah smile. He enjoyed seeing Luc squirm; for all his careful, detailed planning, Luc overlooked the simplest, easiest way to keep his identity from Micah. One simple action and Micah may never have learned the truth.

In the chapel of a small girl, dead for not quite a century, the two men came to an understanding and salvaged what was left of their friendship. Explanations had been made and transgressions were forgiven.

"My brethren number beyond your calculations," Luc explained to Micah. "Any one of us can, upon departing our bodies, become an emissary of the Mourning Light, should we not move on to another existence. We've held the hands of countless people when it was their times to go. I've been in the company of the ones who were there that day in 1958 at Our Lady of the Angels Catholic School, when the fire broke out, trapping those dozens of children in the school. I know the agony they eased, the suffering they alleviated."

Micah, in the depths of the catacombs, listened to his friend describe what happened all those decades ago.

"There was nothing to do but to wait for what was inevitable: the deaths of so many innocents, those children and the nuns. The emissaries did not have the power to stop the fire; all they could do was guide the souls to the Mourning Light. The deaths could not be circumvented, but my brethren cradled those children before a single flame licked their flesh, so they felt no pain; for the ones who sought escape by leaping from the windows, my brethren embraced them so they would not feel the ground. We are not bringers of death; rather, we are who greets you. We are there so you are not alone on the journey."

"Wait. You said the deaths could not be avoided. What about what you did for me? Isn't that circumventing death?"

"It's not the same. There were extenuating circumstances, a huge reason for keeping you in this existence."

"Such as?"

"Let me just say you are part of something bigger and your life should be preserved," Luc said and winked.

"What is it?"

"Telling would be giving you an unfair advantage, wouldn't it?"

"Saving my ass when I should be dead is giving me an unfair advantage, isn't it?" Micah countered. "Tell me."

Luc refused.

Micah's eyes never left Luc. He asked, "Were you there when David Cordone died? Did you take him?"

Luc shook his head from side to side. "I was not responsible for David. I was to be responsible for you."

"Me?"

"You were to be there with Cordone when his house burned."

"I was supposed to die?"

"And not for the first time. A couple times in the past few months I was to have guided you, but I couldn't do it." Luc looked from Micah to the child. "I couldn't do it. Not after feeling the connection between us. Not after getting to know you. I don't think anyone of us have ever directly defied..." His voice trailed off.

"Orders?" Micah said. "Haven't you been called on this? I mean, if I should have been dead months ago, hasn't anyone questioned you about why I'm still alive and kicking? Isn't there someone to whom you have to answer?"

For the first time, Luc smiled. "Let's just say I might be reprimanded for my course of action."

"You took a hell of a risk."

"For the greater good, for the bigger picture, and all that," he said. "No worries about me."

And Micah understood what Luc was saying. He hadn't come only to explain; he came to say goodbye.

"You're leaving."

Luc nodded. "Yes."

"Why?"

Luc didn't answer.

"When?" Micah demanded.

After a few seconds, Luc answered, "Now, my friend."

"Will we meet again?"

Again Luc nodded. "Most definitely we will, although probably not in this existence, Graves."

"And probably not in an underground chamber surrounded by thousands and thousands of mummified corpses."

"Probably not," Luc agreed. And then he said, "Micah, I really do have to go. Truth be told, I should not have come, but I couldn't leave things the way they were between us; I owed you that much. I needed to know that when I left we were back on good terms."

Micah's throat was dry and he coughed. His eyes teared up at the thought of losing such a close friend, even if the friend was an emissary of Death or the Mourning Light or whichever Luc said.

He looked at his friend and said, "Sterling—"

"It's okay," Luc said. "I already know." And he smiled.

The sound of approaching voices caused Micah to look away for a moment. He looked back.

And Luc was gone.

Epilogue

Lights flickered in the windows of the old Victorian. The dark sky was filled with the glittering of stars and solar systems light years away. The night air was cool and a soft breeze blew through the gardens and whistled lightly through the leaves, the sound like silk sheets smoothly shifting against each other.

A host of small animals scampered here and there on the lawns. Rabbits and squirrels and chipmunks frolicked in the gardens.

A full moon cast rays of lunar light down upon the serene scene.

And then came the fog.

It erupted violently over the walls, surrounding the estate like an angry ocean bursting up onto the cliffs, rolling in wave after wave. Undulating wisps and great arms of dense whiteness reached out greedily to touch all, to hold it in its death-grip.

It leaked onto the estate grounds, wrapping its tendrils around anything and everything in its path, coiling and coiling. Wisps curled around trees and plants, licking before it smothered.

It drowned whatever it touched in a sea of white: the brilliant colors of the flowers were eclipsed by the blight. Nothing escaped its tenacious, all-consuming grasp. It entwined everything within reach.

Animals ran in any direction to escape as quickly as they could, fleeing before the syrupy mist could touch any of them. Their fear spurred them on and soon they had all vacated the grounds of the estate, running for sanctuary away from the creepy shroud enveloping the estate.

Inside the house there was cause for celebration.

A great achievement. Part of the goal of a lifetime or two had been accomplished and they were very happy.

They took no notice as the thick whiteness folded itself tightly around the big house and formed a fortress of fog. They didn't know they were the only two living beings left on the property.

The statue, perched on a table in the cavernous room, held the attention of the two people present. It captured their gazes like a snake charmer to the cobra.

"How does it feel to finally have it in your grasp after all this time?" the woman asked the man. "Did you ever really believe, in your wildest dreams, you would have it in your possession when…" her voice trailed off as she gestured toward an upright rectangle recess in the wall.

"The time I spent behind the mirror did nothing to diminish my desire to possess the statue," he said, never tearing his gaze away from the object of conversation. "If anything, being trapped there made me more determined than ever to find a way to be released so I could realize my dream of finding the statue."

Hesitating, she finally asked, "How did you get it?"

No answer. Then he laughed. "From two paramedics who were on the scene of the conflagration, Jamie and Shane. Faithful followers, from families of true-believers who have never forgotten me."

She turned to him with adoration evident in her eyes. "I admire you, your tenacity and your strength. You don't allow anything to come between you and your goal. You are more determined than anyone I have ever known in my life—including myself, and I thought I was damned determined to do as I saw fit."

"When you have a clear vision," he said, "you see the path before you and you know where to walk; your ultimate destination is laid out before you. When you can see everything you can't possibly get lost for too long."

"You're closer than ever to realizing your full potential. You must be buzzing with power just having it in the house."

He laughed and a lock of his dark hair fell down into his eyes. He brushed it back and said, "Perhaps buzzing isn't the correct term," he said. "However, I am feeling more strength than before it was here; I feel its pull very strong. It is definitely increasing the flow of power in my direction. I feel vindicated in my beliefs. My blood is more alive in my veins than ever before."

"Well," she said, "they are not exactly your veins, now are they? Not quite your blood flowing through them, either."

He waved a hand to dismiss her comments. "This body is mine for all intents and purposes now; a new resident in the house, if you will. Nothing will stop me again from accomplishing what I set out to do what seems like forever ago. All the signs are pointing toward the release of the Scarabae. Soon it will come to pass and the world will never be the same."

She thought before asking her next question. "Where is he now? I mean, what happened to him? Where did he go? Won't you give me some details about what happened that night?" She hated it when she thought she sounded needy or like she was begging for a favor. But she wanted to know; the question nagged at her in the wee hours on the nights when sleep wouldn't come to her.

"You'll drive yourself to insanity if you allow such petty questions to occupy your mind and your time. It is of no concern to you. He is but a memory now and it is best if you were to remember that instead asking about what happened to him. I am here and that is what matters most, my dear friend."

"Of course. I apologize if I hurt your feelings in any way. You know I think the world of you. You've done so much for me and I know I can never repay your generosity," she said. "Don't be upset with me. It bothers me to think you'd be upset because of something I've said."

"I'm not upset. This is an occasion for rejoicing; this is our celebration," he said and took her hand in his. "This is victory. The statue is here and I am one step closer to achieving what I set out to do those many years ago. Everything I worked for, everything I endured, everything I sacrificed—family, friends, followers—has all been worth it for this moment in time.

"To see the statue here in the same house with me for the first time is powerful beyond belief," he continued. "And an event many people didn't think would ever happen. They just didn't have enough faith like I did, because I knew it would happen. And I knew I would be the one to call upon the Scarabae."

"How did you know you were the one?" Nannette asked him.

"Ever since I first came across the knowledge of the Scarabae and its awesome powers, I felt deep down inside I was the one who would discover where it was locked away and free it. I was chosen, I knew it somehow, and I would live up to my sacred duty. And the statue being here is proof like never before I'm on the correct path. The statue is here."

"Now you have it," she asked, "what will you do with it? Your first step in gaining control of the world? Conquering the universe? You're so secretive most of the time. Tell me all about your master plan."

"All that information will come to you when the time is right, dear Nannette," he said. He turned to her. "I'm not putting you off. After all, you've been a wonderful friend and confidante to me since I've been back. It's merely that you will understand better when the time is right. Too much information too soon will only serve to confuse and confound you."

"I have faith in you, Alex," she said and then corrected herself. "Storm, I mean." She smiled at him in apology. "I'll have to watch myself. Sometimes it still slips out without me realizing."

He patted her arm. "Completely understandable, my dear. Just take care not to let it slip when others are around; that would be most unfortunate. Vanessa should be here to share in this moment with us. After all, she played a pivotal role in my being here instead of still trapped behind the mirror. But she'll have her opportunity to gaze upon it. There is always tomorrow."

Nannette decided to ask the question burning on the tip of her tongue. "For everything you've told me about it, you still haven't told me what it is exactly," she said. "Can you tell me what it is now or do I have to wait for that information until you tell me the time is right?"

"Not at all," he assured her. "I'll tell you now."

She waited for him to say it, silently knowing the answer already. She wanted him to validate her suspicions. She held several pieces of the puzzle, and she only needed one or two more to be able to fill it in entirely.

"It's the key."

"To what?" she asked, wanting confirmation. The answer would be what she suspected; she just knew it down to the core of her being the answer would be what she thought it would be.

"To everything," Storm answered. "It is the key to it all."

"The key," she repeated.

"Yes. And now I finally have it in my grasp. This is one of the moments to which I have looked forward my entire existence. Finally it's at hand."

Inside she rejoiced. She'd known all along the statue was the major missing piece of his bid for power.

And then she heard a sound behind her. She looked but saw nothing. There was no one in the house save the two of them. She fought the urge to go look. No one would enter uninvited, but something did bother her.

If Storm hadn't sensed it perhaps she was overreacting or overexcited; she made the conscious decision to ignore the feeling someone or something was standing behind her in the doorway.

Storm smiled as he reached out to caress the winged ankh statue. His hands gently moved down the shape of the statue, almost like a lover enjoying his partner's flesh. His finger traced the loop of the ankh.

She was happy for him; she wanted him to be as powerful as possible because she wanted to be on the winning side. She very much enjoyed the many amenities in her life and she knew Storm was the source of it all. She would never risk all she had to stray from him. Never in a million years. By his side, as his loyal friend, she had access to the things no one else could or would ever offer her.

Just as she began to relax, Nannette turned to look over her shoulder because she heard something again from the doorway, some noise she thought sounded familiar. She couldn't quite place the sound.

Nothing there.

When she turned back to look at Storm and the statue, she heard it again. This time she knew exactly what it was she heard…

Something had sneezed.

A Note from the Author:

Here we are again, at the end of another of my novels. I want to say Thank You to all the readers who have enjoyed reading my work and who Keep Frank Working by passing along information about me and my books; word of mouth is the best way to advertise.

Exciting news about my books: In addition to *Into the Mirror Black* placing in the Top Ten of Preditors & Editors Reader Poll for Horror Novel of the Year 2006, *Angels of the Seventh Dawn* placed in the Top Ten in the same category in 2007.

And if that weren't exciting enough, both novels have appeared on the Top 100 Horror list on Amazon.com, along with other great names you would easily recognize. I couldn't have dreamed it any better.

Ready for more? I am officially an International bestselling author. Yes, copies of my books have sold in other countries, and have soared up the charts. Another great Win for me.

I've also had the honor of being included in an anthology titled *Sinister Landscapes*, an international bestseller on Amazon.com; so feel free to check out the collection of stories by up and coming names in horror.

My official website, **The Lair of Author Frank E. Bittinger**, if you will, is up and running at http://FrankEBittinger.com, so drop by and pay a visit. Tell everyone you know. A big thank you to Allen for getting it off the ground for me and also to Chrissie of *CK1 Graphics* for designing and maintaining what you, the visitors, see when you stop by. I will hopefully be learning more about that so I can work on my site, too.

Everything only gets bigger and better as I go along on this journey.

I have come across a wonderful word for a series of six books I would like to share with you: **Hexology**. What an awesome term. It just sounds good and it fits my **Scarabae Saga** nicely. I happened across it by pure accident and it suited me perfectly. So below you will find a list of the novels in my **Hexology**.

Into the Mirror Black
Angels of the Seventh Dawn

Angels of the Mourning Light
Shadows Amongst the Moonlight
Illusions of Darkness: The Forbidden
Lair of the Scarabae

I also have more news about my first novel **Into the Mirror Black**: it's being reissued with a new cover design and a new round of edits; we are looking at an October 2009 release. Graphic designer Laura Meese and I are once again working together to create a great new cover. Laura is the designing force for creating the fantastic cover for **Angels of the Mourning Light**. And Sarah Moses will once again be working her editorial magic on the manuscript. Great friends and two beautiful ladies.

And a heart-felt Thank You to all the people who helped me after the arson fire that raged through my old house, destroying most of my belongings 28 May 2008; many people, friends and new friends, stepped forward to help out or send positive thoughts and energy my way, and encouraged me to continue my efforts. I love each and every one of you and I feel privileged to know you and have you in my life. So many people to thank and so little time. I have great friends and they all lent support and listened to me talk endlessly about my books while helping me when tragedy tried to destroy my world. You are all appreciated and my existence would be less enjoyable without you. Thank you Sean and Stephanie, Candy, R'Chel and Cole, Ronnie, Sue Y, David, Becky, Juanita and Jamie, and my mom for helping clean up the mess so I could start rebuilding.

I have to take time to thank my good friend Teri, who came to my rescue with a laptop so I could continue my writing; she's an awesome lady.

On another note: I will not stop my efforts to help find homes for abused, unwanted, or neglected animals; my goal has always been and will always be to find a safe and happy home for every animal I can save. I urge everyone to please think of the animals and do your best to help in any way you can, whether it be giving a loving home to an animal or a donation to one of many shelters across the world. Remember: spaying and neutering pets goes a long way in the effort to control the animal population.

I was asked to contribute a poem ("**Tonight**") to the collection "**What's It All About…? Alfie!**" to benefit Cornwall's Voice for Animals and Jollity Farm in Cornwall, UK, which gives homes to animals who have no other place to go. I gladly go on record as saying I am up for contributing to the sequel.

To everyone at Hillside Animal Hospital, thank you for coming to the rescue of many of my animal children the night of the fire and for many nights after; I truly appreciate the kindness and care you extended to us.

Everyone should know, there is a **Way to Happiness** and we can all play our roles in making the world a better place for every man, woman, child, and animal; working together, we can and will calm and clear the planet.

And on a final note: Keep in mind my books are written for your enjoyment. Any resemblance to persons, places, things, etc, is strictly coincidental and unintentional. Even if I use the real name of a place, I use it fictitiously. This is fiction, which means I make stuff up.

So read and enjoy.

Nighty-nightmares,

Frank

Please turn the page for a preview of Frank E. Bittinger's next novel

Shadows Amongst the Moonlight

Waking up dead was most certainly the last thing on my mind, something I wouldn't have planned for myself. In fact, I'd always wondered what the damned phrase actually meant.

Exactly how would one wake up dead?

I understood the concept better when I woke up around seven or so one autumn evening, in bed wearing only unbuttoned jeans. My throat felt raw, like I'd been swallowing molten lava or something just as caustic, and I felt both light-headed and heavy at the same time.

Crawling out of bed, I walked to the bathroom and shocked myself senseless when I looked in the mirror. I stared at my reflection in shock. Dark red smears ran down my neck and chest. Dry to the touch, they flaked off when I brushed at them with my fingertips—like specks of rust.

My memory was foggy. I remembered going out. I remembered talking to an assortment of people over the course of the evening. What I didn't remember was a bloodbath. Obviously something had happened to me and it was more than a bloody nose during the night.

And I didn't have a clue.

Try as I might, no memory would come to the surface.

I went back to check my bed. No stains on the sheets. Of course, bloodstains on red sheets would be difficult to detect. Pulling the sheets off, I scrutinized the white mattress underneath. Nothing. No blood on the wood floor either.

After the fire, I had my bedroom done in dark red, black, and brown because I thought it would be sexy and exotic, and it was. The blood red walls gave no clues. If there was blood anywhere in the room it would probably take a forensics scientist to hunt it down and take samples.

Shit. No help at all.

I looked around my big bedroom at all the statues of Anubis and scarab beetles. By far, my favorite piece of Egyptian art in my room was the more-than-life-size statue of Anubis, colored in black and gold and silver. It stood in the corner of the room, towering almost eight and a half feet tall. I'd surrounded myself with images of the Guardian of the Entrance to the Underworld. The dark god guarded me while I slept; his muscles and magic were supposed to keep me safe. But where was he when whatever happened had happened?

If an attack had occurred, surely there'd be some kind of evidence. But nothing was out of place. I looked again. None of the statues were knocked over; none of the scarabs had been moved—not even a fraction of an inch. My nocturnal chamber was as it always was.

After checking the front door, and finding it locked and chained, I decided, if

I was the victim of some sort of assault, I'd either known my assailant and let him or her in and then locked up afterwards or I was the victim of a magician. Either way it bothered me. The classic "locked room" situation and all that.

Not a whole lot I could do about it anyway; and, besides, it appeared to be just a little blood and I didn't seem all the worse for wear, aside from my throat and head. I'd survive.

A long, hot shower seemed like the best idea, so I turned on the water, stripped off my jeans, and stepped under the spray. The heat felt so good against my skin. When I looked down and opened my eyes, I saw the red-tinged water pooling at my feet and draining away. I closed my eyes and stood still, enjoying the hot rain. The steam rose and swirled around me; I felt it circle and press against me, then draw back. Tendrils reached to caress me through the water.

My eyes flew open; my breath caught. It had felt like someone stroking me with their fingertips. I nearly slipped on the wet shower floor. My hands reached out to steady me and instead slid across the tiled walls.

But I didn't fall. From out of nowhere I summoned some inner grace and managed to keep myself upright, executing what probably would have looked like an erratic dance move. I turned off the water and stepped out of the shower, the tiled floor cold beneath my feet.

Screw it.

Something weird was happening, and it wasn't just my nerves.

Wiping the steam from the bathroom mirror, I took a closer look at myself. The smeared blood was gone and some of the color had come back to my skin, or maybe my face was flushed from the hot shower. Whatever. A mark on my neck caught my attention and I leaned in for a closer look.

It looked like a mosquito bite. I rubbed it and felt another one. I searched my neck and chest for others, hoping I hadn't caught a disease or been bitten by insects. None. Only the two on my lower neck. Spaced a couple inches apart.

Interesting.

Then I had a flash of fear: What about, you know, down there? My stomach nearly dropped at the thought, and I slowly looked down. To my relief, no marks were evident. If they were insect bites, at least they didn't sink their teeth into my—

My gaze rose back to my neck and I reached up to scratch at the marks even though they didn't itch. And then I decided to get dressed and go feed the birds. I could hear them chirping happily and I knew they had to be starving since I normally fed them by 11 or noon at the latest.

Sure enough, they began chirping louder when I walked into the room; the little guys loved me to death. Cockatiels have held a special place in my heart, and I don't know why. I had four: Max, Norma, Joe-Joe, and Betty, all named after characters in one of my favorite movies *Sunset Boulevard*. My other favorite classic movie being *Rosemary's Baby*, and I once had a quartet of finches named Rosemary, Guy, Minnie, and Roman.

My birds love to sing and dance around their big cage, and sometimes they'll whistle at you and make kissing noises. They still loved me even though I was many hours late in feeding them.

Norma was sweetheart who sat on my shoulder and Betty was a little bitch who bit. The boys Max and Joe-Joe were very friendly and would perch on my fingers for as long as I'd let them.

This evening none of them were quite as friendly. They came close and made their usual friendly noises, but they wouldn't let me touch them, dancing out of reach every time I attempted to do so. I figured maybe they were a bit more pissed at the late feeding than I originally anticipated and were letting me know it the best way they knew how. They'd come around sooner or later.

My throat still felt raw and the metallic taste in my mouth hadn't gone away even after brushing my teeth twice. My head had cleared up and I felt more alert than earlier, but I wasn't feeling quite like myself.

I walked downstairs to my home office and sat at my desk. An entire day lost. No use calling anyone to see what I'd missed, they'd let me know about it tomorrow. I worked at home, employed by Saint & Sinner, the law firm with the cute logo of an angelic halo above the name Saint and a devilish tail beneath the name Sinner. My grandfather on my mother's side and his best friend were the founding partners many moons ago. Almost everyone in my family had some connection to law, mostly they were attorneys; I was the black sheep who wanted to do something more creative. I didn't know what that was yet, so I worked as a research assistant, meaning I looked up all sorts of obscure laws and judgments and precedents for the attorneys to use. Mostly the law firm was on retainer, a family tradition of some of the older and wealthier families in the area. "Work for old money and you'll be old money" was the mantra of our family. It's not as society sucking as it sounds, not when you consider my family *is* old money.

So, I guess it's true: When you're used to money it's not that big of a deal. Nothing unusual about any of us being chauffeured to an event. My first blowjob was in the back of a limousine on the way to some spectacular gala event somewhere, and it's a good memory. Thank the gods for those partitions that separate the passengers from the driver.

Never have I wanted for lack of money. An inheritance and an allowance from my family has permitted me to lead a nice life to which I'd become accustomed. I'm not a playboy nor am I a jet-setter. I enjoy my job and I do not intend to quit, nor do I intend to become an attorney. My life was pretty much carefree.

And at this point I digress, I never expected to wake up dead…but that's what happened to me.

I figured it out. Granted, it took me a while to do so, but I did. The marks on my lower neck: that's where I was bitten. My raw throat and the weird taste in my mouth: the aftertaste of the blood I ingested from someone else.

The sleeping way later than I ever had before was a direct result of my new lifestyle. And my loving cockatiels acting so strangely towards me: because they sensed something about me had changed and that caused them concern.

Hello, my name is Patrik Saint-Siere—most of my family and friends call me Trik—and I am a vampire.

What?

Vampire. Creature of the night. Nightstalker. Bloodthirst. One of the undead. Master of the dark.

All those wonderfully descriptive words. What did it mean?

Being a huge fan of horror, obviously I've seen most of the movies and read as many of the books as I possibly could. Fiction is fiction and it is far from fact. Most of it was made up, tailored to fit the storyline of the writer creating the script or the manuscript. Manufactured to further the plot.

Mirrors. Mirrors did not frighten me. I could clearly see my reflection—no blank space where I should have been. Lack of a reflection wouldn't be a dead giveaway. No pun intended.

Garlic. Great in tomato sauce and on pizza. Caramelized. Tastes great. Another one bites the dust.

Crosses. Gasp! Just kidding. A collection of thirteen different crosses is located on the wall above my fireplace in the formal living room. No blasphemy, no cowering. I can touch them all I want. Another myth busted.

And I don't roll around in a full body orgasm at the mere sight of blood. My eyes don't roll back in my head nor do I begin to salivate if someone gets a papercut. I hesitate to dispel this next fallacy because it may sound like it's in poor taste, however, I can walk by a woman who has her monthly visitor without falling to the ground and gnashing my teeth. Whoever thought up that one was seriously disturbed.

But I do confess to wearing my sunglasses at night. Not out of necessity but because it looks cool and sexy.

I figured these things out as I went along. Obviously the crosses are in my house so that was one of the first myths I figured out was bullshit. The rest fell into place and made sense.

Taking all the credit would be easy but I can't. Eventually I gravitated to the Seventh Dawn, sort of a club for my fellow more than mortals, which is what I found out we called ourselves. More than mortals being exactly what it says: we are more than mortal. It encompasses vampires, weres, practitioners of the Art, among others.

The Seventh Dawn is where I met many of my new friends.

There and another club frequented by my kind: Shadows. Shadows is more of a rock star club, more of a party club than the Seventh Dawn. Okay, Shadows is a strip club. Men and women entertain the audience by taking off their clothes while sultry, seductive, and, sometimes, pulsing rock music accompanies them. More on that later, but let's just say it's on the sleek and sexy side.

So, I'm Trik. I have dark brown hair, when I don't play around with the color, and brown eyes with green flecks, when I'm not wearing tinted contacts. Must have a chameleon somewhere back in my line of ancestry. I'm roughly six feet, give or take an inch, and I weigh somewhere in the range of 170 pounds. Honestly, I'm good-looking. Not only my opinion, just an insight.

And I'm still attempting to retrieve the memory of who made me what I am or uncover who he or she is so I can find them to ask why?